I PUT A FOOT ON THE TOP STAIR

The tread, which had been silent as cat paws on velvet on the way up, creaked like a rusty violin string. I flattened myself against the wall and waited to see if the mystery person in the study had heard.

Whoever he or she was, the person wasn't deaf. Something crashed. The light went off and the hall became a pit of blackness. I was clinging to the banister, trying to get my bearings when a body hurtled past me. An elbow slammed into my ribs and knocked me to one side. My forearms and fists went up to defend myself, but whoever had attacked me was already gone.

By the time I'd run down the hall to the open window, it was already too late. As I called Jamal's name, I flicked on the flash. Its beam caught a figure fleeing into the tunnel between the houses. It wasn't Jamal. But it was someone I recognized.

RAVES FOR LOUISE TITCHENER'S *HOMEBODY*

"An exciting seat-of-the-pants thriller with so many twists and turns that readers remain in constant suspense . . . an instant hit."
—*Affaire de Coeur*

"Ms. Titchener makes nice use of Baltimore locations. . . . fans of Mary Higgins Clark should enjoy this suspenseful tale."
—*Baltimore Sun*

"*Homebody* is one of the best suspense reads of the year. Populated by a cast of interesting and colorful characters, fast-paced and smoothly plotted, the story unfolds with unrelenting suspense that builds and strengthens, culminating in several pages of nail-biting edge-of-the-chair vicarious terror."
—*Gothic Journal*

Also by Louise Titchener

Homebody

Available from
HarperPaperbacks

**Harper
Monogram**

MANTRAP

◆ ◆ ◆

Louise Titchener

HarperPaperbacks
A Division of HarperCollinsPublishers

HarperPaperbacks *A Division of* HarperCollins*Publishers*
10 East 53rd Street, New York, N.Y. 10022

Copyright © 1994 by Louise Titchener
All rights reserved. No part of this book may be used or
reproduced in any manner whatsoever without written
permission of the publisher, except in the case of brief
quotations embodied in critical articles and reviews. For
information address HarperCollins*Publishers,*
10 East 53rd Street, New York, N.Y. 10022.

Cover photograph by Herman Estevez

First printing: March 1994

Printed in the United States of America

HarperPaperbacks, HarperMonogram, and colophon are
trademarks of HarperCollins*Publishers*

❖ 10 9 8 7 6 5 4 3 2 1

1

Four days after I *moved* into my Federal Hill townhouse, I had burglars.

When I first heard the noises, I thought they came from the street. Federal Hill overlooks Baltimore's Inner Harbor. With the restaurants staying open until all hours and the guys in black fishnet T-shirts roaring around on cigarette boats named Wet Dream, weekends get noisy. But this wasn't a weekend.

Remembering that, I jerked fully awake. Tensed, my heart thudding, I pushed myself up against the headboard and checked the clock on the nightstand. Two. Two o'clock in the morning! Oh, God!

Creak, click, drifted in from the living room. Tinkle, tinkle. Just the faintest of noises, but enough so I knew I had trouble.

What I did next I'd practiced in drills. Quietly, I got out of bed and padded to my closet. When I took the Ruger out of the shoebox hidden under a pile of sweaters, it felt heavy and cool against my palm. Click, creak, click. Were the noises getting closer to the stairs? My bedroom door hung open.

My heart thudded, my breathing came quick and shallow, and my hands were icy. Stiffly, I put a full ammunition clip into the gun and loaded a cartridge into its chamber. Then I headed out into the hall and down the stairs.

At the foot of the steps I paused just before the entrance to the kitchen. I caught the skittering play of a flashlight's beam and heard whispered voices.

"This place a fuckin' mess. How'm I sposed to find anything?"

"Jesus, Jamal, just grab the TV and VCR, so we can get out of here."

"I can't find the fuckin' VCR, and the TV's small. It ain't worth shit."

I took a deep breath and pulled back the slide on the Ruger. Its metallic snick stabbed the darkness, signaling my intruders that they had trouble. I wanted them to hear the noise and run.

Three seconds of paralyzed silence, then Jamal's voice and bedlam. "Get the fuck out!"

I heard a high-pitched yip succeeded by a crash.

My china, I thought, and pictured the unpacked boxes stacked atop the glass coffee table. Unable to stand there in the dark doing nothing any longer, I flicked on the light switch. Steadying the gun, I stepped forward.

Out of the corner of my eye I spotted a skinny blond girl who looked about thirteen. One horrified backward glance at me and she dived through the open window. Though I heard her land with an anguished "oof" on the patch of grass outside, I wasn't paying too much attention. Most of me focused on the small but muscular black youth.

Sprouting cornrows, he lay sprawled on the floor amidst my broken plates and saucers. I guessed his age at somewhere around sixteen.

The kid had knees made of steel. One second he was down. The next, like a duck-walking cossack, he sprang to his feet and crouched to lunge. But plainly, the way I held the Ruger before me gave him pause.

He stood tensed, knees flexed to spring, hands clenching and unclenching. "White lady, you ain't gonna' pull the trigger on that big cannon."

"Take one more step and I will."

"You ain't got the balls."

When I didn't answer, but just stood there with the barrel aimed at his belly, he straightened slightly and shot me an insinuating grin. "That some fine nightie. Show off them sweet titties real good. I hope your man appreciates you."

I hadn't given my flimsy nightgown much thought. I'm proud to say that my eyes stayed fixed on the kid, my hands held the gun steady.

His grin widened. Giving himself an arrogant little shake, he turned and swaggered to the door. When he'd opened it, he glanced back over his shoulder. "Time you straighten up your place. Only a pig would live in a mess like this." Then he closed the door quietly behind him and was gone.

"And you just let him walk off like that?" On the other side of my desk, Maggie Brown splayed her hands on her solid hips. Her milk-chocolate face, framed by its aureole of tight pepper-and-salt curls, grimaced indignantly.

"Mag, it was either let him walk or shoot him."

"Then maybe you should have blasted the punk."

"Mag!"

"Oh, I know, I know." She rolled her eyes at the ceiling. "It's just sometimes I get so, so . . . you won't believe what Intake handed me this morning . . . a nine-year-old caught with his pockets full of crack. Still a baby and already he's dealing."

She pincered a file folder between her thumb and forefinger as if it were contaminated. The big diamond on her ring finger flashed and I caught a whiff of Joy. No matter what, Maggie always smells and looks great. "Now I have to go check out his home situation," she groused. "We both know what that's going to be."

Yes, we both knew. Probably a crumbling rental in an area of the city where drive-by shootings are common. More than likely Maggie's nine-year-old dealer came from a family where drugs and alcoholism, welfare checks, and hopelessness had been a fact of life for two, maybe three generations. Maggie and I and every other juvenile counselor in the department had seen it a hundred times over.

"God, Sally, why do we stay in this rotten profession?" Maggie demanded.

It was an oft-asked rhetorical question. "I know why you do it. It's because you're studying to be a Baptist saint."

Maggie let go of a chuckle. "Yeah, yeah, that's gotta be the truth because I know it isn't my itty bitty paycheck inspiring me. Speaking of inspiration"—she tucked the file back under her arm along with the dozen or so others already clamped there—"saw your ex sitting in his fancy box at Camden Yards last night. He was alone."

"Yeah?" So, while I was being burgled, Joe had been watching a baseball game. At least he hadn't had a date. I felt myself tighten up. Whenever anyone raises the subject of Joe Winder I still go stiff as a lamppost.

Maggie, who can sweet-talk a hornet's nest, but who can also have the tact of a freight train, searched my face. "I don't suppose there's any hope of you two getting back together."

"No hope." I began to rifle through the stacks of files carpeting my desk. I was going to be spending the day out in the field, interviewing teachers, cornering hostile parents. Pointedly, I glanced at my watch.

"Hookay, I know when I'm poking my nose into a nest of bloodthirsty, man-eating fleas." Maggie turned to go, then glanced back over her shoulder. "Speaking of fleas, get yourself a dog."

"What?"

"Child, every woman living alone should have a dog and a gun and—if she's smart—a man she can call in an emergency. You're glad you had that gun, aren't you? If you'd had a dog barking its head off, those kids might never have bothered you."

"I've already called about getting a security system installed."

"Burglar alarms are fine, but dogs are better. Think about it."

I thought about it all the way down to the parking lot. A dog? What would it be like to have a dog? Except for tropical fish, I'd never owned a pet. How much care did you have to give them? What would it cost to feed one? Where did you go to get one? Would a dog really have stopped Jamal and his girlfriend from climbing through my window in the first place?

The late spring morning was windy and overcast and the Bureau of Juvenile Services parking lot, never a beauty spot, looked bleak.

As I headed for my '86 Ford Mustang, I scanned the premises. You never know what you're going to meet in city parking lots these days. Only last week a couple of kids were caught stealing the tires off our supervisor's state vehicle.

I had just slid in behind the wheel when a Chevy Cavalier pulled into the empty space alongside and blasted its horn. My head jerked around in time to see the driver lean across the empty passenger seat and roll down the window.

"Top of the morning to you, Sally."

"Morning, Detective Spikowski." I grinned. "To what do I owe this pleasure?"

Through the open window, Duke Spikowski gave me the once-over. He's a big man in his late thirties with a square, blunt-featured face, short, curly sand-colored hair, and shrewd gray-green eyes that size you up against some yardstick he keeps to himself. I've heard him laugh, so I know he has a sense of humor. He just doesn't trot it out for anything less than Robin Williams and Steve Martin in concert.

It's a little hard to explain our relationship. He's sort of a foster brother, I guess. But since Duke was away in the army when his parents took me in, I never really got to know him well the way I did his kid brother, Peter. We've always been a little wary of each other.

"I hear you had a B and E last night."

"Word certainly gets around."

Ignoring my caustic tone, Duke killed his motor and then got out and came over. He was wearing his detective suit, a boxy gray job set off by a maroon tie with a little diagonal stripe. I swear the man must have a closet filled with copycat gray suits and maroon ties. When he's working I never see him wear anything else. Same thing with his socks. They're always the identical shade of the tie.

Admittedly, I don't see all that much of Duke. Sometimes we go for months without running into each other. Then when we do, it feels as if we're sharing a secret. Damned if I know what the secret is, though.

He leaned an arm on the hood of my car and peered down into my upturned face. "You okay?"

"Do I look okay?"

His gaze flicked my features. "A little pale, maybe. Tough, all you've been through and then just moving into a new place and having something like this happen."

Duke was referring to my assault. It happened nine months ago. A guy tried to rape me. When he found that his weapon of choice wouldn't cooperate, he beat me up instead.

When it happened, I was engaged to be married. The trauma broke Joe and me up. Duke was right. My life, of late, hadn't been Mylar balloons and Tootsie Rolls.

"I'm fine, Duke. I appreciate your concern, but last night was really nothing. Two minutes after my uninvited guests left, I dialed 911. An officer named Miller came by and took my statement. He was very sweet. You should give him a promotion."

"Rookie officers don't get promotions for being sweet. Listen, I read your statement. I'd like to talk to you about it, but I guess now's not the time."

"Sorry." I took my hand off the key in the ignition and patted the bulging briefcase next to me on the passenger seat. "Got work to do."

He straightened and took a step back. "Okay. I'll give you a call and set up an appointment. In the meantime, here's something to mull over. There's been a rash of B and Es in the Federal Hill area. We're theorizing it might be a gang."

"A gang?"

"Yeah. I'd like to hear more about these burglars of yours." He waved. "Have a happy day."

So now I had two things to think about, a dog and the couple I'd surprised in my living room. Not that I hadn't been thinking about Jamal and his blond girl-friend all along.

Every day I work with kids who are in trouble. The city budget being what it is, I sometimes juggle eighty cases at a time. Frankly, a lot of those youngsters don't make that deep an impression. I mean, if they did I'd be in the funny farm by now. Still, all too often, one really gets to me.

This time two had really gotten to me. I'd caught only a glimpse of the girl, yet her image hung in my mind. She hadn't been much to look at. Skinny as a rake with transparent skin stretched over a face that was all bones and eyes. But the blight mixed with ter-ror that I'd seen in her had cut straight through me.

The boy, Jamal, had been memorable, too. I liked the way he'd told her to run and then stayed to cover her retreat. Chivalry is rare these days. What was their relationship? I wondered. He might be her pimp, but somehow I doubted that. What would have happened if I hadn't had the gun? Would he have attacked me, done me serious harm?

I doubted that, too. But here I knew I was on shaky ground. My instincts about people aren't always too good—witness what had just happened with Joe. Intriguing though I found Jamal and his girlfriend, I didn't want to run into them again. Especially I didn't want to run into them again at two o'clock in the morning in my living room.

Several hours later on the way home from work, I veered off the main road into a narrow entrance. I'd seen the sign for the animal shelter many times. On occasion I'd even caught sight of people walking down the steep drive that is its entrance. They'd caught my eye because they'd been holding two or three leashes attached to frisking dogs. How much longer did the ones left in the pound have, I'd wondered. A week? Two weeks?

I guess those questions had made more of an impression than I'd realized. Now I charged my Mustang up that road as if I'd been planning a rescue raid for months.

"I want a dog," I told the girl at the reception desk. Her badge said her name was Suzy.

"Great. What kind of a dog?" She looked me up and down. Through the closed metal doors behind her I heard frantic barking.

"I want a big dog. A German shepherd or a Lab or something like that. It's for protection."

Adopting a pet is a lot more complicated than I would have imagined. You have to sign a covenant that rivals Rumpelstiltskin's. But the worst part is walking down those rows of cages and meeting the eyes of their doomed inmates and having to choose. Halfway, I spotted a German shepherd. I was making for him when I saw the black rag mop in the cage next door.

Curled up tight in a canine fetal position, she was covered with matted black ringlets. Her long floppy ears hung down over her snub-nosed face like beaver tails. When I paused in front of her, she pulled herself up on all fours. Wobbling from side to side, she peered out at me with the biggest, saddest brown eyes in the world.

"What kind is she?" I asked Suzy.

"Just a mix, part cocker, part something else. She wouldn't do for a watchdog. Too small and gentle."

"Yeah, I guess so."

Suzy sighed. "It's too bad. Poor little thing."

"She's so cute. Who would give her up?"

"Oh, it happens all the time. People decide to give their kid a puppy for Christmas. Then when he doesn't take care of her and she gets big enough to need spaying, the parents decide she's too much bother. So they dump her here."

As if acknowledging the cruel scenario, the rag mop gave a little moan. I couldn't stop myself. I reached out and poked a finger inside her cage. Suzy started to warn me against that, but it was too late. I'd already felt the warm, wet pressure of the rag mop's pink tongue. Our gazes met and held, mine weak, hers pleading.

Then I saw the red tag tied around a top bar on the cage. "What does that mean?"

"We keep track of how long the animals have been here with those."

I glanced around and noticed tags on all the cages, but not all in the same colors. Some were yellow, others blue, white and green. "Does that red mean she's in the danger zone?"

"She's been here awhile. We can't afford to keep them long, unfortunately."

"So, how much longer does she have?"

"Tomorrow's her last day."

"Tomorrow?"

I glanced over at the German shepherd. He was a handsome beast and would probably make somebody a great watchdog, but his tag was green.

Well, so that's how I happened to take home a dog that would probably welcome future burglars as honored guests. Doubtless, she would lead them to all the valuables, pointing out any they might otherwise have overlooked, and then escort them to the front door happily wagging her stump of a tail.

By the time I got home with Mopsy—that's what I'd started to call her—it was past eight at night. I unearthed a bowl from one of my yet-unpacked boxes and filled it with some of the start-up kibbles Suzy had provided. Then I shed my business clothes for jeans and a sweatshirt and fixed myself a turkey sandwich and a glass of diet Coke.

While I ate, I watched Mopsy. After delicately nibbling a third of the food in her bowl, she selected a corner of the kitchen next to the refrigerator. She lay down with her paws crossed and regarded me anxiously.

"It's okay," I told her. "I'm a nice lady. You'd have to do something pretty awful before I'd take you back to those cages with red ribbons. This is your new home. Why don't you check it out?"

She made a noise and I laughed. "Yeah, I know. It's pretty messy. Well, see, I just moved in and I haven't had time to get set up. Maybe I'll do some of that tonight. What do you say?"

I rinsed my plate, poured myself another diet soda, and went out into the living room. Mopsy followed, claws going clickety on the bare wood floor. While she threaded a path around the boxes and settled herself in another corner, I stood surveying the clutter.

The broken dishes where Jamal had tripped and fallen still lay on the floor. The boxed VCR his girlfriend had dropped when I surprised them lay wedged against another box at a crazy angle. I relived the scene and my breathing grew ragged. What if I hadn't had the Ruger and known how to use it? Before I was assaulted I'd never even touched a gun. It was only after that, at Duke's suggestion, I'd made myself learn. What if it hadn't been a pair of kids but a guy with a knife, like that other guy?

My aloneness closed around me like a fist. Nobody

here to protect me but me. Taking a deep breath, I told myself to cool it. Then I dropped to my knees and began scooping up the shattered dishes.

An hour later I had the floor swept and four boxes unpacked. "Looks a lot better, doesn't it?"

Mopsy panted and woofed politely. While I'd been working, I'd kept up a running conversation with her. It hadn't all been one-sided, either. She'd whine, or thump her tail as if she actually understood what I was saying. Really, it was almost like having a friend. Maybe this dog thing was going to work out.

I was shaking couch pillows out of a green plastic bag when the doorbell rang. Dumping the bag, I peered over the top of my closed shutters, spotted the maroon Lexus parked under a streetlight, and identified my visitor. "Who is it?" I yelled just to give myself time to get my breathing under control.

"It's me, Joe. I need to talk to you, Sally."

My hands quivered as I undid the deadbolt. He was on the stoop. For a moment I just stood gazing at him.

It's not true that absence makes the heart grow fonder. It is true that when you've lost something you really start to appreciate it.

My ex-fiancé is a tall, well-built Paul Newman look-alike. He's the CEO at C&G, a brokerage firm with an office tower in downtown Baltimore. The hand-tailored English suit he had on told me he must have been working late and come directly from the office. My gaze played over him. His thick silvering hair had been razor cut short and crisp to the micro inch by a master barber. His intent ice blue eyes were a stark contrast in his deeply tanned face.

The silver at his temples is Joe's only concession to having celebrated his forty-eighth birthday. Fitness is his religion. When he isn't locking up million-dollar business deals, he's either working out at a gym, playing tennis, riding horseback, or diving. In fact, the first time I saw him he was scuba diving in a tank full of tropical fish at the National Aquarium. We met because we were both off-hours volunteers there.

Okay, so maybe you're wondering why a thirty-year-old woman is the ex-fiancé of an almost fifty-year-old. All I can say is that Joe is the most vital, exciting man I've ever met. At first the age difference made me a little wary. But he pursued me like a retriever on the trail of a wounded canvasback. Calls, flowers, candy, romantic telegrams. When he rolled up to my door and wafted me off to the opera in a rented white limo, I fell like a crane off a fifty-story building. That night we made love, and Joe proved himself as vigorous and thoroughly competent in bed as he was everywhere else. From then on, the age difference just didn't matter.

After we'd lived together for a year and decided to make it permanent with a small but perfect wedding in the spring, the flame still burned high. Then that guy came at me with a knife.

"What do you want to talk to me about?"

"Can I come in?"

"Yes, sure. The place is kind of messy. I haven't finished unpacking."

As Joe strolled past me, I held myself stiffly. That didn't keep my eyes from straying wistfully to the back of his head. Our separation didn't appear to be doing him any harm.

Seeing him made me feel resentful, even though in a lot of ways the breakup was as much my doing as his. After the assault I was impossible to live with—touchy, depressed, paranoid. Long after my bruises and cuts healed, the wound to my psyche stayed raw.

"Nice little place," he said, glancing around. "I can

see you could use some help. Is there something you'd like me to lift?"

Opportunists are survivors. "Well, in exchange for a cold beer, you could put the TV and VCR back into that cabinet."

He shot me his quick, glinting smile. "Deal."

When I returned with the beer, Joe was on his knees threading wires through the back of my entertainment center. "I'm kind of surprised you've decided to move so close to my place on Warren."

Joe owns two houses, a three-story yellow brick Victorian across from Federal Hill and a big spread in the Greenspring Valley. Monday through Friday he lives in the city close to his office. Weekends he usually heads for the county.

His valley property is gorgeous, with horses pastured in meadows surrounded by white rail fences. While I lived with him he gave me carte blanche to decorate both his homes. Now he has them all to himself again.

"I like Federal Hill, always have. I think it's big enough for both of us."

"I didn't mean it wasn't, Sally. I'm just a little concerned with you living here all alone."

"Well, don't worry your head. Besides, I'm not living alone. I've got protection." I pointed at Mopsy, who was listening with her head cocked.

Joe followed the direction of my glance and laughed. "A dog? Hairy, too. Where'd you pick it up?"

While I explained, he held out his hand. Females respond to Joe like popcorn in a microwave. Mopsy came waddling over, tail thumping. He petted her and she licked his fingers as if they were coated with Alpo.

"How'd you know where to find me?" I asked.

He peered up at me and then gave Mopsy a final

pat before rising smoothly to his feet. "Duke Spikowski told me."

"Duke? You mean you looked him up?"

Joe shook his head. "He stopped in at my office to see me. Wanted to let me know your new place had been broken into."

"Why'd he do that?"

"Sally, for Chrissake, we were engaged to be married. Maybe he thought I'd care!"

"Do you?"

We stood looking at each other, a million unspoken thoughts hanging between us. Joe groaned and laid his right hand on my shoulder. The heat of it burned through the fabric of my shirt and I felt the old familiar ache in my gut and in my groin. It had been months since I'd had sex, or wanted it. Suddenly having Joe standing so close let me know in no uncertain terms that I did.

"Of course I care, Sally." He moved his hand to my wrist and drew me toward him. "I care a lot. I always have, and I always will."

"Oh, Joe . . ." I resisted, but not as hard as I should have. Being with Joe had always made me feel safe, secure, and loved. Desperately, I wanted to feel that way again.

He searched my face. "Duke didn't look me up just to tell me about your break-in."

"What?"

"He was testing the water."

I didn't understand what Joe was talking about.

"Sally, he wanted to find out if we really were quits. Is there something going on between the two of you?"

At that, my eyes widened. "There's never been anything between Duke and me."

"Yeah, I figured that. Of the two brothers, Pete's always been your favorite."

That was true, but all I could think about now was Joe and how close he was standing to me. "Well, I've never dated either Duke or Peter, even before they were each married. I think of them as my brothers."

"Are you dating anyone?"

"I've been out a couple of times, just to prove to myself I could do it. Why the cross-examination? What do you care?"

"Oh, God, Sally—" Joe drew me to him and pressed his mouth down on mine. I started to respond and then caught myself. With all my being, I wanted to kiss him back. The dates I'd had since our separation had been disasters. And not because of the men I'd gone out with. Because of me. I just hadn't wanted to get started again with another man. I hadn't had the heart for it.

The breakup had been Joe's idea, not mine. I missed him and what we'd had together terribly. "Joe," I whispered, turning my face aside, "why are you doing this? What did you come here to talk to me about?"

At that, he stopped. Then he gave a big sigh. "You're right. I shouldn't be doing this. I need to tell you something."

"What's that?" I sensed there wasn't going to be any more kissing now, so I stepped back.

Joe looked slightly embarrassed. He jammed his hands in his pockets and paced to the window and then back. All the time, even when he turned to face me again, he didn't meet my eyes. "I guess this is going to sound pretty funny, but I came to tell you that I've been seeing a lot of Janet lately."

I just stood there frozen. Janet was his ex-wife. They'd divorced two years before Joe and I met. "I thought you and Janet couldn't stand each other."

"That's what I thought, too. But she's changed and so have I. Scott is going to graduate from high school this year. I've been feeling guilty about not seeing him as much as I should. After you and I split, I started going out there. One thing led to another. Sally, I think Janet and I are going to give it another try."

"Another try? You mean, like remarry?"

Joe shifted his stance. Finally, his eyes met mine. "Well, not right away, of course. But it's a possibility. I just thought the decent thing was to tell you before you found it out some other way."

"Decent!" I balled my hands into fists and struggled for breath. When I found it, I gasped out, "You come here uninvited, start trying to kiss me—Jesus Christ, Joe!" I grabbed the beer he'd set on the coffee table and threw it in his face.

All those sessions at his executive health club have given Joe quick reflexes. He yelped when the can struck his forehead and caught it before it could fall on the floor. Nevertheless, the beer splashed out. It wet his eyelashes and dripped down his cheeks.

"You son of a bitch!"

"Now, Sally—"

"Don't Sally me! Get the hell out of my house, ass-hole!" I yanked the door open and glared at him.

I was so steamed that at first I didn't notice his gaze had gone beyond me and he had a funny expression on his face. I turned and saw Duke Spikowski standing there on the stoop.

He, too, wore a funny expression. "I just thought I'd drop by to talk to you about your B and E," he said. "Guess I caught you at another bad moment. I'll try again tomorrow." He nodded at Joe and then turned and walked back out to his car. As he got in, he was whistling.

2

There I was, *alone* in my living room cursing Joe and pacing like a windup toy. Mopsy whimpered and scratched at the door I'd just slammed.

"So, what's your problem? Don't tell me you're sticking up for that jerk! Listen, he didn't walk out in your time of need. He didn't sweet-talk you and then go back to his wife when things got rough."

I glared at Mopsy, but she only scratched at the door again. By that time I'd figured out her problem. I sighed. "Okay, okay. I gotcha. Time to water the grass."

Outside, Mopsy finished up and looked at me inquiringly. I glanced back at the house and shook my head. My insides were too scrambled over what had just happened with Joe to want to coop myself up. I needed exercise. "How about we take a little walk," I told her. "Get some fresh air."

You might wonder what a woman traumatized by a near rape was doing strolling around a city at night. Well, the irony is that even though I spend my working life in all the worst city neighborhoods, I was attacked while jogging in the early morning on a tree-lined country road about a mile from Joe's Greenspring Valley paradise. Truth is, now I actually feel safer on a city street than I ever will in the country again.

As Mopsy tugged me along, I tried not to think about Joe. Instead, I reflected on how unhealthy the life I lead is. Five days a week I'm either downing gallons of coffee at meetings in stuffy office buildings, or waiting to testify in courtrooms, or riding around in a car trying to track down delinquent parents, overworked teachers, service officers, or cops.

Lunch is usually what I can grab at a McDonald's and cram down my throat while I steer one-handed. I'm medium height with a wiry build and have always been skinny and strong. But I'm never going to see twenty-nine again. Pretty soon my decadent ways will catch up with me.

Gradually, I got into the rhythm of strolling with Mopsy. While she sniffed trees and cracks in the narrow sidewalk, I relaxed some and took pleasure in the cool night breeze riffling my hair. I kept an eye out for potential muggers, but saw only couples strolling arm in arm and other people walking dogs.

Still not wanting to think about Joe and his announcement, I started speculating about the burglary ring Duke had mentioned. Even now Jamal and his girlfriend might be picking out their next mark. That set me to musing. I found myself sizing up each townhouse Mopsy and I passed. How close were the windows to the ground? Did they have grates or closed shutters? Any signs of a burglar alarm? Was the place well enough kept to suggest that it might have good stuff inside? What kind of car was parked at the curb?

Now, there was an easy gauge, I thought. BMWs,

Mercedeses, and top-of-the-line Japanese sedans caught my eye and I started taking special note of the houses they were parked closest to. But if Jamal and company used that yardstick, why had they burgled my place when I drove an aging Mustang? Oh, yes, my neighbor had a new Camry and he'd been parked practically at my door last night.

Pleased at my powers of deduction, I gave a satisfied chuckle that made Mopsy turn around and look at me again. We'd walked several blocks. Without consciously intending to, I'd directed my steps to the high-rent district at the top of Federal Hill where not so long ago I'd lived during the week with Joe. Big old Victorian brick townhouses gazed serenely out over the park and the harbor. Below the end of the street where I stood, the water from the bay wound like a skein of shiny black silk. Lights on the streets and on the boats moving back and forth caged it in a changeable web of diamond glitter.

Once, twice, I filled my lungs. I felt bad about the way I'd yelled at Joe. A scene like that could only make the pain of our parting worse. In fact, maybe I should work at making things better. Maybe I should tap on Joe's door and wish him well. Why say good-bye forever on such a sour note?

Five minutes later I stood on the sidewalk outside Joe's house and stared up at his living-room window. It was unshuttered and brightly lit. Framed against it, I saw Joe and another man. I recognized Joe's guest from his shock of reddish hair and slump-shouldered posture. He was Frank Leftwich, an accountant who worked for C&G under Joe and who was also a volunteer at the aquarium. This must not be my ex's night for tranquillity. He and Frank appeared to be having an argument, or at least a heated discussion.

Frank was a fussy bachelor. It was hard to imagine him getting up the nerve to argue with anybody. And indeed, he looked even more upset than Joe. He hung his head like a frightened kindergartner tattling to the teacher about a rough playmate and not getting a very good reception.

What is it about watching people on the other side of a lighted window? Strangers are interesting, but ex-lovers are truly fascinating. Since he had company, I'd abandoned any thought of tapping on Joe's door. Yet I must have stood there staring at him for a good five minutes. Then Joe and Frank moved away.

I gave myself a shake. "C'mon," I told the patiently waiting Mopsy. "This is not the time for a final reconciliation scene with the ex-love of my life."

Several times during the next few days I thought about calling Joe and burying the hatchet. Yet I didn't. That Sunday night I sat curled on my couch in my bathrobe and slippers, going over case files, listening to the eleven o'clock news. A news item made me jerk my head around and gape at the screen.

"Tragedy here in Baltimore tonight. A prominent C&G executive plunged to his death from the Chase Street Bridge."

It was Joe.

After work the next day, still in shock over Joe's death, I stopped off at Mama Spikowski's. In the living room I found her younger son, Peter-the-candidate, meeting with half a dozen eager campaign workers. After I'd given Pete a weak high sign and he'd waved back distractedly, I tiptoed past and closed the door between the kitchen and living room.

"Sally, doll, whatcha' been up to?"

"Nothing much." After pecking Mama on the cheek, I dropped my briefcase on the floor and perched atop a creaky red-painted stool. Dumbly, I sat breathing in the fragrance of canned peaches and fresh bread.

Mama, who likes to bake and never gives calories or cholesterol a thought, was sprinking brown sugar and chopped nuts over a thick slab of dough slathered with butter. Maybe I'd better explain that her real name isn't Mama. It's Pat. But I've never heard anybody call her that.

She's a big woman, built like a pear on stilts, and imposing. The neon knit tops she wears upholster an impressive pair of canteloupe breasts. Her marshmallow face, with its kohl-rimmed blue eyes, is marvelously expressive. Atop it, she sports a pile of bottle-blond hair.

Back in the sixties Baltimore was famous for its beehive hairdos. Mama's coiffure isn't exactly a beehive, but it is elaborate, a varnished cornucopia of complicated curls and waves that testify to her skill at her calling. She operates a beauty shop down on Eastern Avenue called The HairStop.

Mama is my foster mother. Vivian Dunphy, my birth mother, is an alcoholic. I lived with her until I was twelve. Well, to oversimplify a complicated story, I ran away. When I was caught, I got turned over to the Spikowskis, and I've been on the straight and narrow ever since.

"Sally, you look like the world's been beating up on you," Mama said as she clomped to the refrigerator. "Still pining over Mr. Fancypants?"

"Joe? I guess you haven't heard."

"Heard what?"

"He committed suicide last night." Even as I said the words, I still couldn't believe them. Joe, dead? It couldn't be possible.

Mama stopped what she was doing and stared at me. "I didn't know. Are you sure about this?"

"It was on last night's news. I called the police right away and they confirmed it."

"They didn't want you to identify the body or anything?"

"His ex-wife's already done that."

Mama rubbed her chin. "I'm surprised Duke didn't tell me. He was out of town yesterday. That must be the reason." She looked at me hard, that searchlight look she used to give me when I was a kid coming home from school after something rotten happened. "Are you all right?"

I nodded. "Guess it hasn't really hit me yet. I just feel sort of numb."

"You don't sound so good. Disjointed, like. You don't look too hot, either. When you first came in, I thought maybe you had a bug, you're so pale."

I'd been sitting there like a lump. Now I started to wring my hands. "Oh, Mama, I don't know what to do. Joe's dead and I wouldn't even have known if I hadn't heard it on the news. It's so crazy."

Tears leaked down my cheeks. I took a swipe at them and then hugged myself and shivered.

"Sally, you poor baby." Mama wrapped her arms around me and let me cry into her soft, floury-smelling bosom. While I sobbed and hiccupped, she stroked my hair.

"I can't believe he did it," I kept saying. "I just can't believe he killed himself."

When I finally let up some, Mama said, "You aren't blaming yourself, are you, Sally?"

"I don't know." I lifted my head and leaned away. Mama got a box of tissue from the top of the refrigerator and handed it to me.

"What do you mean, you don't know?"

"Mama, the last time I saw Joe we had a terrible fight. I felt bad about it afterward. I was going to call him and try and set things right. But I never did."

Mama rolled her eyes. "For God's sake, Sally, I don't believe what I'm hearing. You honestly think Joe Winder committed suicide because you had a fight with him?"

"No." I blew my nose. "I just can't believe Joe would commit suicide over anything. He wasn't the type to kill himself at all. I certainly can't picture him taking a dive onto the Jones Falls Expressway. I mean, Joe dressed in five-hundred-dollar suits. He was vain about his appearance and meticulously neat. It sounds awful to say it, but he wouldn't want to risk getting messed up."

Mama peered at me. "What do you know about what a man will do when he's feeling low? From all I know of men, they're an unpredictable breed. He could have had a million troubles in his life that he never told you about."

She sighed and patted my shoulder. "Speaking of trouble, what about this break-in I hear you had?"

I didn't want to talk about Joe anymore, either. My eyes still felt hot and scratchy, but at least they were dry now. I sat on the edge of the stool tearing my tissue into tiny shreds. "No big deal. Just a couple of kids looking to rip off a VCR."

"Kids today." She shook her head with such vigor her fleshy cheeks bobbed. "When I think how you've devoted your life to helping them. And this is how you get paid back!"

"Mama, I'm not looking to get paid back. Besides, nothing was stolen."

Mama kept on shaking her head. "Tell me, Sally,

what is it with you? I mean, here you are—young, beautiful, educated, and with a good job. Yet you always seem to wind up with guys who give you trouble. I thought with Joe things were going to work out, but—"

"Yeah, I must put out the wrong brand of pheromones."

"What's that, some kind of perfume?"

Idiotically, I started to laugh. "You might say that."

When I left Mama's kitchen, Pete was just doling out good-byes to the last of his campaign workers. All the Spikowskis are big people. Pete's six foot four dwarfed the row house's tiny living room.

"Staying for dinner?" he asked as I paused by the open door.

I shook my head. "Not tonight. Think I'll mosey on down to Greektown and get myself a feta cheese salad."

"Mind if I join you?"

"Of course I don't mind. I'd love it."

I really meant that. If Pete Spikowski were my flesh-and-blood brother, I couldn't love him more. I've adored him from the moment I first saw him hooking basketball shots in the family's tiny backyard. At the time I was a twelve-year-old misfit and he was a seventeen-year-old high school football hero. Peter can't have liked his parents taking on a problem waif like me. Yet he was never anything but the ideal big brother.

"Tell you what," he said after he let Mama know where we were headed. "You drive."

"Sure, then afterward I'll drop you off at your car."

"No. After dinner I'll go to my campaign headquarters.

It's only a couple blocks from Ikaros. We are going to
Ikaros, aren't we?"

"Of course. Where else?"

When we walked outside we bumped into Duke,
who'd just pulled up. He got out of his car and pushed
open the rusted little gate that didn't do much of a job
protecting the postage-stamp yard. Watching us come
down the steps, he stood with his hands on his hips.
"Well, well," he drawled, "if it isn't my two favorite
Balti-morons. You two going somewhere special?"

"Dinner at Ikaros," Pete answered cheerfully. "Want
to join us?"

"Maybe I might." Duke looked from my face to his
brother's and then back at me. Something in his
expression told me he knew about Joe. I looked away.
Maybe from that he guessed I didn't want to talk
about it. He asked, "Whose car?"

"Sally's the designated driver."

"That okay with you?" I queried.

"I don't know. That neon heap of yours doesn't look
safe to me."

We had started down the sidewalk together. "Just
because it's old and I had it painted red doesn't mean
it's unreliable."

"Repainted red cars with white stuff sticking up out
of torn upholstery make me nervous."

Pete guffawed. "C'mon, big brother. Remember
that '58 hearse you used to cruise around in during
your glory days?"

"I remember it well."

I looked from one Spikowski to the other. It was
something to see them together. Duke is three years
older than Pete and looks more. Yet you couldn't mistake that they're brothers. Both are tall and heavily
muscled, with short, tight blond curls that have only

lately begun to darken from coin gold to the color of oak leaves in autumn. In other ways they're a complete contrast. Pete has his hands manicured and wears pinstripe suits. Duke cuts his nails with kitchen scissors and, for all anyone would know, dresses himself blindfolded.

I had just unlocked the passenger side when Duke's beeper went off. He crossed the street and used his car phone. When he came back, he looked rueful. "Scratch dinner for me, I'm afraid. Duty calls." He gave me a quick, hard look. "Talk to you later, Sally. Okay?"

"Okay, sure."

Inside my Mustang, Pete leaned back against the headrest. He laced his fingers together, extended his long arms, and stretched until I heard his shoulder joints crack. "Too bad about Duke, but that's what he gets for being a cop. What did he want to talk to you about?"

I opened my mouth to tell Pete about Joe, then closed it. I didn't feel up to talking about it again yet. "Tell you later."

Pete and I cruised down Eastern, the avenue that strings together Little Italy with Greektown and the Polish community in Dundalk. It was a warm night in May and my air-conditioning system had long ago given up the ghost. Through the open windows we breathed the exhaust from buses, jalopies, pickup trucks, and restaurant-bound suburban sedans.

Mixed with the acrid fumes came the punctuation of horns and tire squeals and the chatter of voices from the street. I caught whiffs of fried food and hot tar. Now and then my gaze was distracted by a particularly garish or provocative storefront.

"I see Sister Olella is still reading palms. How long has she been on that corner?"

"Ever since I can remember," Pete said. "Ever go to her?"

"No. You?"

"Once. Just before I married Joyce. I asked her if I was doing the right thing."

A car pulled out from a meter a block from the restaurant and I darted in.

"You've always had good parking karma," Pete commented.

"Yeah, but there are things I'd trade it for. What did Sister Olella say?"

"She said it was a serious step. I'd be wise to give it some more thought." While I pulled the key out of the ignition, he changed the subject. "I heard you bought a house."

"Yeah. Listen, how about coming to see my new place? I have a rooftop deck. Bring Joyce and the kids. I'll barbecue steaks and we'll eat outside."

He grimaced. "Sounds nice, but you know how Joyce is."

I knew, all right. Peter's wife is a pretty redhead he met and married right out of college. She and their fresh-faced, fair-haired, eight- and ten-year-old boys live in a five-bedroom colonial-style demimansion in Columbia. In theory, Peter lives there, too. But not in fact.

From a socoiologist's point of view, I guess, it's an interesting phenomenon. Peter is definitely the Spikowski son who made good. I mean, I'm sure Duke draws a decent salary working as a burglary detective for BPD, but his marriage to a Korean girl he met in the service didn't last. He has no children and is kind of a reclusive curmudgeon when he's not out chasing criminals.

Peter, on the other hand, is a partner in a big-time law firm in Baltimore where he earns the kind of money the other members of his family hardly know exists. When he married Joyce and moved out of the city and into sqeaky clean Columbia to raise his kids, I figured he'd joined all the other well-heeled suburbanites and we'd lost him.

Not so. Never underestimate the depth and tenacity of the root system here in Dundalk. The place isn't much to look at. Congested streets. Storefronts that need a fresh coat of paint. Down-at-heels Formstone row houses that march the streets, glued at the hip like multiple pairs of siamese octoplets.

Still, generation after generation of immigrant families have lived in each other's pockets here. The women have worked together in the canneries, telling each other their woes while they shelled peas and peeled tomatoes. Shoulder to shoulder, the men have endured the blast furnaces at Bethlehem Steel. They go to the same churches, belong to the same bowling leagues, hang out in the same bars and beauty shops, and know each other's business as well as they know their own.

I guess, for someone brought up in that kind of community, the suburbs are a sterile environment. Peter kept coming back to the old neighborhood and trying to bring Joyce and the boys with him. Maybe the kids in their younger days would have accepted it. But Joyce thought of Baltimore as Gotham City. She looked down her nose at the Spikowskis' homy townhouse with its plastic-covered couch and painted statues of the Virgin. On the street she kept peering over her shoulder expecting to be attacked by a crazed drug dealer driving by with an Uzi slung through the window.

Eventually Peter bought a little house close to his parents' place, using the excuse that when he had to work late in the city he wanted a place to stay. Now he spends more time in that cramped little row house than he does in his big fancy bogus colonial. The latest is that he's planning to run for city council.

"Campaign headquarters, poll watchers, the whole bit—hey, you're really serious about this getting-elected thing, aren't you?" We'd just been seated at a corner table. I'd ordered a Greek salad and lemon soup. Peter had gone for the moussaka.

He widened his big blue eyes at me. "Damn right! Do you have any idea how much time and money I've already invested in this thing? Sally, I started putting out feelers last year when Ralph Lowecki died."

I nodded. "Yeah, while Lowecki was around, no other candidate had a chance. He's had the council seat in this district sewed up for decades. But now that he's gone—"

Peter nodded. "Since he died, I've gone to more receptions than Miss America. Don't tell me you haven't noticed."

"Of course I've noticed, and I'll do anything I can to help. But I have to wonder about your motives. I mean, it's not as if you need the job. And aren't you jeopardizing your position at the firm?"

Peter frowned down at the martini the waiter had just set in front of him. "You sound like Joyce."

I toyed with my fork. "I gather she's not too thrilled at your plunge into politics?"

"She hates it. It's driven another wedge between us. Lately, we barely speak."

"Oh, Peter, then why . . ."

He went dull red. "I'll tell you why. Somebody has to, somebody who really cares about this city, who has enough education to know the score, and who can dredge up some honesty and integrity. These days, by the way, it's the last two that are in shortest supply."

"You don't think the people we've got on the council now are honest?" I was fascinated by the passion he'd summoned.

Peter slammed his drink down. "Oh, Sally, I think a lot of them are good people and mean well. But it kills me when I see what's going on out there—kids dealing drugs because they can't find a job, the crime, the hopelessness. Seems like every day a new drug rehab program gets cut, or mental institutions lose funding and release more vagrants onto our streets. Baltimore needs more leaders who can swim with the sharks."

I laughed. "You mean without being eaten by them or turning into them?"

"Down at Juvenile Services you deal with the scum of the earth, right?"

"Thieves, pimps, child molesters. You might say that."

"Okay, so you probably think that because my clients and associates are high-priced lawyers, stockbrokers, CEOs and the like, I hobnob with a better class of people. Well, hon, let me tell you something." He took a swipe at his brow. "Something that I never would have believed when I first collected my law degree but that I've finally had to recognize. There's no real difference between the moral mind set of most of the lily-white guys in the pinstriped suits and the drug dealers doing business around Pimlico."

"Oh, Peter, c'mon."

"I'm telling you, it's true. They're all out for number one, see, and they don't give a damn for anything or anybody else. Let the world go to hell. So long as I've got mine, that's all that matters."

I stared across the table at him, thinking I'd never seen him so wound up, so positively aflame with righteous indignation. St. George charging the dragon must have looked the way Pete did now. "Well, you're not like that."

"No, I'm not. And I'm not going to be. Though I have to admit, a couple of times I've felt myself come close."

"How do you mean?"

"Oh, just deals I found myself involved in, things I've seen." He looked embarrassed. "Nothing illegal," he said hastily, "just stuff that made me feel slimy. I didn't like that feeling. I like the way I feel about what I'm doing now a lot better."

The waiter appeared at our table carrying our food. As he set our dishes down in front of us, I mused that poor Joyce didn't stand a chance of talking Pete out of his self-appointed mission. I knew his downtown law firm dealt with some pretty high-powered business types—people who wielded influence not only in Baltimore but in D.C. and all over the world. It shouldn't come as any surprise that some weren't exactly upstanding characters. That made me think of Joe. When I told Peter that Joe had committed suicide he stared at me.

"Joe Winder? Guy like that jumping off a bridge? I can hardly believe it."

"Me, neither."

"Sally, I'm sorry. I know how crazy you were about him."

That seemed to open some kind of floodgate. I started talking about my feelings, about the stuff that led to Joe and me calling it quits and about our last scene together.

Peter listened and chewed. When I finished spilling my guts, he shook his head. "It's a mystery to me. From what I know of the man, he had everything to live for. Did he leave a note?"

"Yes, but the police wouldn't tell me what it said. You don't think his suicide could have had anything to do with me, do you?"

"Come on, Sally. You're a great gal and all, but Joe Winder could never be more hung up on a woman than he was on himself. It'll be interesting to see who moves into his spot at C and G. That's a power-broker position. Whether I get elected to the council or go back to my firm, I'll probably find myself dealing with Winder's replacement." He gazed down at his plate. "Ain't life strange."

"Very strange," I agreed. "Maybe too damn strange."

After I dropped Peter off, I drove back to my place. I locked the car and then stood under a streetlight weighing my keys in the palm of my hand and gazing at the mellow brick facade of my tiny Federal-style townhouse. I was thinking about Jamal and Joe.

I told myself that the two incidents were totally unrelated. It was pure coincidence that two such things had happened within less than a week of each other. I do believe in coincidence, but I also believe in fate. Sometimes your life takes a turn into a dark alley and you get the feeling that you might not come out the other side in the same shape you went in. I knew that had happened to me. I could feel that metaphorical dark alley pressing in on me.

It was after nine and I had another long day tomorrow. But Mopsy needed her walk and, once again, so did I. This time I strolled her across Key Highway to the harbor.

The night was still warm, with only a light breeze coming off the shiny black skin of the water. As I cut past the Science Center the deserted merry-go-round still churned out music. It was in the midst of a Stephen Foster medley. "Swanee" wheezed mournfully out over the marina on the other side of the carousel's striped canopy.

One of the charms of the harbor is that on warm summer nights people linger in the cafés that line its twin pavilions. Even without Mopsy dragging at the leash two yards ahead of me and wagging her tail like an overwound metronome, I'd have felt safe walking without a male escort.

Leisurely, I strolled, sniffing the gamy fragrance of the breeze from the bay, listening in on snatches of conversation as people passed me by. I checked out the fashion statements. A gorgeous black couple with perfect posture glided past, he in peacock blue silk pants and shirt, she in a silk ensemble tie-dyed in shades of purple, yellow, orange and parrot green. Three teenage girls on Rollerblades caromed by and made Mopsy bark in fear and wonder.

A game had just finished at the stadium and the harbor was full of fans. I glanced to where the stadium's vapor lights haloed the sky and thought of Joe. He'd really been looking forward to the season this year.

Which set me thinking of what Pete had said about the guys in the pinstriped suits, the guys who live to grab power and ride around in Mercedes Benzes. Joe had been like that and he'd loved every minute of it. How could such a man throw himself off a bridge?

As I often do when I walk this way, I headed for the aquarium. Since Joe and I split, I'd stopped volunteering at the aquarium. It's still one of my favorite places, though, particularly the seal pool. The seals were all hauled out on rocks. They preened themselves, arching their fat, sleek bodies seductively. Their eyes opened and closed dreamily.

Seal scent started Mopsy growling low in her

throat. I bent over to shush her. Through the slats of the fence I saw the doors to the members' entrance slide open. A man stepped out. He wore the royal blue T-shirt and khaki slacks of an aquarium volunteer. I recognized Frank.

He hurried past without seeing me, and I followed him with my eyes. Then, on impulse, I started to stroll after him, dragging a reluctant Mopsy. I wanted to ask him what he'd been arguing with Joe about, but he was walking much faster than I. I would have lost him, but as he rounded the corner of the promenade and headed toward the World Trade Center, another, taller, man stepped out of the shadows and stopped him. He was thin and dark with a hawk-nosed profile.

I stopped, too, angling myself behind the ship moored nearby. At first, as I watched their conversation, I was merely curious. Who was Frank talking to and why? There was no reason to connect this conversation with the one I'd seen Frank having with Joe. Yet, gradually, a sense of danger overcame me. My stomach tightened and my knees began to tremble. Mopsy must have picked it up from me because, after shooting me a troubled look, a low growl rumbled at the back of her throat again.

The stranger had clamped his hand over Frank's shoulder. Something in Frank's posture expressed the same irrational terror that I was feeling. He broke away from his assailant's grasp and started to run out toward Pratt Street. The stranger didn't follow. He stood watching. Then, abruptly, he turned and looked directly at me.

3

The next morning I called Volunteer Services at the National Aquarium and told them I'd like to start coming in again on weekends. Why? I wasn't sure why.

Work that day was tough. In the morning I had two home visitations with welfare mothers living in the public housing on East Pratt. One was fourteen, the other a year older. They were both having the kinds of sad problems that children trying to raise children are prone to.

As I approached the building I spotted a ten-year-old riding a bike one-handed through oncoming truck traffic. In his other arm he clutched an infant with a bottle. He was one of the windshield-wiper kids I sometimes give quarters to when I get stopped at this intersection—a frequent occurrence in my line of work.

"Tyrone," I called out, pulling over and sticking my head out to eyeball him with proper severity. "What are you doing out of school and whose baby is that?"

Tyrone slowed by dragging his Reeboks on the curb so hard I expected to see smoke. He gave me a worried look, not sure whether to speak to me or pedal on past. Then, recognizing me, he flashed a sweet smile. Under his tight curls, sweat glistened. "Hello, Miss Dunphy, how you doing?"

"I'm doing fine. It's you I'm worried about. Why aren't you in school?"

"I got to take care of my baby sister. This is Keesha." He juggled the baby in the crook of his arm. She was a fat, dark-eyed beauty. Above her bottle, she gazed at me solemnly. Clearly, the cars, semis, and oil tankers honking their horns as they roared past at the change of the light bothered her not a bit.

"Tyrone, do you realize how dangerous it is to ride in a street like this with her? I mean, this is a major truck route."

His brows knitted. "My mother, she got things to do, so I gotta take care of Keesha."

"And miss school? How often does that happen?"

He put his chin down like a turtle withdrawing into its shell. "Keesha and me, we get bored shut up alone in the apartment all day. We going down to the harbor to play on the slides."

"How about letting me give you a ride so you'll get there in one piece?"

"No, thanks. We be fine. I ride this way just about every day."

Before I could react to that charming piece of information, Tyrone was already pedaling off in the opposite direction, his skinny calves pumping beneath his ragged cutoffs. As he wove through traffic, I stared after him in frustration.

Watching him take on the rushing cars while he clutched that baby and tried his best to keep her safe,

I thought he made a fine visual metaphor for all the kids I dealt with. The odds were stacked against them so bad it made you want to weep. Yet, even with the worst ones, there was always something to like, something to admire, something that made you want to pull for them and that broke your heart when they didn't make it. Tyrone, I'll keep my fingers crossed for you and Keesha, I thought as I went on my way.

Later that afternoon, I was dragging. So I can't really say I was thrilled to find Duke Spikowski's unmarked Cavalier lining the curb in front of my townhouse.

"That's my space you're hogging," I pointed out after I took two passes to pull into a tight spot across the street.

"Sorry." As he got out and followed me in, he didn't sound sorry. He was wearing the suit. In the dying afternoon light his curls gleamed like old gold and his green eyes studied me with hidden humor. Picture a six-foot-two-inch Spencer Tracy always silently laughing at you and you get the idea. "You can take it back after I leave," he said.

I jammed my key in the lock. "After you leave I'll be too tired to take anything."

"Hey, don't overwhelm me with girlish charm. Bad day?"

"Bad life. A kid I've been working with and had high hopes for just got sent to Hickey for vandalizing a library." I tossed my briefcase on the couch and stalked through the living room to the kitchen. Duke's leather shoes creaked as he followed. "Then there's Norman."

"Norman?"

Feature this. A seventeen-year-old with a personality disorder that has him trying to get attention from his parents any way he can. His folks can't stand the sight of him, have institutionalized him, so we set up an evaluation meeting with them. "Can I go home, can I, can I?" he begs. Mom and Dad shake their heads. "The last time you were home, son, you wrecked the car, smashed in all the windows and lopped off the heads of all mom's favorite roses." "Well, nobody's perfect," the kid argues.

I knocked back the lock of hair that always wants to dangle over my right eye. "I mean, if it weren't so tragic I'd be laughing. Want a beer?"

"No, I'm on duty."

I already had my head in the refrigerator, painfully aware that I'd been babbling about problems at work because I didn't want to talk about Joe. "Mind if I have one?"

"Why should I mind? It's your place. Make yourself comfortable."

Back out in the living room, I flopped on the couch next to my briefcase and sipped at my Coors. "I'm sorry, Duke. I really have had a bad day. That doesn't give me a license to take it out on you."

He dropped onto the chair opposite and cradled his big hands between his knees. "If you come home this irritable from that job of yours every day, I can see why you and Joe split."

Joe, the sound of his name was like having a nail dug into raw flesh. "Joe and I didn't split up over my job."

"Oh? I heard he was trying to get you to quit."

"He was and I refused. But that's not what broke us up." All of a sudden, I started to cry. Just like that. No preliminaries. "God, I have to stop doing this," I muttered as I set the beer down and took a useless swipe at my eyes.

Duke offered me his handkerchief. "Tough luck about what happened to Joe. You're in no shape to go to work at all. You should stay home for a few days, take it easy."

"Yeah, sure. Tell it to my mortgage company." I blew my nose. "I just can't believe Joe would commit suicide. There was no reason."

"He'd lost you."

"He didn't lose me. He dropped me the way you would a can of tomato soup with a cockroach doing the breaststroke on top. Are the police certain it was suicide?"

"You mean, did someone push him off that bridge?" Duke shrugged. "It's not my department, but far as I know, there was no sign of foul play. I'll check around, if you want."

"Yes, I do want. I'd appreciate it. Duke, what did his note say?"

"I can't give you the exact wording. Something to the effect that he couldn't go on."

"There was no mention of me?"

"No." Duke frowned.

I felt a second or two of incredible relief. Then other questions crowded it out. "What did the note look like? Where was it found? Was it scribbled in haste, or did it look as if he'd written it carefully?"

"The investigating officer found it in Joe's pocket. It was typed on C and G stationery."

"Typed! Joe wouldn't type a suicide note."

"He was an executive. They use their computers and laser printers for everything."

"Not a suicide note."

"O'Dell, he's the man in charge of the case, found the note in a file on Joe's office computer." Duke was obviously registering the shock and disbelief on my face. "Sally, don't start making complications for yourself."

"What do you mean?"

"Joe is gone now. Don't start getting all hung up about how he died and why he died. I realize you cared for the guy. The fact is, he's dead and you're not. See what I mean?"

"Maybe." I stared at Duke coldly.

My frigid glare didn't faze him. "I suppose you know that his funeral is tomorrow?"

"Yes. I saw it in the paper. Is that what you came here to tell me?"

"One reason."

"So, to what else do I owe this pleasure?"

I expected him to start asking me about my burglary. Instead, he gazed at a print I'd hung above the couch. "I'm glad you think my dropping in on you in your new place is a pleasure. We don't see much of each other."

"No, though we've been bumping noses quite a bit the last couple of days."

"Last night at Mama's was pure coincidence. I'm sorry I couldn't join you and Pete for dinner, by the way."

"So were we."

"Yeah? You didn't exactly look depressed when you drove off together. You two do that sort of thing a lot?"

"Do what? Go out to dinner together? Hardly ever. Last night we just happened to feel in the mood."

"Pete's a married man, Sally. He might not act like it a lot of the time, but he's a married man with kids."

Now I really stared at Duke. "Pete's my brother, for crying out loud."

"Pete's not your brother and neither am I." The statement hung between us like a spider that had just dropped from the ceiling. He cleared his throat. "Now let me ask you another question. Any possibility this break-in you had could be connected in some way with your other trouble?"

I picked up my beer and took a careful sip. "If you're asking about the assault, no. It was totally unconnected. Totally."

"Okay." He held up a palm. "I guess I'm just worried about you. Call it misguided brotherly concern, if that makes you happier."

He reached into his pocket and took out a crumpled notebook and a tired-looking ballpoint. "Run the events of the night of your break-in past me, will you?"

Curtly, I described my encounter with Jamal and company. When I finished, Duke studied his notes. "This Jamal was nobody you know?"

"No."

"He couldn't be a kid you've worked with or the brother of a kid you've worked with?"

"I can't be sure who he's related to, but I don't know him."

"And the girl?"

Again, I shook my head. "If I'd ever seen her before, I'd remember."

"Unusual?"

"There was just something about her. Her face haunts me."

"I'd like you to stop by and look through our family albums."

"Sure. Glad to." I hated the very thought of thumbing through mug shots of kids.

Duke tucked his notebook into his suit-coat pocket. "Like I mentioned before, there's a ring operating in this area. Yours isn't the first house to get ripped off. However, you're the first to have actually seen the burglars. Always before they've picked places where the owner was out of town."

"How do you know it's the same robbers?"

"Because they always come through a first-floor window on Sunday night and snatch the same things. VCRs, TVs, computers if they happen to be lightweight. No Oriental rugs or art objects have been stolen. Apparently the little munchkins don't realize those are valuable. They do raid kitchens. One guy found three cans of Coke and a box of Snickers bars missing. I'm not surprised it's kids."

"Can you tell me what houses have already been hit?"

"Why do you want to know?"

"Oh, I have a theory." At his look, I added, "a kind of game I've been playing about what houses I'd pick to rob. One of the determiners is the make of car parked outside. If you'd tell me which addresses have actually been broken into, it would help me test out my theory."

Duke shrugged and reeled off a list of numbers. Not being the digit queen of the East Coast, I was able to memorize only three. "Maybe I shouldn't tell you this stuff," he said, stopping abruptly and scowling. "You're not going to try and do anything stupid, are you?"

"Stupid how?" I was beginning to resent his attitude. If Duke didn't think of me as his little sister, why was he treating me like Sandra Dee with a lobotomy? I'm an old movie buff. Recently, I'd caught *Gidget* in a late-night rerun.

"You're not going to try and catch these kids, are you?"

I laughed. "Duke, I'm not that dumb. Believe me, I never want to see those two again."

"Most likely you won't. I doubt they'd come back here."

"Why? Pickings too slim?"

Duke glanced around my sparsely furnished living room and smiled. "Your TV is the size of a postage stamp and your VCR is one of the cheaper models. That Chagall lithograph above your couch is worth something and so are the Aaron Sopher's on either side of the fireplace. Kids wouldn't know them from bubble-gum wrappers."

"You're very observant."

"That's what I'm trained to be. If a cop doesn't notice things, he's worthless and possibly dead."

"If those kids keep breaking into houses they could wind up dead, too. I didn't pull the trigger on my automatic, but if they'd done anything to scare me more, I might have."

Duke grimaced. "That's the risk our younger generation takes when they decide on a life of crime."

I gazed at him, thinking I shouldn't let his attitude make me angry. He had a dangerous job and a lot of responsibility. "Duke, tell me something. Why'd you join the BPD?"

"Not because I wanted to follow in my father's footsteps. I didn't see myself as a knight in blue, if that's what you're asking. When I got back from my second tour of duty in Korea I applied for a dozen jobs. The BPD was the first place that wanted me."

"I'm sure you could have found something else if you'd waited."

"I couldn't wait to get tossed out on the street. I had a wife I wanted to send for, and I needed to pay my rent."

"You could have lived at home until you could afford to send for Young Hee, for a while at least. You know Mama loves it when the family's all together under her roof."

He shook his head. "When the family's all together

it's more fun than being spritzed with honey and staked on an anthill. Not for me, Sally. I like my privacy."

"Any special reason for that?"

"Besides my being an unfriendly SOB?" Duke rose to his feet and stuck his hands in his pants pockets. "Tell you what, Sally. Someday I'll tell you my sad story, but only after you tell me yours. Is that a deal?"

"I don't know. I'm not big on true confessions."

"Neither am I. So let's leave it at that. Okay?"

"Sure. Okay."

The next afternoon I took off and went to Joe's funeral. After debating with myself about going at all, I sat in the back row. When it was over, I darted around a knot of people so I could leave without shaking the widow's hand. I mean, I knew my presence was not improving the day for his ex-wife and son. But I'd had to go. I still couldn't believe Joe was dead. I'd needed to see him buried.

Afterward, naturally enough, I felt a bit low. I got back at dusk, changed clothes, and snapped a leash on Mopsy. Our long walks were getting to be part of my routine. I stayed in Federal Hill, threading the streets systematically. Up Warren, down Hamburg, up Battery, down Church.

Mopsy ambled, stopping to sniff cracks and fire hydrants as if they'd recently been doused in doggie ambrosia. I studied the houses along my route, once again pretending to be a thief prospecting for a likely hit. I told myself I was just playing. But I've never been much good at playing. Sooner than I should, I always start taking things seriously.

I paused in front of each house that had already been burgled and studied it. All had been rehabbed and had a certain look. *Prosperous* was the appropriate adjective—the brick carefully scrubbed free of Formstone, brass carriage lights, a handsome knocker on the painted door. The swags at the windows were lined. Through the lighted cracks between drapery and shutters I caught glimpses of oil paintings, Chinese bric-a-brac, candlesticks. Potted geraniums sat on the stoops. And the cars parked in front were carefully maintained and cost $25,000 or more.

It didn't take me long to pick out others with the same look. By the time Mopsy and I had wended our way back home, I'd selected six likely candidates for robbery. Joe's place was one of them.

As I unlocked my front door, it occurred to me that if I were watching those houses, I'd be attracted to the ones that went several days without showing lights. Which made Joe's a promising prospect.

Now that he was dead, the place would probably sit empty for weeks. What would happen to the things inside it, I wondered. In particular, I worried about his saltwater tank. There were some gorgeous fish in it. They'd be okay for a while. Fish aren't like Mopsy. They don't need to be fed and exercised daily, but a saltwater tank does need regular care and adjustment.

I got through the rest of the week by working so hard that Friday night saw me almost caught up on my cases. Saturday I started in at the aquarium again. That afternoon my job was to stand in front of the open ocean display of a shark jaw. Whenever a likely-looking youngster walked by, I showed off the rotating rows of triangular teeth in the jaw and let him or her feel their razor-sharp edges. My impromptu nature lectures were all the more effective with live tiger sharks and brown sharks cruising past the Plexiglas window behind me.

When Frank Leftwich came down the ramp on his way to the stingray pool on the first floor, he did a nervous double take.

"Sally! When did you come back?"

"Today's my first day."

He rubbed his skinny hands together and looked down at his feet. "I guess you know what happened to Joe."

"I went to his funeral."

"Oh. Yes. Well, I had to miss it, I'm afraid. I'm sorry. I mean, I guess you must be feeling pretty upset."

"Sort of. That's why I asked to be down here with the sharks instead of up with the angelfish in the coral-reef tank. It's hard to walk past the coral reef without picturing Joe swimming around in it, giving the kids a show while he fed the fish."

Frank nodded. His eyes skittered to the sharks. "We sure do miss Joe at the office."

"I can't believe he'd kill himself," I blurted. "I just can't believe it. I mean, what reason could he have?"

"Yeah, well, we'll miss him," Frank repeated. Without another word, he hurried past.

Staring after him, I tightened my grip on the shark's jaw in my hand until the pain made me look down and see a spot of blood on the pad of my forefinger.

When I left the aquarium late that afternoon, I stopped off at Harborplace for a crab-cake sandwich. Back home, I killed the rest of the evening trying to put my house in order. By nightfall I felt as if I'd cleaned a hundred cupboards, stacked a thousand dishes and knocked down a million cardboard boxes.

Exhausted, I sat in my kitchen sipping coffee and telling myself not to think about Joe and a suicide that just wouldn't compute.

You've got an overactive imagination, Sally, I told

myself, and tried going to bed early. I wanted a
dreamless sleep and no trouble. I didn't get it. About
one o'clock I woke up from a nightmare featuring Joe
and those two kids. In my dream Jamal and Blondie
had been laid out on slabs next to Joe. Like him, they
were cold as ice, any future they might have dreamed
of blasted clean away by some angry householder
they'd made the mistake of robbing.

I jackknifed, blinked into the darkness, and ran a
hand through my tangled curls. My hair, which I'd had
cut short after I was assaulted, clung damply to my
sweaty forehead. The rest of my body felt chill with
anxious perspiration. I glanced at the clock, hating the
green numbers. They told me that in about half an
hour Jamal and company might be breaking into
someone's house and getting shot as in my vision and
that if I wanted to do something about it I had time.

What? I asked myself. What could I do? How am I
responsible for those two?

But already I was out of bed and searching for a
pair of black pants and a sweater to match. Mopsy,
who'd been sleeping on the bed with me, whined anxiously.

I stroked one of her floppy ears. "I'm not taking you
walking with me tonight, babe. I'll let you out into the
backyard. Okay?"

It wasn't okay and Mopsy made that very clear. I
ignored her angry barks. Outside, a cold wind whistled
down the street. Shivering, I considered going back for
my jacket. I also considered going back for the Ruger.

What I planned seemed harmless enough—to
check on all the houses I'd picked out just to make
sure nothing was actually happening at any of them.
But suppose I had the bad luck to find a robbery in
progress? What then?

Also, wandering the city alone at this time of night could be dangerous to my health all by itself. That didn't mean I wanted to carry a loaded gun in my belt like some sort of urban Calamity Jane. I left it behind.

This is dumb, Sally, I kept repeating in my head as I hurried down the street. The night was several shades darker than on my earlier evening walks. The sky was overcast, so no moon. You get used to the background noise in a city. Now the quiet felt unnatural—only the occasional car swish or truck rumble breaking the ominous silence. A bum clutching a bottle in a paper bag slept in a doorway on Light. He looked up and mumbled something incoherent when I hurried past.

I rounded the corner on Hamburg and began my circuit. All quiet at the first four houses. The fifth showed a light in a third-floor window that was probably a bathroom. Studying it, I decided it didn't mean anything more ominous than diarrhea. Heading up Warren to the last house, Joe's, I honestly didn't expect to see anything. Yet as I got within striking distance, a shiver prickled up my spine. Instinct drove me into the deeper shadows of the street, and I slowed so I could place my sneakered feet more quietly.

Joe's house was as dark as the rest. Yet I couldn't get rid of the feeling that something was wrong. A narrow arched passageway separated his place from the one next to it. Cursing myself for an idiot, I peered into it and then took cautious steps along its claustrophic concrete walk. It led to a small courtyard similar to the one I had, but much more elaborately landscaped. The moon slid out from behind the clouds long enough so I could make out the trellised deck and hot tub.

Like the front, the back of the house was dark and deserted. Probably, Joe's ex-wife wouldn't get around to dealing with it for several days yet. Janet came from a banking family, old Baltimore aristocracy. Her taste ran to antiques and original oils in gold-leaf frames. My tastes were eclectic and sometimes funky. I could imagine her walking around turning her nose up at the way I'd decorated. What would she do with the fish in Joe's saltwater tank? I wondered. Poor little guys must be getting pretty hungry by now.

My hand went to the pocket where I'd stuffed my keys and a pocket flash. The key to Joe's house was still on the ring. This might be my last chance to take a look around the place where we'd lived together, and to feed the fish. While this thought ran through my mind, I was already walking toward the back door. Before I even knew I'd made the decision, I had it unlocked and was climbing up the steps to the kitchen.

Inside, it was cool and stale. Already the place had the tomblike feeling of an abandoned residence. I felt guilty enough about being there that I didn't flick the light switch in the kitchen. Anyhow, I knew the house so well that I could have found the floating Victorian staircase in the hall blindfolded.

It was a beauty, curving in a tight spiral to the third floor with a tented skylight at the top. As I stood at the foot and looked up, I could see the moon and the ambient light from the streetlamps. If the curtains aren't drawn, it doesn't get all that dark in a city house at night. That's why I didn't notice the thread of artificial light coming from beneath Joe's study door until I was standing on the second-floor landing.

For several seconds I heard nothing above the piledriver thud of my heart and the roar of my breathing. My skin prickled. If I'd been a porcupine, my needles would have been erect and ready to fire.

The only intelligent thing to do, of course, was to

get out before whoever it was noticed me. As I took a cautious step back, I heard papers rustling, drawers shutting.

If it was Jamal and Blondie, why weren't they downstairs carting away VCRs and raiding the refrigerator, I wondered. Maybe they knew the house was empty, so they were taking their time and going through it room by room. And maybe whoever was in there didn't happen to be those two misguided children. Who, then? Janet? The last thing I wanted was a meeting with her.

I put a foot on the top stair and shifted my weight. The tread, which had been silent as cat paws on velvet on the way up, creaked like a rusty violin string. I flattened myself against the wall and waited to see if the mystery person in the study had heard.

Whoever he or she was, they weren't deaf. Something crashed. The light went off and the hall became a pit of blackness. I was clinging to the banister, trying to get my bearings when a body hurtled past me. An elbow slammed into my ribs and knocked me to one side. My forearms and fists went up to defend myself, but whoever had attacked me was already gone. I heard the rattle of feet on the staircase.

Pushing myself upright, I followed down the staircase, taking it a little more cautiously than whoever had preceded me.

By the time I'd run down the hall to the open window, it was already too late. I arrived in the back bedroom just in time to hear a body thud on the courtyard below. Grabbing the small flash I carried in my pocket, I stuck my head out.

As I called Jamal's name, I flicked on the flash. Its beam caught a figure fleeing into the tunnel between the houses. It wasn't Jamal. But it was someone I recognized.

4

I *was so surprised* I dropped my flashlight. Fussy, old-maidish Frank Leftwich breaking and entering? Surreal.

I had met Frank at the aquarium before I ever got to know Joe. Volunteers there are a mismatched lot, either retirees, high school kids, or singles looking to fill the blank spaces in their lives with an educational activity.

Frank fell into the blank spaces category. Until his mother died a few months back, he'd lived to cater to her many eccentricities. So far as I knew, he had no girlfriends or even close pals. He did have a hero, and that was Joe. For all his twelve years at C&G, Frank had been Joe's devoted servant.

Joe had been everything that Frank wasn't—charismatic, outgoing, athletic, handsome, and a lady's man. In fact, it was through Frank that I'd met my ex-fiancé. "Who's the diver with the great bod?" I'd asked Frank.

"That's my boss," Frank had replied with pride of ownership. "I'll introduce you to him."

He had, and that's how it had started between Joe and me. One date and we were both smitten. Frank, oddly enough, seemed smitten by the two of us as a pair. It was almost as if he'd felt we were the closest he'd ever get to a real romance himself. Whenever he could, he'd followed us around like a loyal retainer.

So what had he been up to in Joe's office at this hour? And why had he slammed me out of his path as if he were afraid I might be the devil?

In Joe's study, the desk and file drawers hung open. Paper confettied the floor. Frank hadn't been up here for reasons of sentiment. He'd been searching for something very specific.

At this point I remembered the bit of paper I'd managed to tear away in our collision. I still clutched it in my hand. When I glanced down, the torn scrap didn't yield much information. Printed on it was only one word and a letter. "Departure S."

Baffled, I stuck the ragged corner of paper in my pocket. Let me tell you, I was feeling pretty antsy. I wanted to get out of there. But I still had the plight of Joe's fish in my mind. It wouldn't take much time to feed them. Then, I'd split. I flipped off the light in the study and walked down the hall.

Joe's tank is a beauty. It has reef fish darting around in jewel colors so bright and beautiful they make you blink. It's set up in his bedroom. A lot of nights after making love, Joe and I would lie in bed gazing through the darkness at the softly lit tank and talking. Before I was attacked, Joe was a tender, dynamic lover. Afterward—well, afterward everything seemed to go bad. I don't know if it was just me reacting to what had happened, or if it was both of us.

As I stood in the doorway to the bedroom, my eyes burned. I averted them from the bed and walked over to the tank. It didn't look any the worse for having been neglected. On second glance, an orange-and-black striped clownfish was dead and floating on the top. His fellows had taken several nips out of him. Sadly, I scooped him out and flushed him down the toilet.

"Hey, guys," I crooned when I got back. "No need to start eating each other. "Your faithful dinner provider is back." Being fish, they didn't cheer. But they were plenty hungry. As I scattered the food they gobbled it down double time.

I watched for a minute or two and then replaced the supplies and headed for the door. Out in the hall I passed Joe's study. It occurred to me to stay and straighten the room up. But why? What would be the point? Joe was never coming back to it.

My eyes had adjusted to the darkness, so I had no trouble negotiating the stairs. I stopped in the kitchen and fingered a three-inch ceramic bird I'd purchased with Joe on a vacation in Ocean City. On impulse, I pocketed it. The bird wasn't much of a memento of the years we'd spent together, but at least it was something.

I heard the back door open. Like a fool, I'd left it unlocked when I'd come in. There was a squeak as it swung inward. Then the barely audible impact of a rubber-soled shoe on the tile threshold. Then a long, ominous silence.

While my breathing stopped, my heart went into overdrive. So much adrenalin slammed through my already sorely taxed system that I felt dizzy. Who could it be? Frank coming back to retrieve what I'd torn from him? Jamal and his blond girlfriend? Janet?

None of these people did I wish to encounter. And there was always the possibility that it might be someone considerably more sinister.

As still happens at stressful moments, I flashed back to the time I was almost raped. It didn't happen in a dark house, but out in the fresh air with the sun shining and the early morning birds twittering in the trees. A guy in a pickup passed me while I was jogging.

He must have pulled over right away and then cut through the woods. When I heard him pounding after me, I looked over my shoulder. Even if I hadn't just jogged five miles, I doubt I could have outrun him. All I remember is the ugly expression on his face and then the way his hand smelled of grease when it clamped over my mouth while the other hand jammed a knife against my throat.

Now in Joe's kitchen, my mouth went dry as the inside of a brick oven. Whoever was down there wasn't making a move. Just waiting. I inched around the table and pressed myself against the wall closest to the stair. The figure on the threshold was a mass of darkness standing between me and the exit.

I decided to use the same technique Frank Leftwich had just used so successfully on me. I rushed down the stairs and tried muscling the intruder out of my way. I might as well have tried to brush aside a refrigerator. Whoever it was felt just as solid. Instead of giving ground, he shoved me down against the stairs. Panicking, I drew up my legs and fists to kick and punch. He slammed a trunklike knee across my thighs and used the heel of his hand to snap my head back against the edge of a step. Then the beam of a flashlight blinded me.

"Sally? Holy hell!" Immediately, the pressure was lifted.

"Duke?"

"Yes, it's me. Are you all right?"

"No, I'm not all right, King Kong! I'll probably never dance the tarantella again." If my legs weren't broken, they were at least paralyzed.

Gently, Duke lifted me to my feet. As if I were a favorite niece's Barbie doll he'd inadvertently stepped on, he began patting my hair and straightening my clothes. "How's your back?"

"What back?" Still seeing stars, I started to sag.

Duke scooped me into his arms and carried me up the steps to the kitchen. After he flicked the switch with his elbow, he headed toward the table. "One of these chairs okay, or would you rather I find a couch?"

I moaned.

"Sally?"

"Oh, for crying out loud, just put me down and leave me alone."

He set me on a chair and then stood back and eyed me with a worried frown. "How do you feel?"

"Terrible! Don't you get enough fun beating up criminals? Do you also sneak around at night tackling women?"

"The women I tackle don't usually complain. You're the one who came after me. I was merely defending myself. Now, what was that all about? What are you doing here at this hour of the night?"

"I might ask you that." I ran a hand down my legs just to make sure no jagged pieces of broken bone were sticking out. "I have a hell of a lot more right to be here than you do. I used a key to get in. You just barged through an unlocked door."

"I saw a light and thought I'd better check it out."

"Saw a light? You mean upstairs? That was twenty minutes ago. What have you been doing prowling around Joe's place? I know it's not part of your job. Are you even on duty?"

"No." For the first time Duke looked a bit sheepish. "I was just taking a walk."

"Taking a walk? At two in the morning?"

"I'm an insomniac."

I peered at him, noting that he wore baggy jeans and an Orioles sweatshirt. So something did hang in his closet besides those suits. "You live in Charles Village. That's not close to here."

"I drove."

"You drove across town to take a walk in my neighborhood at two in the morning?"

He shrugged as if this were normal behavior. "I got to thinking about that theory of yours. Figured maybe I'd check it out for myself. I was strolling around looking over the houses with fancy cars parked in front when I saw a light in the upstairs window here. You know the rest. Now, what about you?"

Figuring my midnight perambulations couldn't possibly sound any more bizarre than his, I gave him the full story. When I got to the part about Frank, Duke insisted on going upstairs to take a look at Joe's study. I still felt battered enough that I didn't follow him. Instead, I sat massaging my aching temples and thinking dark thoughts. When he came back down he wore a scowl.

"The squirrel was definitely after something."

"I think he found it and I tore part of it away from him." I dug out my scrap of paper.

Duke gave it a cursory glance and handed it back. "'Departure S.' That could be anything, even a train or airplane schedule from a travel agent. They print them out on computer paper like that sometimes."

"I suppose. But if it were only an airplane schedule,

why would Frank come here in the dead of night to get it? Are you going to arrest Frank for breaking and entering?"

"It's not worth the time and effort to arrest either of you for trespassing on private property," Duke said pointedly, "but maybe I'll have a talk with him."

"While you're doing that, how about finding out where Frank was the night Joe died."

"Joe's death was judged a suicide, Sally."

"Just because you guys call it suicide doesn't make it so."

Duke gave out with a heavy sigh. "You're doing it, aren't you."

"Doing what?"

"What I warned you against. You're getting all hung up over how and why Joe died."

Wanting to punch him, I balled my fists. "Thanks so much for the manly wisdom. I'll decide what matters to me and what doesn't. Suppose Joe didn't commit suicide? That typed suicide note might have just been a plant. Suppose he was deliberately pushed over that bridge?"

"By who? This Frank Leftwich guy?"

"It's not inconceivable that Frank could have had a motive for murder," I retorted stiffly. "He's an accountant. He juggles figures and deals with large sums of money. He would have access to Joe's office computer. What if he was up to something crooked and Joe caught him? I did see the two of them arguing a couple nights before Joe died."

Duke paced to the sink, gazed out at the shadowy courtyard, and then turned to face me. "How tall is Frank Leftwich?"

"I don't know. Five six maybe."

"Strongly built?"

"No." Frank was strung together along the lines of one of Santa's elves.

"Tell me something, Sally. Since Joe died, have you gone over to take a look at the Chase Street Bridge?"

"No." My denial whooshed out breathy and shocked. It hadn't even occurred to me to want to look at that bridge. In fact, driving around the city, I'd been going out of my way to avoid it.

"Maybe it's time you did."

"Why?"

Duke reached for my wrist. "Come with me and I'll show you why."

I resisted when Duke pulled me up out of the chair, and not just because I'd had enough of being man-handled. "Take it easy," I complained as he led me outside and then around the house to the sidewalk. "Remember, I'm a fragile little female and I've had a hard night."

Duke snorted. "Fragile as the arming mechanism on a rocket launcher. You're no sissy. Mama used to tell me about the notes she got from school. They complained about you beating up on boys who gave you trouble. And that was a tough neighborhood and an even tougher school."

"Yeah, well, that was then. I've changed."

As Duke unlocked his car door, he glanced at me shrewdly. "Back there in the dark, were you afraid I was a rapist?"

"The thought crossed my mind."

"If you bit and scratched the guy who tried raping you like you just did me, I can see why he lost interest."

"It might have been a mistake to fight him. When he became impotent, he was so mad he nearly killed me."

"You were lucky he didn't."

"When I woke up in the hospital, I didn't feel lucky."

Duke's lashes hid the expression in his eyes. "You haven't been feeling lucky for a long time now, Sal. Time you got over that."

We rode in silence through the night. Late as it was, the brightly lit harbor was eerily quiet. There was no traffic on the Jones Falls Expressway, either. The Chase Street Bridge is the first exit off the expressway.

The bridge is interesting in that it's one of the city's many undeclared territorial boundaries. West is the historic neighborhood of Mount Vernon with its elegant Victorian townhouses, its museum, art galleries and Peabody Music Conservatory. To the east are some of the poorest streets in Baltimore.

Duke pulled up to the curb and we got out. Even during the day the bridge feels like a prop for a World War II devastation movie. Though it's a solid concrete structure, it sees very little traffic. Trash litters the gutters. In the background the bleak spire of the state prison dominates the night sky.

"I would never come here by myself at night." I pulled my collar up around my throat. "I don't think Joe would, either."

"Is that part of what's bothering you?"

"Yes." We were standing on the concrete that bordered the left side of the bridge. We'd picked our way through bits of torn newspaper and bottles. In the dark the broken glass wasn't always easy to see. Several times I heard it crunch beneath my sneakered feet.

"You never know where a guy will go to commit suicide. But that's not what I brought you here to discuss. Sally, look at that guard rail."

It was a waist-high concrete wall with a wide lip. A four-foot metal fence backed with mesh, probably to keep vandals from throwing rocks and bottles down on passing cars, had been sunk into the lip. "What about it?"

"Can you picture a five-six guy forcing a man Joe's size to jump off it?"

Duke was right. Joe had been muscular and athletic. He'd worked out regularly. There was no way skinny little Frank Leftwich could have physically forced him to do anything. "Frank might have used a gun. Joe might have been drugged. More than one person could have been involved."

"Picture the effort it would take to climb up over that fence and jump to your death. Would you do it if someone threatened you with a gun?"

I looked down at the road below. "No." A bullet would be preferable. "Do you know if the autopsy revealed any sign of a drug?"

"There was no autopsy."

"No autopsy?" I was shocked. "Why not?"

"Several reasons. There was a double stabbing in a row house that night and a shootout in Lexington Terrace. The ME had bodies coming stacked up like apples on an overloaded fruit cart."

"You're telling me the Medical Examiner didn't bother to autopsy Joe because he was too busy?"

"The procedure is expensive. The ME doesn't order it where cause of death is obvious. I checked his report. It said Joe's injuries were consistent with his fall. There were no knife wounds or bullets, no sign of foul play."

"There's something you aren't telling me, isn't there?"

Duke looked away. "Before Joe's body was retrieved from the Jones Falls, it was hit by several cars. He was pretty messed up, Sally. An autopsy wouldn't have revealed much."

"All right, already! Let's get out of here."

Back in the car I leaned against the headrest and closed my eyes. Duke switched on the heat and the flow of warm air against my chilled ankles felt good. The bridge, so bleak and lonely, loomed in my mind.

I kept imagining what it must be like to plunge to your death off it. Then I pictured being forced over it. No, that isn't the way it would have happened with Joe. He had too much fight in him. First he would have been knocked unconscious or drugged. Then he would have been tossed. But that would take two assailants. Either that, or someone as large and muscular as Duke. I shot him a sideways glance. That was silly. What motive would Duke have for killing Joe?

"You're shivering," Duke said after he pulled up in front of my house.

"This has not been one of my better nights."

"You need a hot drink. Got serious alcohol inside?"

"Over the sink."

"Good." Duke handed me onto the curb and guided me up the steps to my front door. I was so out of it that I let him maneuever me like a sick puppy, even gave him my house key. It wasn't until we were in the kitchen that I began to gather my wits. By that time he'd let Mopsy in, filled her bowl to overflowing, and was now rummaging through my cupboards.

"Duke, do you realize it's four A.M. and we have to go to work in the morning?"

"Good thing we're both young and vibrant."

"Speak for yourself."

He slid a cup of hot cider laced with brandy across the table. "This will put hair on your chest."

"That's what your dad always used to say to me and I hated it. God, I really miss him."

"Yeah, me too." Duke sat so we faced each other,

and took a sip of water he'd drawn from the tap. Duke rarely drinks alcohol. Ruminatively, he studied his water. "You know something, Sally? I think you took it harder when Pop died than either Pete or I did. You got something special from having an older man in your life that you could count on."

My wilted antennae started to creep back out. This was something new. "So? Everyone needs a father figure."

"Yeah, but Pete and I had one growing up. You didn't. Your old man walked out on your mother before you even knew him. After that there was just her string of loser boyfriends."

I could feel my forehead puckering. "Hey, what's going on here? I'm the one who majored in psychology, Duke, not you."

"You've always dated guys older than yourself. It doesn't take a college course to see that you're hung up on older men, Sally. Nor to figure out why. You know what I think? All your life you've been trying to find a daddy."

I'd had about enough of Duke's reverse charm for tonight. "Are you implying that Joe was some sort of surrogate father figure?"

"Well, wasn't he? Wasn't that the real attraction between you two?"

"Joe was an exciting, fascinating man."

Once when I was a kid Duke teased me by outstaring me. Now he tried the same rotten trick. "What made him so exciting? His money and success? The security he could offer you?"

"His money and success weren't exactly negatives. But that wasn't it. I really cared for Joe."

"I don't doubt that. But you know what I think? If you two had got married, it wouldn't have worked. You would have outgrown being Joe's little girl. You're too much of a woman for that."

"You didn't like Joe much, did you?"

"Not much."

I pushed my cup at Duke so hard he had to grab it to keep it from going off his side of the table. "You know, this is really bizarre. The man I lived with for over a year is dead. After beating me up, you've just dragged me to the spot where his life got smashed on an expressway and made me relive what must have happened. At this point, the least you could do is say a couple of kind words and then leave me in peace. Instead, you're hassling me about a love affair that was dead even before Joe was killed. Where do you get off being the most tactless lonely-hearts counselor on the East Coast? I mean, so far as I know, your own love life is not exactly up for an excellence award. Correct me if I'm wrong, but your wife walked out on you, didn't she?"

Duke drained his water. "That she did, darlin'. Young Hee experienced culture shock in Baltimore."

"Maybe what she experienced was Duke Spikowski shock. Maybe she married you and came over here because she expected more in the way of a living standard than a Baltimore cop can provide."

"Maybe." Duke stood. His face looked closed up tight, his chin impregnable. "Time I shoved off. You okay now?"

"Just great. Absolutely wonderful." There was a long pause. "Listen Duke, I'm sorry if I—"

"Forget it, Sally. You're right. I was out of line. Don't forget to lock up after me." And with that, he stalked out.

*   *   *

I went to bed feeling bad. I woke up feeling worse. I regretted the way I'd lashed out at Duke—not that he hadn't deserved it. But still . . . Several times at work I picked up the phone and almost dialed his office. On each occasion I stopped myself. What was there to apologize for? He'd started it with his lousy remarks about my relationship with Joe. So all right, Joe had been rich and successful and old enough to be my father. That didn't mean I'd lived with him because of what he'd represented, instead of because of what he was. I'd cared for the man and what had happened to him hurt me.

I managed to leave work early enough to arrive at the C&G office tower just as the five-o'clock exodus started. Secretaries wearing sneakers and trench coats and account executives toting heavy briefcases stampeded out onto the pavement. Horns honked and buses spewed evil-smelling exhaust.

Stationed to one side of the revolving door, I kept my eyes peeled for Frank. As time wore on, the crowd thinned considerably. I'd about given up on him when he came through. He had his head sunk between his shoulder blades and carried a briefcase the size of a file drawer. He didn't see me, so I had to run after him and tap him on the arm.

"Wait up, Frank!"

His head jerked around. His eyes widened and his shock of pinkish red hair seemed to lift like a rooster comb. "Sally!"

"It's me, all right." I fell into step next to him. "How are things at C and G?"

"Fine."

"Well, then, how are things with you? Personally, I mean."

"Fine."

"They can't be all that fine, Frank. Otherwise you wouldn't have been skulking around in Joe's place last night."

Frank turned a delicate shade of green and quickened his pace. "I don't know what you're talking about." He was looking everywhere but at me.

"I saw you, Frank. I was there. I'm the one you slammed into the wall when you ran out."

He kept his profile averted. His mouth thinned. "Are you responsible for sending that policeman around to my office?"

"Policeman? You mean Duke Spikowski? Did he question you today?"

"I don't appreciate this, Sally. He interrogated me as if I was a common criminal. It was embarrassing, humiliating. I don't have to stand for that kind of harrassment." Frank broke into a run. He veered to the right and dashed across Charles. Horns blared and brakes screeched as he scrambled heedlessly through rush-hour traffic. On the curb, I stood staring after him while an eerie coldness prickled at the base of my skull.

5

After my latest brush with Frank, I walked home feeling like the little guy with the black cloud over his head. I had been feeling that way for the last nine months.

Before that wannabe rapist, life had seemed sweet. Afterward, everything was poisoned—Joe's and my happiness together, our hopes for the future. Now Joe was dead, killed supposedly by his own wish. Mama had scoffed at the idea that I might be to blame. I wasn't so sure.

Against all logic, victims tend to blame themselves, especially when sex is involved. I was no different. My brain told me it wasn't my fault. My emotions were a different matter. Maybe I had been picked out because my jogging shorts were too brief. Maybe I had inadvertently made eye contact with the guy in the truck and given him the wrong idea. Maybe I was just too damn independent, running around by myself in a lonely wooded area.

I'd felt that if I was thinking like that, so must everyone else be—including Joe. I became withdrawn and defensive. I bristled at every supposed innuendo, every doubtful look. The result, finally, was that Joe left me.

Now I asked myself if his death might not be the end of a long chain of events I had somehow started. So far, Frank Leftwich's peculiar behavior was the only clue I had. All my instincts screamed that he knew something about Joe's death. Running away from me wasn't going to do him any good, I decided. Somehow, I was going to shake the truth out of him.

I wended my way around the harbor and across Key Highway. As I climbed toward Federal Hill, I took the long way around. Maybe I was punishing myself, but Joe's house drew me like a magnet.

When I was within half a block, I saw someone sitting on the stoop. For a moment I considered turning back. Then curiosity got the better of me and I pressed on. Another few yards and I recognized Joe's son.

"Hello, Scott," I called out and quickened my pace. Scott Winder was a good-looking seventeen-year-old and everything a hard-driving perfectionist like Joe could have wanted in a son. Now in his last year at private school, Scott was captain of the lacrosse team, an honor-roll scholar and first trumpet in the school band. Last I'd heard, Johns Hopkins and Yale had already accepted him.

"Oh, Sally . . . hi."

He didn't exactly look or sound thrilled to see me. Not that I'd expected him to shout with joy. When Joe and I lived together, Scott had spent quite a few weekends with us. We'd all got along fine together. But it had to have been hard on the kid going back and forth between his mother and his dad and me.

Except for a few bitter remarks about their divorce settlement, Joe had never talked much about Janet. According to Joe, the breakup had been as much her idea as his. They'd divorced long before he met me. Yet, from my few encounters with her, it was clear she resented me.

"How are you doing, Scott?"

"Okay, I guess." He didn't look okay. He was sitting hunched up on the step, oblivious that city grime smudged his Dockers. Between his fingers he twiddled a ballpoint pen.

"Scott, I didn't get a chance to speak to you at the funeral. I'm so sorry about your dad."

"Yeah." He glanced up from his pen, then looked down again. A nervous frown tugged at his eyebrows. "My dad and my mother were going to get back together again."

"Yes, he told me."

"He did?"

"Yes, Scott, he did." I tried to make my voice sound neutral. I didn't want to think about that awful last scene Joe and I had. I'd have given almost anything to make it play differently. "What are you doing here at the house?"

Scott jerked a thumb back over his shoulder. "My mom's inside looking things over.

"She is?" Actually, I'd already taken note of Janet's pale green Mercedes parked at the curb. Knowing she was prowling around inside Joe's house didn't give me a good feeling. As his ex-wife and the mother of his son, she had more right to it than I did. Still, since I'd lived there with Joe for so long, I couldn't help feeling proprietary. "I'd like to speak to her. Do you think she'll mind if I go in?"

"Don't know. Door's open."

Gingerly, I stepped past him. I rapped on the door frame and peered inside. No one in sight. I crossed the threshold and stood listening. Faint noises filtered from upstairs.

"Janet," I called out.

The noises stopped. High heels clicked and then Janet appeared at the top of the stairs. Her face went blank when she spotted me. "Yes?"

I had to stand with my head thrown back, staring up through the tight coils of the staircase. It wouldn't take much of that to give me a queasy stomach. "Hello, Janet. Would you mind if I came up?"

"For what?"

"I'd just like to speak to you about something."

"Very well." She retreated out of sight.

I didn't see her again until I reached the second floor. She was waiting a little way back in the hall with her arms folded across her chest. Though Janet doesn't work, she always dresses as if she were about to go for a job interview. She wears her hair in a smooth, shoulder-length pageboy. Beneath its shining brown sweep her makeup is faultless. She is the kind of woman who makes other women feel as if they ought to check their fingernails for dirt.

"Janet, I don't know what to say about Joe. I'm so terribly sorry."

"Naturally, everyone feels terrible." She bit her words off. This wasn't going to go well.

I glanced around the empty hall. "Do you mind telling me what your plans are here?"

"No, I don't mind. Goodwill is coming tomorrow. After they shovel the place out, I'll put it up for sale."

"You're going to give everything in the house to Goodwill?" I was aghast. I knew how much some of the furnishings had cost.

She waved an encompassing hand and then pointed at the handwoven Navajo runner beneath her feet. "This sort of stuff isn't my taste."

It had been mine, though, and still was. When I didn't comment, she added, "I've already spoken to Joe's lawyer. He left everything to me and Scott."

This came out like a slap in the face. Steadying myself, I leaned a hand on the railing. Not that I was surprised. After we got engaged, Joe had talked about changing his will to include me. But he'd never done it. Naturally, he wouldn't have done it after we split. I cleared my throat. "Janet, I came in because I wanted to ask you about the fish."

"The fish?" Her eyebrows tented. "You mean that tank in the bedroom?"

"Yes. It was a hobby that Joe and I shared."

She pivoted and marched smartly to the bedroom door and through. I followed. Inside, I saw that she'd been busy. The sheets and quilt had been torn away from Joe's bed and heaped on the floor. His suits, slacks, and sport coats were slung helter-skelter on top of the mattress. The sight shocked me. Joe's clothes had been so important to him. He'd picked them out so carefully. I averted my eyes and turned toward the tank.

I didn't like the look of the cloudy water. The fish hung in suspended animation or swam around in listless circles. On closer inspection, I saw another dead clownfish.

"If you have no use for the tank," I said, "I'd appreciate it if you'd let me set it up in my place."

Janet stood a few feet behind me, tapping her foot lightly. "That's how Joe and you met, isn't it? At the aquarium."

"Yes."

"I never did understand his passion for fish."

"Well, it's hard to explain." I turned back to her. "I think you either feel there's something magical about an aquarium or you don't. They've always fascinated me."

"I bet. You and Joe must have had a great view of this one from that bed."

With an effort, I kept a rein on my tongue. Janet intimidates me with her society manners and prom-queen grooming. But she also pisses me off. If she was going to be jealous of another woman in Joe's life, why didn't she hold onto him in the first place? It isn't as if I stole him from her. "It's pretty at night when it's lit."

"I can imagine." She looked from the tank to the bed and back. I kept my mouth shut tight.

"Of course," she went on, "it was really the diving that Joe liked more than anything else. That's why he gave so much of his time to the aquarium down here."

"That's true. He was great in a wet suit." I remembered a trip we took to Cozumel, Joe swimming through a school of yellow fin tuna and beckoning me to follow him into an underwater cave. Though I was a poor swimmer and a novice to scuba diving, I did follow. At that time I'd worshiped him and would have followed him anywhere.

"He was always a wonderful athlete. That's how we met, you know. In college we were both on the tennis team."

"Oh?" I could just picture Janet in a white tennis skirt. Smashing. "Well, Joe was good at everything he tried. He was just one of those men who are born to succeed."

"That was certainly true while I was married to him," Janet shot back. "Afterward, I don't know."

"What do you mean by that?"

She gave a sharp smile. "After you left him, he

came around and talked to me about his feelings. He was quite depressed."

It hurt that Joe had talked about me to Janet. "Breakups are never easy."

"Yours with Joe must have been unusually harsh. Joe wasn't an easy man to depress."

Now I saw what was going on. Janet had decided that I was responsible for Joe's suicide. She was doing her subtle ice-water-down-your-back damnedest to lay a guilt trip on me. I went rigid. "I didn't leave him, Janet. It was the other way around."

She tapped the smooth toe of her Ferragamo. "Not according to his suicide note."

"What?"

"I'm keeping the contents of that note private. Not even Scott has seen it. But maybe you should know what it said."

"Maybe I should."

" 'Too many things have gone bad for me lately. Life isn't worth living when you're unlucky in love.' "

For a moment I was too shocked to speak. So Duke had misled me about Joe's letter. "I thought you and Joe were getting back together," I finally managed.

"We were, and I thought he was over you. But apparently not." Her mouth turned down. "I never could see what you two had in common, other than fish, that is. It didn't surprise me one little bit when you broke up. What surprises me is how much it hurt Joe. I thought he was over you. Then this happened."

"You're blaming me for his suicide?"

"Who else is there to blame? Everything else in Joe's life was fine. He was a healthy, successful man with a great future. The only worm in his apple was you."

I had started to tremble. Janet's accusations were like having my worst nightmare confirmed. I took a steadying breath. "Janet, I realize you don't like me. You're wrong about Joe and me, but it's pointless to discuss it. Believe me, I wouldn't be here bothering you if I weren't concerned about the fish. As you can see, some of them aren't doing so well. A tank like this needs a lot of care. If you'd be willing to let me take it, I'll have it out of your way by tomorrow. You won't ever have to lay eyes on me again. That I can promise."

Janet stood there gazing at me like the sphinx, her toe tapping away. "Just a minute." She went out of the room and called down the stairs.

"Scott. Scotty! Come up here, please." There was a long pause and then the grumbling thumps of Scott's sneakered feet pounding up the stair treads.

"Yeah? What?"

"Come into the bedroom, please. I want you to do something."

"What?"

"Just follow me."

Janet clicked through the door with a sulky Scott in tow. When he saw me, his neck turned bright red. Through the fog of my own misery, I felt sorry for him. It's rough to be a kid that age, old enough to feel your manhood is in constant need of proving yet still under a parent's thumb. I couldn't even guess what effect Joe's death was having on him.

Janet picked up the dip net that lay on top of the tank, opened the hood, and scooped out the dead clownfish along with two live angels. She handed the dripping net with the fish still squirming inside to her son.

"Scotty, flush these down the toilet for me, please."

"What?" Scott drew back. "Mom!"

"Do as I say, please."

"But Mom!"

"Janet . . ."

She whirled on me, her hand raised and her teeth bared. "Sally," she said, her words clipped icily, "you're right about the fish in that tank. They're all half-dead. It's noble of you to want to move them and care for them, but I think the time has come to put all this behind us." She glared at Scott, who was still standing there holding the net. Inside it the fish wriggled and gasped. I felt I could almost hear their anguished cries.

"Scott."

His face went dull red. "Ah, Mom . . ."

"Do as I say, please."

He looked from his mother to me. "Go ahead," I told him. "Do whatever your mother says." Then I left the room. A minute later I was out of the house and I knew I was never going back.

That night Duke called. "We've got him?"

"What? Who?"

"Jamal Bassett, African-American male, age sixteen, one-hundred-and-twenty-two pounds, caught passing a television set through a window on South Harmony."

I took a deep breath, reliving for an instant that moment when I'd faced Jamal in my living room. "You think it's the same kid?"

"Fits the description."

"Any priors?"

"Not on our records."

"Who was he passing the set to?"

"Probably his girlfriend, but she got away."

I rubbed my forehead. After a minor is booked, he's

only kept overnight if the crime is serious or if there's some reason why he won't be allowed back in the home. "Is he in Detention?"

"Yes."

After Duke hung up, I called Maggie who I happened to know was handling Intake that night. "Maggie, have you received a file on Jamal Bassett?"

"Let's see. Hmm. Yes, here it is. What's up?"

"Would you mind if I stopped in at lockup and spoke with him?"

"I guess not. Why? What's this about? Hey, he isn't the kid who tried ripping off your place, is he?"

"I think he might be."

"Then what do you want to fuss with him for?"

"I'd just like to talk with him."

She heaved a big sigh. "You know what, Sally? If God arranged for you to spend your life in Disneyland, you'd find some way to bust out and head for the nearest war zone."

"You're probably right, Mag. I wouldn't be a colleague of yours if I wanted to spend twenty-four hours a day with Tinkerbell, now, would I?"

An hour later I walked down a corridor decorated in out-of-date dismal. Why do police stations always look like gray concrete overkill? By law the police are not allowed to lock up juveniles within sight or sound of adult prisoners. That doesn't mean they try to make kids comfortable. When I walked in to Jamal Bassett's holding room he was handcuffed to his chair.

He looked pretty much the way I remembered him, only smaller and a lot less threatening. When he recognized me, he rolled his eyes. With elaborate unconcern, he leaned back against the frame of his wood chair. Ignoring his manacled wrist, he let his free arm and legs dangle like an unstrung marionette's.

I'd seen that defiant sprawl in so many kids. It was their way of declaring, "You and your system don't scare me." I always feel like answering, "If you're not scared, you should be. You're getting caught up in something that can grind you into dog meat."

My job is to try to see that this doesn't happen. Sometimes I succeed. More often than I like to dwell on during the wee hours of the night, I fail.

I put my briefcase on the table. "Hello, Jamal."

He took one look and then stared at the wall to the left, showing me a profile set in stone. Despite his indolent pose, I could see the pulse in his throat jumping. My gaze ran over him, taking in the cornrows, the outthrust jaw, the expensive black warmup threads, gold chains, and Jordan sneakers. Doubtless, the spoils of his nefarious doings. He was a good-looking kid. He also looked intelligent.

I sighed. "C'mon, Jamal, let's not play games. We've met before."

Slowly, his head swiveled and he glared. "You tell the cops about that?"

"After you broke into my place, sure. But they didn't need me to identify you this time around. Caught you red-handed, huh?"

"What do you want with me?"

"I came to talk about your future."

"What future? I got no future."

"On the contrary, you haven't used up all your luck yet. Legally speaking, this is your first offense—though we both know otherwise. Jamal, your case has been formalized. That means it will be sent to the State's Attorney. He'll decide whether or not to prosecute. I think chances are good you'll be assigned to a juvenile counselor instead. There's time for you to turn things around."

His dark eyes smoldered. "You talkin' about probation?"

"You might call it that."

"Oh, fuck!" He threw his head back and stared stonily up at the ceiling.

"You could do a lot worse."

"Yeah, there's always worse. I could be spittin' out worms six feet under. That big white-ass cop in the suit did this, didn't he? He's the one made sure I didn't get to go home. Well, tell him to go fuck himself."

I might be having the same thought regarding Duke Spikowski, but I wasn't about to pass it along to Jamal.

"How'd you get into this mess, Jamal?"

"Sheeit."

"Jamal, let's stop wasting time with the big bad words. Let's start talking about how you're going to dig yourself out of this hole you're in."

"I ain't no mortician. Diggin' is not my bag, lady."

"From now on, you bet your ass it is. Nice warmup suit you've got there. You must be making quite a bit of money stealing TV sets."

"Matter of fact, until tonight I was doing pretty fine."

"Did you ever consider that every time you break into somebody's house you risk getting killed or winding up in prison being molested by perverts?"

"That's just a risk someone's got to take, you know?" he drawled insolently.

"There are other ways to make money. A job, for instance."

"What jobs? People like me don't get decent jobs in this city." His dark gaze smoldered.

"That's not true. It's especially not true for a smart

kid like you who has the brains to stay in school and keep his record clean."

"Yeah? Well I wouldn't know nothin' about that. Since you're so strong on that fact, why don't you take your tail out of here and prove it?"

"Maybe I might."

Two days later I threaded my way through the murky cavern of an underground municipal parking lot. One good thing about having your Mustang painted tomato red, it makes it easy to spot. After I climbed in and locked the door, I leaned back against the headrest and just sat there with my eyes closed.

I jumped when I heard a tap on my glass. The face peering in at me was Duke's.

I rolled down my window. "Where did you come from?"

"Spotted your car and decided to wait for you." He gestured over his shoulder at his BPD Chevy. Maybe it's not so great that my Mustang stands out in a crowd, I thought.

"I hear you got yourself assigned as Jamal Bassett's juvenile counselor. That's not kosher, Sally."

I eyed Duke coldly. "I already discussed the conflict-of-interest issue with my supervisor."

"What did she say?"

"Warned me not to let my emotions get in the way of my judgment. Not that it's any of your business, but I pointed out that I'm a seasoned counselor who never lets emotion interfere with judgment."

"Yeah, well, I wish I agreed." He walked around to the passenger side and stood with his hands on his hips, waiting for me to let him in. I leaned across and flipped the lock.

Once he'd folded his large self into the passenger seat, I felt like a sardine inside an eight-ounce can that had just been packed with sixteen ounces of vital protein. As Duke swung toward me, I pressed my back against the door just to give myself an inch or two of extra space.

"Why are you so hostile? I thought you'd be happy that I caught the kid."

"I am happy."

"Then why do you want to get yourself involved with him?"

Since I couldn't explain it very well to myself, I felt irritated at having to explain it to Duke. "There are judges in this system who like nothing better than to pack young kids off to Hickey. Bassett needed an advocate."

"You haven't answered my question."

"When I look at Jamal, I see a kid who has brains and guts and who could be turned around. When I recognize that in a kid and I don't do the best I can for him, I don't sleep at night."

"Are those bugles I hear in the distance? I should have known you'd come charging back at me like Joan of Arc. Okay, let's change the subject. Tell me this. Did Bassett give you any information about the girl who was with him the night he robbed your place?"

"No."

"Did you ask him?"

"No. It's not time for that yet. Right now I'm still trying to establish some sort of rapport with him. He's still staring at me as if I'd crawled out of a drain."

"Good thing neither of is in this business because we live for popularity." Duke rubbed a forefinger down the crease between his eyes. It gave me a chance to look at him without having him stare back. I've always been fascinated by his eyebrows. They are thick and touched with glints of gold that shimmer in certain lights. Now, close up, I detected a couple silver ones. I also saw signs of his parents in his square jaw and broad cheekbones—Mama's direct gaze, his father's thick neck. Yet it struck me that Duke with his blunt, stubborn ways was like no one else in his family. It also struck me that he was a very attractive man. I wondered what he would be like in bed, then pushed away the thought.

He said, "We couldn't get anything out of him about the girl. Question is whether they're part of a gang, or operating alone. My guess is, they're alone, in which case we've solved the problem."

"No problem will be solved until those kids and the ones like them have a chance to be something other than jailbait," I retorted.

Duke's nostrils flared. "Right. Your pal Maggie feels the same way. Why couldn't you arrange for her to get Bassett's case?"

"Maggie's already up to her ears in problems."

"And you're not?"

"My life is a bed of rosebuds. Haven't you noticed? Speaking of which, I saw Joe's ex-wife the other day. Why did you lie to me about Joe's suicide note?"

"I didn't lie. You asked me if your name was mentioned and I told you it wasn't."

"You didn't tell me it said life wasn't worth living because his love life was messed up."

"Is that what it said?"

"You know damn well what was in it, Duke."

"So? Don't tell me you're taking a vague piece of typed craziness like that personally."

"How can I not?"

"Use your brains, Sally. Joe Winder and whatever happened between you two is history. Forget it."

My nails dug into my palms. "Fat chance. I stopped over at C and G to see Frank Leftwich the other day. He told me you'd already paid him a visit."

"I had a few words with the man."

"He made it sound as if you'd beaten him with a rubber hose."

"He overstated. I rarely carry crude instruments of torture into classy downtown office buildings. The chief frowns on anything so unrefined."

"Well, did you learn much?"

"Leftwich said he was at Joe's place looking for some files that belong to an account he's working on. He claimed you scared him. He thought you were a burglar. That's why he pushed you and ran out."

"Did you buy that?"

Duke reached out and laid a large hand on my shoulder. "Sally, take it easy."

I stiffened, crowded by the physical contact and ready to explode with all the emotions roiling inside me. "What do you mean, take it easy?"

"You have enough to worry about without trying to do the police's work. Leave Joe's death alone and get on with your life."

"What if I can't do that until I know what really happened?"

Duke met my trapped glare squarely. "In all likelihood, what really happened is that the man threw himself off a bridge because he was unhappy about a lot of things in his life that had nothing to do with you."

"Then I have to know what made him so unhappy."

Duke took away his hand. For a moment he just looked at me. "Okay." With a sudden movement, he slammed a hand against the door latch on his side and eased out. Just before shutting it again, he peered in at me. "I know I'm wasting my breath, but stop making yourself unhappy, okay?"

"Okay."

Duke shut my door with exaggerated gentleness and strode back to his car. Through my rearview mirror, I watched him. After he climbed in, I turned on the ignition and peeled out of there. All the way to the exit, I could feel his eyes on the back of my neck.

Since my head buzzed with tiredness, I should have headed home for a frozen noodle dinner and an early night. Instead, I aimed the Mustang east toward Keester's, a Highlandtown tavern I know on Conkling Street. It's not much, just a bar and a lot of Formica tables and tubular chairs with Naugahyde seats that probably date back to the fifties.

When I walked in, I stood adjusting to the gloom and the stale perfume of beer and dead cigarettes. The bartender caught my eye. He cocked his thumb and mouthed, "She's over there."

I'd already seen her, a slender woman in a pale blue sweat suit. Her thick hair, dyed so black it looked like a Dynel Halloween wig, hung in a mass of permed curls down her back. She was standing mesmerized in front of the poker machine. To either side of her, a row of neon-lit video gambling devices lined the wall.

Loudly, she banged the flat of her hand against the machine's side and yelled at the bartender. "Hey, Wally, I'm outa' quarters. Let me go home and get some from my old man. I gotta hit soon." Then she spotted me and did a double take. "Well, whaddya know!"

"Hello, Mom," I said as I walked toward her.

6

I *go see my mother* about once a month. Sometimes we meet for lunch, but usually I drop in on her at Keester's. Every cloud has it's silver lining. In a way it's convenient that video poker has her so hooked. Since I can usually find her planted in front of a machine, I don't have to knock on her door and deal with whatever jerk she happens to be living with.

Ever since I can remember, Mom has been hooked up with one Mr. Wrong after another. It was because of a Mr. Extremely Wrong that I ran away and got placed in foster care. One afternoon when I came home from seventh grade and Mom lay sleeping it off on the couch, the creep approached me with more on his pea brain than checkers. I bit his hand and streaked out of there never to return.

Now, after I gave her ten bucks for quarters and bought her a Coke, she said, "I'm glad you showed, Sally. If I had to go home and wake Jeffie up for some money he'd probably blow straight through the roof.

He's a musician. Works all night, sleeps all day."

"Jeffie, so that's your new guy's name?" All I knew about Jeffie was that my mother had met him at AA. She'd been living with him for just over a month. "What's this one like?"

"Oh, I don't know. Like a man."

"Uh-oh."

She snorted a laugh. "Yeah, I know. I haven't had too much luck in that department. You neither, right?" Taking her eyes off the game, she shot me a grin.

"You might say that trouble with men is the one family tradition we've really kept up."

"Like mother, like daughter. Hey, I heard about what happened to that ritzy boyfriend you used to have. Fell on his head off a bridge." She shook her head. "Well, at least you didn't get pregnant when you were just a kid like I did."

"No." My mother had me—out of wedlock, of course—when she was seventeen. The responsibility was too much for her. Still is. She never seemed to blame me for agreeing to live with the Spikowskis. In fact, I think she was relieved.

She stuffed another quarter into the slot and worked the lever. "I have some great news for you."

"Oh?" My mother's idea of great news and mine don't always mesh, so right away I got tense.

"First, in case you stopped by to check, I haven't had a drink since Taylor Manor. Here, smell my breath." She jammed her face up close to mine, opened her mouth and sent me a blast of air. I whiffed fries and a burger with onions, but no alcohol.

"Mom, naturally I'm concerned about you."

Last year after a boyfriend she'd lived with for two years walked out on her, my mother really hit bottom. She would call me up and tell me her garbage bags were singing to her. She drank so much she nearly died from liver damage. I arranged for her to be detoxed. It wasn't the first detox she'd been through, but this time it seemed to have taken. Since she left the program she's stayed straight, so far as I know.

"Well, Sal, you can relax and stop worrying about me. Your mom's getting married to someone who'll make sure she never touches alcohol again as long as she lives."

"Married?"

"Yeah." She stood there enjoying my astonishment. I couldn't have been more surprised if she'd told me she'd won a Miss America contest.

"Are you talking about this Jeffie guy?"

"Right. I'm going to be Mrs. Jeffrey Spadea."

"But you just said—"

"I said he was a man. Well, that's not so bad. Hey, don't look like that. Jeffie and I are good for each other. Honest. We both have a drinking problem and we're both in AA, so we keep each other on the straight and narrow. Besides, it's time I settled down, wouldn't you say?"

Actually, I thought it was too late for her to settle down. She's never stuck with a lover and some of the guys she's lived with have been nightmares. For a long time now I've felt more like my mother's parent than like her daughter.

Seeing the doubt all over my face, she clutched at my hand. Her eyes glistened up at me hopefully. "Be nice. Wish me luck, Sally. This may be my last chance."

"Of course I wish you luck."

"That's my girl. Will you come to the wedding?"

"You've actually set a date?"

"Not yet, but it'll be soon. Maybe next month."

"Sure I'll come." I managed a little laugh. "I'll even

give you away if you want." The moment the words were out of my mouth, I regretted them.

"Oh, my sweet baby!" She gave me a big hug. "You've got a deal."

The next morning I went to see Jamal's mother, Carrie Bassett. The family lived in a row house near the prison. Major hurdle—I had to cross the Chase Street Bridge to get there.

I knocked on the Bassetts's door figuring I wasn't going be welcomed with flowers and a parade. A curtain twitched. No answer to my knock, though. I rapped again. Still nothing. Then I heard a baby cry. Rat-a-tat-tat with the knuckles one more time. The knob turned and the door cracked open.

"Yes?" The smooth, dark face of a young African-American woman peered at me. Her hair had been straightened into an ear-length pageboy and she wore jeans and a green cotton blouse.

"Miss Bassett?"

"Yes?"

"I'm here about your son, Jamal."

"What about him?" She asked belligerently, but terror flickered behind her eyes. I felt sorry for her. This must be tough.

"If you'll let me come in, I'd like to talk to Jamal. Is he at home?"

"He's upstairs. Seems like he's been sleeping all the time."

Uh-oh, a bad sign. Jamal didn't need to sleep. He needed to be kept constructively busy.

"Let me in, Ms. Bassett. We need to talk."

She took a reluctant backward step. "Okay, but the place, it's a mess."

It wasn't any messier than you'd expect a place to be when you were raising five kids on welfare and had a three- and five-year-old bottled up inside all day. Carrie informed me that she was afraid to let her two youngest children, Antwon and Lateesha, out. A few weeks earlier a stray bullet from gunplay in the neighborhood had wounded a baby who lived only a few houses away.

"The boy who shot the gun, he was just thirteen. Seems like the kids today are just going crazy."

Upstairs, I found Jamal lying awake on a bottom bunk. Judging from the toys and clothes scattered around, he shared the room with one or more siblings.

I knocked on the open door. "How's it going, Jamal?"

He had headphones clamped to his ears, so he couldn't hear me. He could see me, though. He delivered what the cops around here call an "eyefuck." It's an ocular assault that's been perfected to an art by the ghetto kids in these parts.

I walked in and lifted the phones from his ears. A beat like a sledgehammer thunked into the walls.

"Hey!" He scowled and jerked into a sit, all primal posturing gone.

"I said, how's it going."

"Terrible." He kicked at a tangled sheet.

"You bored?"

"Yeah, I'm bored. Nothin' for me to do round here. They don't want me back in school till I get things straight with you."

"Well, here I am. Let's get things straight."

We eyeballed each other, then he flopped back and put his hands behind his head. "Way I see it, things in my life won't never be straight."

I pulled over a chair and pushed a pile of socks and sneakers in various sizes off it. "Know something, Jamal?

In the long run, that's really your call. Now, here's the way I see things. You've got a chance here to turn your life around. Take it, because you may not get another."

"Yeah?"

"Yeah. Now, I want you to answer some questions for me."

"Before I answer you any questions, how about you answer me one? How come you got my case when I robbed your house? Wouldn't that be conflict of interest or something?"

"Yes, actually it would. And normally I wouldn't have your case."

"Then, how come—"

"I asked my supervisor for it. She granted it to me as a special favor."

He bristled with suspicion. "Why?"

"Because I wanted it so much, Jamal. I really wanted it."

"You asked for my case so you could make my life a living hell, didn't you? You're out to get even with me." He looked at me hard, his dark eyes knowing.

"That's not it at all. I'm not here to get even with you. I'm here to help you."

His nostrils flared. "Why is that? You tellin' me you liked the way I broke into your house and tried to steal your VCR?"

"No. Actually, I didn't care for that at all. But I did like the way you helped that girl you were with get out so she wouldn't be caught. Who was she, by the way?"

Like a threatened clam, his expression snapped shut. "What girl? You're imagining things."

"You know, Jamal, I even like that. You don't see too many guys wanting to protect women these days. I figure one who does can't be all bad. Now let's see if I'm wrong. Let's get started."

*   *   *

I spent the rest of that day and the one after digging
into Jamal's life. I visited the minister at the church
where he'd once attended Sunday school and knocked
on some of the neighbors' doors. I talked to all his
teachers and his school counselor. My conversation
with his biology instructor was the most productive.

"Jamal's a smart boy," she told me. "Nature is interesting to him, not that he gets to see much of it living
in the city like he does. Why I remember, we had a
school trip on the *Lady Maryland*, you know the old-
time sailboat that takes kids out to see the wildlife on
the Chesapeake Bay. Jamal was in heaven. He asked
so many questions. We couldn't shut him up."

That got me thinking. The next morning I picked up
the phone and reported on my progess to Duke. "Any
luck finding Jamal's partner in crime?" I asked first.

"The mysterious blond? No. So far she hasn't
turned up. What about you?"

"No one I've interviewed knows anything about the
girl. At least, that's what they told me. She's not a
classmate of Jamal's. There aren't that many white
kids at his high school, so she'd be easy to identify."

"How's it going with Bassett? You think you'll be
able to do him some good?"

I twirled my ballpoint between my fingers. "Maybe.
Anyhow, I've got some ideas. Do you know about the
Living Classroom?"

"It's a program for delinquent boys. They do a lot of
hands-on stuff down at the Maritime Institute, building boats and learning seamanship."

"Right. Well, I've spoken to the resource director
down there. He's agreed to let Jamal participate in the
program on weekends."

"Why not full time?"

"I considered that, but it's vocational with a GED program. Jamal's teachers say he's doing well in school. I think he should stay there. I just think he needs to be kept busy at something he likes and finds meaningful."

"Don't we all? So, okay, what about after school?"

"I've got some ideas about that, too."

Duke chuckled. "Okay, Supergirl. I give up. Want to get together for lunch and talk about it?"

I let my breath out slowly. "Is this business or a date that we're talking about here?"

"If I say it isn't business, you'll be scared off, won't you?"

I sat up very straight. "Doesn't matter. I can't make it anyway. Too busy."

There was a little pause. His voice, which had been warm, dipped a degree. "Well, that lets me know where I stand, doesn't it."

"When I say I'm too busy, Duke, I mean it."

"Sure."

Pretty quickly after that, the conversation ended. For I don't know how long, I sat rolling my pen back and forth between the palms of my hands.

"Trouble?"

I swiveled and saw Maggie's head poked around the corner of my cubicle. "Uh, no, why?"

"You were sitting there looking meaner than a cat trying to eat a cement canary. I know you can't be trying to solve the mayor's budget crisis. You wouldn't waste your time on a math problem even Einstein couldn't deal with."

I gave myself a little shake. "I just had a strange experience, that's all."

"Did one of the kids you've gone to bat for call to thank you for straightening out his life?"

"I said strange, not unheard of. I think Duke Spikowski is coming onto me."

"Are we speaking of the BPD's gorgeous golden sphinx here? Well, now, aren't you the one." Maggie winked. "I hear quite a few lady cops have made a heavy play for Señor Spikowski and fallen right on their faces. What's your secret?"

"I don't have a secret, Maggie, and I don't want one. Getting something going with Duke doesn't interest me."

"Am I missing something here? Have you been on down to Johns Hopkins for a sex-change operation?"

I threw my pen at her. She fielded it neatly. "The guy is my foster brother. I don't think of him that way. Besides, even if I did I wouldn't want to get involved with him. He's a difficult, complicated man."

"So? You're a difficult, complicated woman. In that department, the two of you are a matched pair."

"Yeah, well, that's reason enough for us to steer clear of each other, isn't it?"

I skipped lunch to drive down to The HairStop. I needed a haircut, but that was just an excuse. What I really needed was a little TLC. The minute I walked in, however, Mama started telling me her troubles instead of the other way around.

She was just finishing up with her best friend, Peg Rigowski. The Rigowski men have been longshoremen at the Port of Baltimore for five generations. They're big, bull-necked, raspy-voiced guys with beer bellies and nicknames like Puddleduck, Toadface, and Little Frog.

Peg's husband, Little Frog, grew up admiring Rita Hayworth, Susan Hayward, Maureen O'Hara and the other Hollywood redheads of the 50s. Peg, like most wives of a certain age in Highlandtown, aims to please her man. Though pushing sixty-five, she sports a head of flaming tresses that waterfalls down her back almost to her waist. For thirty-some years now, Mama has kept them red and rippling.

"Oh, hon, I'm glad you're here," Mama exclaimed as I set down my purse. "The worst thing just happened."

"What?"

Mama patted one of Peg's scarlet waves into place. "Joyce just called."

"Pete's wife?" This was unusual. Communication between Joyce and Pete's family was rare these days. The troubles in her younger son's marriage were a constant source of heartache for Mama. Of course it made her proud that Pete wasn't shunning his roots and spent as much time as he did back at the old homestead. On the other hand, she adored her grandchildren and wanted to be close to them. Since Pete had all but moved back to the city, Joyce had kept the boys away.

"She called to say she's fed up with Pete and his politicking. She's going to divorce him."

"Oh, no!" I glanced at Peg who was listening avidly and who had obviously already heard the story. Mama is not one to keep secrets, especially her own. Spend an hour at The HairStop and you leave knowing a whole lot more about goings-on in Baltimore than you'd ever learn from reading the newspaper.

Peg met my gaze in the mirror and shook her head. Her rouged cheeks and wattles jiggled dolefully. "Girls. These days, I just don't understand them. When a woman has herself a decent man who don't drink too much or beat her up, she should hang onto him. If Pete wants to live in the city near his folks, his wife should come live with him. I ask you, what's this world coming to when a woman turns her nose up at her husband's neighborhood?"

Peg left and I took her seat in front of the mirror. If I didn't know it would wound Mama to the quick, I'd have my hair done at one of the trendy salons downtown. Going to her is safe only if you are vigilant. Falter for a minute and you walk out looking like a 60s Marie Antoinette.

"All this gorgeous ash blond hair, and you just want me to lop it off and not curl it?" Mama shook her head. "Seems like such a waste."

"I like it plain, Mama. Just a little trim, please. Hey, what's this I hear about you and Peg taking a cruise to Bermuda?"

She smiled softly. "It was a birthday present from Pete. Sometimes that boy can be so thoughtful."

I agreed. Too bad his wife doesn't appreciate him, I thought.

While she shampooed my hair, Mama talked unhappily about Pete's marital troubles. "It all comes from this running for city council business. I wish he'd never got into that."

"You're against his political campaign?" I was surprised as I'd figured all this time she must be for it.

"All I've ever wanted for my boys is that they should be healthy and happy. How can either of them be happy with no proper home of their own and separated from their kids?"

"Duke doesn't have kids."

"No, and that's just my point." Mama unwrapped the towel around my head and picked up her scissors. "At least I thought Pete was settled. Now he's going to be just like his brother, floating around like a barge without an anchor." She snipped at the hair above my ear. "Because that's how a man is without a good woman. Just like a big old barge heading for nothing except trouble."

I cleared my throat. "I'm sure they'll both find themselves the right sweetie eventually."

"Duke don't show no sign of it and all Pete can think about is votes." She took another snip and then shot me a considering look. "You know, Duke thinks the world of you, Sally."

"He does?"

"Maybe you haven't noticed. He's the quiet type and don't show his feelings. But I can see it when he looks at you."

"Duke and I have known each other for years and years. He's never—"

"I know what you're going to say. But you always had someone else before. Now that you've lost Joe—" She stopped cutting. "Sally, honey, what's wrong? Did I nip you with the scissors?"

"No, Mama. I'm sorry." At Joe's name, my eyes had filled with tears. Appalled, I grabbed a corner of the towel around my shoulders and blotted them. I'd thought I'd stopped doing this. "I'm just upset, I guess. The other day I heard what Joe wrote in his suicide note, and I haven't been able to get it out of my mind."

When I quoted the note to Mama, she threw down her scissors. "If that man weren't already dead, I'd horsewhip him. To think he'd write such nonsense, and him the one walked out on you."

"It doesn't even make sense. Just a couple of days before he died, Joe told me he was going back to his wife. He seemed happy about that."

"It's enough to make you lose your faith in the whole love thing altogether," Mama commented. "Hey, I'm just going to fluff you up a bit with the curling iron."

"Yes," I muttered, wondering if I'd ever again have any faith in the love thing.

As Mama busied herself, she said, "Hey, I was just

kidding. Don't let this make you cynical. Sometimes love works out great. Look at your mom."

"My mom?"

"She was in here just the other day. Told me how she was getting married. Seemed happy as a lark."

"And just how long do you think that's going to last?" I grimaced, thinking of all my poor mother's pathetic love affairs.

"Oh, you are in one lovely frame of mind, my lady. Listen, don't let this business with Joe get you down so bad you see everything in the negative. Could be this man your mom's found is just what she needs. Lord knows, she's been looking long enough."

"That's certainly true. It's been a long Easter-egg hunt."

Mama tweaked a strand of my hair. "C'mon, give her another chance. Everybody deserves another chance. That goes for you, too."

I didn't answer. All this time I hadn't paid attention to what Mama was up to with her curling iron. Now I took a good look at my reflection. A Kewpie doll stared back at me. "Oh, Mama," I moaned.

"You look beeyootiful, hon. Just beeyootiful."

When I got home from work, I'd pulled up to the curb and come around the back of my car before I noticed I had a visitor.

I felt my eyes widen. Joe's son perched on my front steps. "Scott, what are you doing here?"

"Hi, Sally."

He pointed at the huge carton in front of his loafered feet. "I brought Dad's saltwater setup."

"You did?" I was flabbergasted. "I thought your mom wanted to get rid of it."

"She did. She thinks I took it to Goodwill. But I felt so bad about what I did the other day. You know, flushing the fish and everything." He stood up. "I just thought maybe you'd like the tank and the equipment. It's good stuff."

"I know it is. Your dad never had anything but the best."

He smiled sadly. "Yeah, that was dad all the way, wasn't it? Nothing but the best." Scott's gaze dropped to his feet. He swallowed hard, and I saw his Adam's apple bob. "He wanted me to be the best, too. You know what? I don't think I ever really made him happy."

"Oh, you're wrong about that, Scott. He was very proud of you."

"Yeah, well . . . Listen, do you want the tank? I'll carry it in for you and help you set it up."

"Why, yes. Sure. Thanks."

Really, I didn't want it anymore. It was only the fish I'd been fond of. But I didn't have the heart to say no to Scott. I unlocked the door and then held it open while he wrestled the box through. In the living room, I cleared a small table. Together, we lifted the tank out and onto the flat surface. Without the fish and water, it looked dirty and smelled rank.

"You want me to help you clean it up and fill it?" Scott asked.

"No. I'll do that myself later. Getting a tank balanced takes some time and right now I'm kind of tired."

"Yeah, you look sort of washed out." He eyed my overelaborate HairStop curls. "I guess maybe you're not doing so great, either. You gotta' forgive my mom for the way she acted. She's real upset."

"I can imagine."

Uncomfortable in this new role of family mediator, Scott reached down and petted Mopsy. Since we'd come inside she'd yoyoed between us, whimpering and wagging her stumpy tail frantically. "Love me, love me!" her lolling tongue begged.

"I guess you work pretty hard in your job."

"Yes, I do. Hey," I said, "would you like a soda? I've got Coke and Pepsi."

"No, I better go or my mom will start wondering what I'm doing." Balanced on the balls of his feet, Scott shifted his weight from foot to foot. "Sometimes, are the kids you work with in trouble because they don't have dads?"

"Sometimes that's part of it."

"I guess I know how that is."

"I guess you do. Scott, I'm so sorry about Joe. I wish there was some way I could go back in time and change what happened."

"You mean talk him out of it?"

"Maybe."

"Me, too." He shook his head. "I couldn't believe it when my mother first told me. I mean, I just couldn't believe it." Though Scott was close to six feet, his eyes had the look of a lost child's. I patted his shoulder.

For a second his fingers curled around mine. Then he took a step backward. I was the enemy, after all, the woman his mother blamed for his father's death. "I've gotta go now." Still, he hesitated. "I wonder, maybe you could meet me sometime for lunch and we could talk—like we could talk about my dad?"

"Sure, Scott, I'd be glad to. You're not the only one who misses Joe."

"You won't say anything to my mom about this, will you?"

"Of course not, Scott. Your secret's safe with me."

"Thanks."

I stood on my stoop and watched him drive away.

Poor kid, I thought. Poor lost kid. Then I thought about Jamal. Superficially, he and Scott couldn't be more different. Underneath, though, weren't they just bewildered children coping with loss and change and surging hormones and the pressures of a world that was more than anyone could figure out these days? I felt sorry for them both. Me, too, I thought then. I feel sorry for me, too.

That was my mood when, after washing the curls out of my hair, I took Mopsy for her evening walk. Needing a little color and activity, we headed down to the harbor. It was warm and a game night, so people were out in force.

White families from the suburbs pushed strollers through little knots of black kids from the projects. Japanese and Korean tourists chattered while they swung cameras and snapped pictures. Indian women in saris led beautiful ebony-haired children with solemn brown eyes. Latino couples flirted at the water's edge, the boys in tight pants pretending to shove the girls in short skirts into the bay.

Everyone laughed and talked and rubbernecked at the visiting German tall ship moored in front of the Light Street Pavilion. From its deck young blond sailors stared down in wonder at the rich human soup flowing along the brick promenade below them.

Someday I'm going to get my act together and carry a notebook and pen. Then I'll be able to jot down some of the snatches of conversation I overhear during these nightly strolls.

"I just feel that there's meaning in everything," a lanky brown-haired youth confided to his pretty red-headed date as he passed by me.

"If he tries that one more time, I'm going to put his ass in a sling," a woman in tight jeans and three-inch heels informed her girlfriend smartly. "Just because he's bought me a lousy burger doesn't mean I have to jump into the sack with him."

I was savoring this last pearl of dating wisdom when I spotted Pete sitting at one of the tables outside Paolo's. Since he was deep in conversation with a man I didn't know, I would have passed by without bothering him. But at that moment, he glanced up and saw me.

"Hey, Sal!" He grinned, waved and then motioned me over.

I shortened Mopsy's leash and led her up the steps. Since Pete and his friend had a corner table, I could say hello without invading the restaurant's cordoned-off turf.

"Sally!" Pete leaned over the planter that separated us and hugged me. Still holding my shoulders, he leaned back and looked into my eyes, for signs of grief, I suppose. "How're you doing?"

"I'm doing fine. Not as good as you, though. Hey, you look great!" He really did. His skin smelled of lemon and looked freshly shaved. He'd shed his jacket, but the lightweight gray wool pants and silky blue shirt he wore fit him the way only very expensive clothes can. "Why don't you try giving your older brother a lesson in good grooming?" I joked.

"Yeah, why don't I try getting my head knocked off my shoulders?" Pete's gaze wandered to Mopsy. She was tugging at her leash, panting to get at him. "Don't tell me this is your new watchdog. She doesn't exactly growl at strangers."

"That's just a fiendishly clever ploy. Meet my new secret weapon, Mopsy, the fierce beast of the jungle. First she smothers you by shedding hair all over you, then she drowns you with saliva while licking you to death."

"Sounds like a great way to go," Pete's friend drawled.

All the while Pete had been greeting me, I'd been aware of the other man at the table. His business suit didn't look as if it had ever seen a rack, either. Propped against his chair was a leather briefcase that instantly made me visualize a five-hundred-dollar price tag. However, that wasn't what had really snagged my attention.

He had the kind of looks I've always been a pushover for. Black curly hair, snapping dark eyes, an air of crackling masculinity. I wished that I had on something a little nicer than jeans and a baggy T-shirt. I'd come out with my hair still wet and wondered how it had dried. The way Pete's companion's eyes were wandering over me, though, what he saw couldn't have been all bad.

"Aren't you going to introduce me to the lady, Pete?"

"Why, sure." While the man at the table rose, displaying a trim, athletic figure, Pete took my left hand and turned toward him. "Mike, this is my foster sister, Sally Dunphy. Sally, meet Mike Theologus, a friend and benefactor."

"Benefactor?" Mike and I were staring at each other. I wondered if he was married but couldn't drag my gaze away long enough to check out his ring finger.

"Mike's vice president of the Webster Company," Pete said, naming a major development company in the area. "He's backing my race for city council."

"Well, then he must have good taste in candidates," I murmured as Pete passed my hand to his friend's.

"Among other things," Theologus said with a grin. I glanced down at our entwined fingers and smiled. No ring.

7

Pete and Mike asked me to join them for a drink, but I used Mopsy for an excuse and declined. Mama says I was born looking for a flea in my sweater. I don't like to jump into a situation with both feet until I've had a chance to mull it over.

The more I thought about Mike Theologus, though, the more I approved what I'd seen. If Pete liked him, he couldn't be too bad, and I hadn't felt such instant attraction to a man in a long time. Better yet, the vibes signaled that it was mutual.

"Interesting," I muttered to myself, "veeery interesting."

The next afternoon Maggie promenaded into my office with a stack of phone messages. I'd just returned from a marathon meeting with the staff at Charles H. Hickey, Jr., the correctional school for delinquents where too many of Maryland's juvenile cases wind up. Seeing their problems firsthand had made me more determined than ever to keep as many of my kids out of there as possible.

"What are you? This Jamal Bassett's guardian angel?" She handed over her collection of pink slips. "I see from these calls that you're looking into day care for his younger brothers and sisters and a job training program for his mother."

"You know what they told us in graduate school about healing the whole family," I muttered as I sorted through the messages. I paused, eyeing the slip with Duke Spikowski's name on it.

Maggie broke into a raucous giggle. "Girl, if you could see the expression on your face."

"I'm so happy that I've sprinkled sunshine over your drab day, Mag. What did Detective Spikowski want?"

Maggie's grin threatened to split the lower half of her face. "Said he was lonesome for the sound of your sexy voice. I tell you Sally, that big hunk is smitten."

"He was just joking. Duke and I have known each other forever."

"Maybe all that means is 'ol Detective Spikowski's been waiting just about forever for his chance." With a wicked flounce of her ample hips, Maggie strutted back to her desk. As I watched her go, I wondered if she and Mama were swapping matchmaking info. Hadn't Mama said almost the same thing?

Though I didn't return Duke's call, I'll admit that every time the phone rang, I lifted the receiver with my ear cocked for his voice. I decided it was just as well when I never heard it.

I stayed late at the office catching up on paperwork. Around six, I headed my Mustang down to Fells Point. It's Baltimore's historic seaport neighborhood. A century and a half ago Baltimore Clippers jammed Fells Point's harbor. Chandlers, sailmakers, shipbuilders, and warehouses once lined its docks. Now entrepreneurial types have converted the warehouses into condominiums. Bars teeming with yuppies and college kids crowd the waterfront.

Happily, among the bars and fancy restaurants that have sprung up to cater to the tourist trade, there are still some old-time Baltimore eateries. Jimmy's is my favorite. It's nothing fancy. Some of the tables under their plastic tablecloths have probably been in use since 1922. It's the only local place I know about where you can get a monster dish of shrimp creole for $4.50. Ordering a glass of wine there means you get asked, "You want a large or a small, hon?" The large goes for a buck and a half.

After I ate, I walked down Thames to Ann Street. Frank Leftwich has a house on Ann. Joe and I went there for dinner once when Frank's mother was still alive. Together they spent her declining years restoring it. I remember how proudly she'd showed me around and how solicitously Frank trailed after her to make sure she didn't stumble on a rug or have trouble with the steps.

During the little history lecture she'd given me I'd learned the house is eighteenth century and among the oldest in Fells Point. It once belonged to one of the privateers who got the English so riled up they called Baltimore a "nest of pirates," and started the War of 1812.

My stomach fluttered as I approached the front step. But I've had plenty of practice knocking on front doors where I know I'm not welcome.

"Who is it?" I heard Frank's footsteps slapping the tiles in the hall.

Not too sure he'd open the door if he knew I was on the other side of it, I leaned on the bell.

"All right, all right, all right." The scowl on Frank's face deepened when he saw me. "Sally, what—"

"I need to talk to you."

As I shouldered past, he moved to block me, but he was too late. I was already in with my back pressed against the corner wall so he couldn't easily shove me out again. We were in a dark little passage between floors. It was obvious that I'd interrupted him in the middle of his evening meal. He wore slippers, a baggy pair of sweats and a stained sweater. The fragrance you get when you microwave a Hungry Man frozen dinner drifted down the stairs. I could hear the faint drone of a television news show.

"Sally, what's this all about?" Frank shot a quick, anxious look up and down the street and then pushed the door shut. In the gloom, I could barely see his face.

"You know what this is all about, Frank. There's something funny going on, and I think you know what it is."

"Funny?"

"Not ha-ha funny, wrong funny."

"I don't know what you're talking about."

"What were you really doing in Joe's apartment the other night?"

His mouth made an unhappy popping sound. "I've already explained that to the police. I don't need to explain it again to you."

"Frank, you may not think of yourself as my friend, but I know you liked and respected Joe. Do you know something about his death that you haven't told the police?" There, I'd said it. Now that the question was out of my mouth, I felt stronger.

In the shadowy light, Frank's skin had turned dishwater gray. "No. Of course not."

"Do you have any reason to think it might not have been an accident?"

"Sally, please, I don't have anything against you. But you have no right—"

"Frank, listen to me. I cared for Joe much more than

you did. I need to know what really happened to him. You were in Joe's apartment that night to get a document. When you ran past, I tore off a corner of it. It said, 'Departure S.'"

Frank let out a little squeal of strong emotion, whether of terror or rage, I couldn't tell. "Why are you hassling me like this? What do you want?"

"The truth, just the truth. If you know something that might suggest Joe didn't really commit suicide, please tell me." I was pleading now, some of the guilt I had about the possibility that Joe had killed himself over me bleeding through into my voice.

Not answering, Frank threw open the door and grabbed my arm. As he yanked me close, I could smell stale beer on his breath.

"Frank!"

"What are you doing here? What are you accusing me of?"

"I'm not accusing you. I just need to know—"

"I had nothing to gain from Joe's death," he screeched. "I wasn't in line to get his job." With that, he shoved me out the door. Stumbling off the step, I just barely saved myself from falling flat on my face. Behind me, I heard the door slam. Righting myself, I turned and pounded on it. "Frank!" I yelled. There was no answer. When my knuckles went raw and my voice got hoarse, I gave up and headed back to my car.

Back home, I stomped upstairs, tore off my clothes, and ran a tub full of hot water. While I lay back steaming in it, I reviewed the situation.

I'd left the bathroom door ajar. Mopsy pushed it open and came in.

"Hello. Want company?"

She stared at me and then lowered her haunches and gave a little whine.

"Had a lonely day, huh? Well, there are worse things. Just be glad you don't have my problems." I stuck out a wet arm and petted one of her silky ears. "For instance, I just had a nasty fight with a man. Usually when I do that, I know what it's about. This time I'm mystified."

After running some more hot water, I reached over my head and grabbed a washcloth. While I rubbed soap into it, I rehearsed the scene with Frank. He hadn't been happy to see me and I certainly hadn't endeared myself by pushing my way into his house. But he hadn't turned really nasty until I mentioned what I'd seen on that scrap of torn paper. That had horrified him. "'Departure S. Departure S.'" I turned to Mopsy. "What do you think it means?"

She didn't have the answer and my mind had already got off on another track. I was remembering what Frank had said as he shoved me outside his door. *I had nothing to gain from Joe's death. I wasn't in line for his job.* Who *was* in line for Joe's job?

The more I mulled this question over, the more interesting it became. I cut my hot soak short. Back in my bedroom and wrapped in a terrycloth robe, I got out my Rolodex.

Cocktail parties and big dinners are part of a CEO's way of life. During Joe's and my engagement, I'd been his hostess and got to know a lot of the C&G bigwigs. When I came home from the hospital after I was assaulted, our social life fell apart. I hadn't been able to handle the smiling hostess role anymore. Maybe that was part of what finally broke us up. Joe was a man who took his social obligations seriously.

To be fair, they were an important element of his job and he'd loved his job. He'd loved it a lot more than he'd loved me. On the other hand, he'd accused me of loving mine more than him. Now I could admit that he'd probably been right.

I flipped through my Rolodex until I came to Brenda Bowen's number. She had been Joe's private secretary and was a very talkative woman. Unfortunately, when I dialed, I got her answering machine. After leaving a message, I moved on through the alphabet until I came to the Placers. Bruce Placer was a lawyer for C&G. His wife Laura taught elementary school in the city system. Of all the people Joe had introduced me to, I'd liked her the best.

"Sally, is that really you?"

"It's me, all right, Laura. I know it's been a long time."

"A long time? It's been months."

"Yes, well a lot has happened."

"It certainly has. Oh, Sally, it's so awful about Joe."

"Awful." I closed my eyes and pressed a forefinger between them. With an effort, I steadied my voice. "Laura, I hope you don't mind my calling you out of the blue."

"Mind? Of course not! In fact, I was thinking about calling you."

"You were?" I doubted this.

"Since Joe died, I've been thinking about you and all the good times we had."

Laura and I both worked with children for the city, so that had given us a common interest. I'm sure this can't be true, but the way I remembered it, the other corporate wives had wanted to talk only about their kids and their clubs and their latest shopping spree in Cancun.

"Anyhow," she hurried on, "Bruce and I are having a little party a week from Friday. Why don't you come?"

"Is it going to be a C and G thing?"

"Well, yes." Laura gave the wry laugh that I remembered. "You know how it is with these guys we're married to. They mix business with everything. Still, a lot of good people will be there that you and Joe used to know. I know they'd love to see you. Please come, Sally."

I fingered the telephone cord. I doubted Joe's old business associates were anxious to see me. Still, this was an opportunity to find out what I wanted to know. "That's nice of you, Laura. I'll think about it."

"Don't just think about it. Come."

"Okay, maybe I will. Thanks."

I'd just put the receiver down when the phone rang. Surprised, I picked it up half expecting to hear Laura's voice again. Maybe there was something about the party she'd forgotten to tell me. Or maybe Bruce had just told her to disinvite me. Could I really blame him if he didn't want the ghost of past powers-that-be hanging around to cast a pall on the festivities?

The voice that flowed into my ear was deep and very masculine. "Sally?"

"Yes?"

"Mike Theologus here."

For a split second my mind went blank.

"Pete Spikowski introduced us last night. This *is* the Sally Dunphy who walks a little black dog with the longest ears since Bugs Bunny, isn't it?"

"Oh. Oh, yes." The handsome guy I'd met down at the harbor unfolded in my memory. I smiled. "Of course, Mike. Mike Theologus. How are you?"

"Much better now that you still haven't hung up on me. Since I haven't been able to get you out of my head, I thought I'd take a chance you might still remember me and call."

"How could I forget you? We only just met yesterday."

"That's true. So why does it seem much too long since I've seen you?"

"Aren't you laying it on a little thick?"

"I'm only aiming to please."

"Well, I'm flattered." I was. Mike Theologus was not the sort of man who needed to demean himself with such an outrageous line and my ego could use a little polishing.

"I was wondering if you had any free evenings in the near future? I'd like to get together."

"For what?"

"Oh, dinner, drinks, maybe a night out at a club or at the theater. Anything that sounds good to you. What about this Saturday?"

I cleared my throat. "Mike, I'm busy this Saturday. But I have another suggestion. I've been invited to a party next Saturday. I wonder if you'd like to go with me?"

Brief pause. "Sure. What kind of party?"

When I explained, his voice warmed. "Certainly. Sounds like fun."

Baltimore's National Aquarium sits like a concrete-and-glass jigsaw puzzle on piers three and four of the Inner Harbor. Really, in some ways, it alone fueled the renaissance of the harbor. All summer, mobs of people wait in monster lines to get inside. Mostly they're tourists from everywhere, the States, Japan, Korea, India, Europe, and the Middle East. We're very global down in my neighborhood.

I theorize that the aquarium owes its popularity to beleaguered parents. No matter of what ethnic or cultural background, they will do and pay just about anything to escape being cooped up with their kids in a crowded car. When your sanity is on the line, entertainment with educational value for ten dollars a pop is a bargain.

Still, I think there's something special about a place that glorifies water, the sea, and its creatures. There is for me, anyhow.

The next afternoon I felt strange heading down to the offices on the lower level. I wasn't dressed in my blue-and-tan volunteer outfit and sneakers but in a pale pink linen suit and white pumps. I'd gussied myself up to look as professional as possible in hopes of impressing Mavis Greenwich, the aquarium's assistant director in charge of program coordination.

"It's not our policy to hire juvenile offenders," Mavis informed me after I'd explained my reason for being there.

She's a tall, slender woman who wears her pepper-and-salt Afro cut close to her elegantly shaped head. Though her background is in business, she's beautiful enough and chic enough to be a model. She can be warm and charming, but her manner to me now was crisp.

"I know it's not your policy, but this is a special case." I took out a file. "Jamal Bassett is a very bright boy with potential to be an asset to this city. Unfortunately, he's growing up in a neighborhood where he hasn't much chance of realizing that potential."

"Ms. Dunphy, I know you're a volunteer here, and I appreciate that. Naturally, we want to accommodate our volunteers in any way we can, but—"

"Ms. Greenwich, I'm not here as an aquarium volunteer, but as an officer working for the city. Since you work for Baltimore, too, we're colleagues and we should be allies."

When Mavis's eyes narrowed, I hurried on. We both knew where I was going to apply pressure. Of course, she didn't want to saddle the aquarium staff with a possible troublemaker. On the other hand, the aquarium owed its life to the city's support. This facility wasn't benefiting from bond issues and hogging its valuable municipal waterfront property solely to entertain people from out of state. Its purpose was to help Baltimore's struggling citizens. At least, that was the argument I pressed the buttons on.

"Just what are you proposing?" she asked. "You want us to hire him as a security guard, or as a crowd handler? C'mon."

"Nothing like that." I shook my head. "Look, he's been accepted for weekend training at the Maritime Institute. I'd like to coordinate the training he gets there with community service that would feed into his interest in biology."

"Can you be a little more specific?"

"Lately, you've involved your mammal staff in a lot of rescue operations for stranded baby seals."

"True."

"Surely with those people as busy as they are, they could use some extra help caring for sick animals."

Mavis raised her eyebrows. "Okay, tell me exactly what you have in mind."

Twenty minutes later Mavis and I stood and shook hands. "You're quite a negotiator," she said. "If I ever get into serious trouble, I hope I'll have someone like you going to bat for me."

I grinned. "Looks to me as if your batting average is just fine."

"Now, maybe. When I was a kid I had some rough strikeouts. Believe me, I sympathize with this Jamal you're trying to help. It's just that—"

"Oh, I know. He's a risk. But aren't we all risks? And there's so much to be gained if this works out."

"One less criminal on the street?"

"One positive, contributing citizen. Look, if something bad happens with Jamal, you can blame me."

Mavis threw up her hands. "Oh, great. What am I going to do, fire you from your unpaid volunteer position?"

"You can complain to my supervisor. That will get me in deep trouble. It might even get me fired."

Mavis shook her handsome head. "People like you shouldn't get fired, Sally." Then she squeezed my hand and sent me on my way feeling like a million bucks.

In fact, my mood was so up that instead of leaving through the members' entrance, I took the elevator to the first floor. There I ambled through the lobby. I planned treating myself to a couple of minutes with the bubble columns.

The first thing visitors see when they walk into the aquarium are these stately rows of floor-to-ceiling clear Lucite columns filled with blue liquid. Compressed air bubbles through them and speakers pipe out the bloop-bloop sound. Kids love the bubble columns, and so do I.

I was planted admiring them when I spotted an aquaintance at the information desk. Steve Hufford is a retired insurance agent who volunteers several days a week at the aquarium. He's actually much more typical of volunteers than I am or Joe was. Most are older, retired folks.

"Hi, Steve, how's it going."

"Oh, fine. I think I've answered the same question a million times."

"What's that?"

"Where's the ladies room?"

I laughed. Then, on impulse, I asked, "Have you seen Frank Leftwich today? I know he walks over on his lunch hour sometimes so he can use the computer." Even last night's unpleasantness wasn't going to stop me from trying to get some straight answers out of him.

"I think I saw him come in earlier. You know where he hangs out?"

"Yeah, down in the library."

On the north side of the lobby there's an auditorium the staff opens up for guest lectures and volunteer training. The library is a concrete cubicle underneath the stage. It's a dank, windowless cell that feels so isolated it might as well be at the bottom of the sea. The place gives me instant claustrophobia. Frank stays walled up down there for hours.

The empty auditorium was dark and the narrow concrete staircase leading to the library even darker. "Frank," I called out when I came to the metal door that seals in the library and its computer.

Though my voice echoed off the slick walls, no one answered. After tapping a couple of times, I tried the door. Finding it unlocked, I heaved it open. The sickly light of the library's overhead fluorescent bounced off metal racks stuffed with marine biology texts.

"Frank?" When I took a step in, the door clanged shut behind me, which made me jump. I peered around the corner of a stack. Humming faintly, the computer sat on a small desk. I glanced at the glowing amber screen. Frank had been entering data about magazine articles.

Knowing Frank, he would never leave the light and the computer burning if he didn't intend coming back. So he must be around someplace close. The airlessness of the library gave me the heebie-jeebies. I decided to go looking for him.

First, thinking he might have gone for a cup of coffee, I tried the volunteer lounge and the snack room around the corner. He wasn't there and no one had seen him. I went back to the library and checked it again. Still empty. At that point, I consulted my watch. Really, if I was going to catch any lunch before my afternoon appointments, I ought to get going.

I have this irrational stubborn streak. Instead of heading for the exit, I took the elevator up to the fourth level and then started down through the ring tanks.

Most people agree that the coral reef and open ocean tanks are the aquarium's most spectacular features. They sit stacked on top of each other like huge coiled doughnuts. A ramp winds through their cores. As you walk down the top section of the ramp a coral reef surrounds you. The coral is fake, but the fish are real. While gentle music plays, a giant turtle paddles past a school of chubs. Filefish follow him leisurely. A pair of five-foot silver tarpon swim the opposite direction, scattering a cloud of yellow-and-black striped sergeant majors. It's like being embraced by another, far more beautiful world.

For a minute I stood admiring the cleaning station an enterprising blue tang had set up for a swarm of porkfish. Then, somewhat reluctantly, I strolled that last few yards toward the darkened area that separates the brightly lit coral-reef tank from the shadowy open ocean display.

It feels like descending from the sunlit waking hours to the phantasmagorical span of the night. For me the open ocean display is an icon for that terrifying time when monsters of the id ooze out of hiding to swim freely through your nightmares. The monsters in the display, of course, are the sharks. There are browns and tigers, bottom-feeding nurses with feelers that hang off their blunt snouts like hairless worms, and twelve-foot-long sawfish.

I gazed at a sawfish. One swipe of his toothed rostrum could cut a man in half, Joe had told me. Once while cleaning the tank, Bill, their keeper, had gotten caught behind a barrier with one and nearly been beheaded.

All day long the sharks swim around the endless doughnut-shaped tank. They stare straight ahead. Their eyes never blink. Their jagged mouths stay agape and their sinuous gray bodies barely move. Feeding time is just about all that interrupts this gloomy monotony. A couple of times a week Bill throws them fish from the catwalk.

A commotion at the other end of the tank made me lift my head. Figuring that I'd stumbled on a feeding period and curious to see it, I meandered over to where I spotted a shark's tail churning up a wake. Since it was early in a weekday, only a half dozen sightseers were down with me in the open ocean display. They, too, began to gather in the area where all the activity was going on.

As I approached I sensed that something was wrong. I heard a gasp and then a horrified scream. Sharks came speeding from the other side of the tank, adding to the thrashing tails. A cloud of dark fluid stained the water. Then I saw a leg hanging down. It wore a shoe. Suddenly, I knew what had happened. My heart pumped crazily. I couldn't move, couldn't speak. The upper half of Frank's body appeared between the milling sharks and turned a slow cartwheel. Upside down, his drowned eyes stared at me.

8

"When was the last time you stayed home from work?" Duke asked.

"Sunday."

"Cute. Okay, not on a vacation day."

"Nine months ago."

"When you were attacked?"

I nodded and he said, "Guess that must mean you're pretty shook about this thing with Frank."

"Guess so." I hugged my knees tighter to my chest. I was wearing a T-shirt and an old pair of gray sweatpants. I hadn't slept too well the night before, and when I'd finally crawled out of bed I hadn't even thought about bothering with makeup. "It's upsetting to see the dead body of somebody you know floating in a tank full of sharks. Sort of ruins your afternoon."

Duke perched on the chair opposite the couch where I'd huddled most of the day. When he'd come banging on my door, I'd been tempted not to let him in. He looked so big and solid and healthy, it was offensive. Then he'd shouted through the mail slot that he wanted to question me about Frank's death.

"I thought you were on the burglary detail. Since when did you get involved in homicide investigations?"

"Since you became a suspect in a murder."

I straightened and let my bare feet drop flat to the floor. "I'm a suspect in Frank's murder? You're kidding."

Duke didn't look amused. His green gaze stayed steady on my face. "You were on the scene, Sally. Day before yesterday you were seen having a violent argument with the victim. You're familiar with the aquarium environment. You had motive and opportunity."

"You're actually serious, aren't you?"

"Don't fly off the handle. For the moment, I'm exaggerating. No one's accusing you of knocking off Frank Leftwich. No one's even sure his death was murder. For all we know, he took a dive into the shark tank accidentally."

"Did the medical examiner do an autopsy?"

"I haven't heard the result of that yet. The preliminary report cites a blow to the skull that probably knocked him unconscious. It could have come from a blunt instrument. But it could also have come from knocking his head against the frame of the catwalk as he tumbled over."

I shivered. Every new aquarium volunteer gets a behind-the-scenes tour, and the catwalk over the shark tank is one of the highlights of that tour. It's a narrow metal platform that projects out over a section of the tank. To my knowledge, no one before Frank had ever fallen off it.

"I gather you've had a look at the place where Frank went in?"

Duke nodded. "I gather the door is normally locked tight."

"Bill Morse manages the open ocean exhibit pretty carefully. Someone must have got hold of his keys. He showed me once how he feeds the sharks from the catwalk."

"Can't take too much expertise to toss them dead fish."

"Actually, it's more complicated than you'd imagine. They like live food, so Bill has to fool them into thinking that's what they're getting."

"Fool them?"

"All living things give off a weak electric field. Sharks have sensors on their heads that detect electric fields. Bill uses a long metal pole with a sharp wire on the end. He sticks a fish on the tip of the wire. When it comes in contact with water there's a slight electric discharge."

"And the shark goes for the dead fish thinking it's still wriggling?"

"Something like that." I had seen Bill nourish his pets. I remembered the blank stare of their eyes and their gaping mouths. I knew all about the rows of razor teeth designed to rip and shred. As I pictured their merciless, thrashing gray bodies, I remembered Frank's drowned face staring out at me from behind the Plexiglas. I put my head in my hands.

Within seconds, I felt the weight of Duke's palm on my shoulder. "Hey, try not to let it get to you."

"How can I not let it get to me?" Through the protective fence of my fingers, my breath felt unnaturally feverish. "You didn't see the way Frank looked in the water. I did."

"I did see him. After they fished him out, that is."

I choked back a gag and lifted my head. I had to know. "Was he, did they—"

"The sharks only got in a couple of nibbles, Sally. They weren't what killed him."

"Then what did?"

"Drowning. The guy drowned. Like I said, there was a bruise on his left temple. How about telling me what went on between you and Frank before yesterday?"

Fighting nausea, I gave Duke the story of my last two encounters with Frank Leftwich. While I talked, Duke sat opposite. His face stayed blank and his mouth tight. When I finished, he shook his head. "I warned you, Sally. I told you to let it go. But would you ever listen? Oh, no, not you."

Resentment finally put some starch in my spine. "It's the most natural thing in the world that I would try to get Frank to tell me what he knew about Joe's death."

"It's not natural for you to meddle in police business. Why couldn't you leave it to the people who are responsible?"

"So far as I can see, everyone at the BPD believes Joe committed suicide, even you."

"First off, it isn't my case. I'd be stepping on Homicide's turf if I tried pretending it was. Second, I talked to Leftwich once and I intended talking to him again."

"When?"

"When I had the time."

"Well, I had the time day before yesterday."

"Yes, and so one of his neighbors saw the two of you brawling at his door and reported it. That looks pretty when the guy falls or gets pushed into a shark tank the next day with you standing around watching."

I had to admit that it was an unnerving coincidence. I swallowed. "Do you believe my story?"

"About being at the aquarium to get Jamal Bassett a job? I don't have to believe it. I happen to know that

Johnny Perski, who's the investigating officer, already checked it out."

"Oh, thanks a lot."

"Don't get on your high horse, Sally. I would've believed you even if Johnny hadn't talked to Mavis Greenwich. I know you're not a liar."

"Just out of morbid curiosity, do you also know I'm not a murderer?"

"Under ordinary circumstances, sure."

"Ordinary circumstances? What's that supposed to mean?"

Duke raked a hand through his curls. "Just that I know how crazy you were about Joe. If for some reason you'd come to believe that Frank Leftwich was involved in his death . . ."

The sentence trailed off, but I had no trouble completing it mentally. "First off," I snapped, "I was crazy about Joe, past tense. We had been finished for months when he died. Second, even if I believed that Frank had personally thrown Joe off that bridge, I would never have wanted to see that pathetic little man's dead body floating in a pool of hungry sharks."

"They couldn't have been all that hungry or they would have taken more than a few nips."

"Duke . . ."

He leaned forward. "Tell me the truth, Sally. Were you really over Joe?"

The intense way he fired the question startled me. "I still feel bad about how the relationship ended, but I wasn't in love with him when he died."

"I guess I thought you still were. I figured that's why you're so standoffish with men."

I was offended. "I'm not standoffish."

"You are with me."

Exasperated, I said, "Duke, I've had a rough couple

of years and I'm still healing. At least, I was until all this started up. Anyhow, what standard of standoffishness are you applying here? Why is it that when a woman doesn't instantly invite a man into her bed he decides she's unfriendly?"

"I asked you for lunch, not a session in bed, and you turned me down."

"I know how men operate. Lunch was just a preliminary."

"Lunch was lunch. Anything that followed would have been up to us both."

"I was not interested in making any mutual decisions of that nature."

"Let's be honest. If it's not because you're still hung up on Joe, then is it because there's something wrong with me?"

"There's nothing wrong with you."

"Okay, prove it. Let me come over here tonight and cook dinner for you. You wouldn't think it to look at me, but I'm a reasonably good cook. I make a garlic sauce that goes great over grilled fish."

"Duke, no."

He straightened and leaned back. "Okay. So maybe, under the circumstances, fish is a bad choice. How about pasta? I'm a whiz with that, too."

"Duke!"

"Sally, if I were baby brother Peter suggesting dinner you wouldn't hesitate, would you?"

"That's different. Pete isn't, he doesn't . . ."

"Doesn't what?"

"There's nothing sexual between me and Pete and never has been."

"And there is between me and you?"

He looked too satisfied. Exasperated, I snapped, "Duke, whether there is or not is beside the point. I don't want it. Right now I'm a mess. I'm wracked with guilt over what happened to Joe and not too sure I want to get emotionally involved that way with a man for a while. What I need is a friend, not a lover. You're my brother, my family, and I want things to stay like that."

"We may be family in a strange sort of way, Sally, but I'm not your brother. I never have been. As far as the sex thing goes, it's been there for a long time and we both know it. There's just never been any opportunity to do anything about it. Until now, that is." He stood. "Yeah, yeah, I'm going to leave you in peace. Before I go, there's just one more thing."

"What?"

"You haven't done yourself any favors playing girl detective the last forty-eight hours. I don't think Perski really believes you're involved in Frank's death. Even if he did, there's no evidence. That doesn't mean he won't get around to questioning you, and questioning you hard. So be prepared. In the meantime, stay home today and get your head together. Go to work tomorrow and do the job you were trained for."

"And stay out of trouble and out of the BPD's hair."

"That's my message exactly."

I didn't see Duke to the door. I just stayed on the couch staring at the window until his car rolled away down the street. Then I leaned back against a pillow and groaned. When he'd shown up, I'd already had a headache. Now it was worse.

I schlepped to the kitchen and got myself a couple of aspirin. Downing them, I returned to the couch and waited for the throbbing to subside. After a while, I dozed. Between nasty dreams, I woke up long enough to hear the postman push mail through the brass slot in the front door. It wasn't until shadows had thickened in the corners of the room that I summoned enough energy to get up and check the little pile of envelopes and cards heaped on the floor.

I wasn't expecting to find anything interesting—an announcement about a gallery opening, my telephone bill, possibly my bank statement. So when I came across a plain white envelope with no return address, I turned it over curiously. When I slit it open, the contents gave me a chill.

It was from Frank Leftwich. Just a brief note written neatly on a card. It was postmarked yesterday morning, so he must have written and mailed it immediately before he died. "If anything happens to me," it read, "check with my sister, Mona. I've left a letter with her explaining all of it." Underneath Frank's signature was Mona's address and telephone number.

All of it, explaining all of it. My heart pounded against my rib cage. I headed to the phone, my first impulse to tell Duke about this. Yet when I picked up the receiver, I hesitated. I didn't care for the way Duke had treated me, telling me to keep my nose out of police business. Really, he seemed unnaturally determined to thwart my tries at learning the truth. Frank had sent me a message from the grave. Me. This was my business, too.

Mona Leftwich lived in Frederick and taught biology at Hood, a private women's college in the area. I dialed Mona's office number. She answered on the fourth ring.

"You don't know me, Professor Leftwich, but I was a friend of your brother's." Considering the unpleasantness of my last meeting with Frank, this felt like a lie. On the other hand, the poor man hadn't had many friends, so maybe I qualified. After I expressed sympathy and shock over what had happened to Frank, I told her about the card I'd received from him. "Did he leave a letter for me with you?"

"No, there's nothing like that." She didn't sound like a woman recently bereaved. Her voice was crisp.

"Are you sure?"

"Of course I'm sure."

"Did Frank ever talk to you about his boss, Joe Winder?"

"I haven't heard from Frank in ages. After Mother died, we hardly spoke. He thought I didn't pay enough attention to her."

"Well, perhaps he mailed that letter the day he mailed me the card and it just hasn't arrived yet."

"That's possible, I suppose."

"If you're coming to Baltimore for Frank's funeral, could you bring the letter with you?"

"There won't be any funeral. I don't believe in that sort of primitive nonsense. As soon as the police release Frank's body, he'll be cremated and his ashes promptly buried." This lady definitely did not come across as the sentimental type. I pictured her a female version of Frank himself, down to the watery eyes and Coke-bottle glasses. How do biologists spend their day? Dissecting motherless kittens?

"Oh. Well, then, if you get a letter for me, would you let me know?"

"Certainly, Ms. Dunphy, I'll be glad to."

And that ended our conversation.

For the next several days I debated saying something to Duke about Frank's card. Maybe if the opportunity had come up, I would have. But I was still smarting from our last tête-à-tête and the feeling that Duke was out to sabotage me. Also, I was very busy.

Spring seems to bring out the criminal tendencies in our youth.

Nevertheless, the letter was on my mind. I called Mona back twice to ask if she'd received it. Each time she answered with an incisive no.

I began to think that poor Frank had only intended writing this mystery letter. He must have fallen into the shark tank before he got the chance. Surely, if he'd written it and not mailed it, the police would have found it in his house or office. I knew they'd searched both places.

Saturday rolled around and I went out and bought myself a new dress for the Placers' party, a sleek black number with a thigh-high hemline that molded my hips like a stocking. During my time with Joe, he'd encouraged me to be a snappy dresser. Since then I'd lost five or six pounds and none of my old clothes fit quite right. Now I felt nervous enough about going back into that environment with a new man that I wanted to look good.

Judging from Mike Theologus's reaction when I opened my door to his knock, I succeeded.

"Hey," he said, after giving out with a low whistle, "you were cute in jeans. In that outfit you look like a model."

"Thanks."

"I like the blue stone in those earrings. Gives those gorgeous big gray eyes a bluish cast."

"Thanks again. You're looking pretty presentable yourself." This was an understatement. In his gray linen sport coat and open-throated pearl silk shirt, Mike looked like a younger, sexier Richard Gere.

Guilford, where Bruce and Laura live, is one of Baltimore's oldest and poshest neighborhoods. This was attested to by the Mercedeses, BMWs and

Lexuses squatting in most of its tree-shaded drive-ways. The curbs outside the Placers' columned front porch teemed with expensive automotive hardware. Mike's gleaming black Infiniti, as he pulled up behind a bottle green Jaguar, fit right in to the thoroughbred stable.

They say Baltimore is really just a big small town, and it's true. At least, it always amazes me how people who hold any kind of power or who are in any way in the public eye all know each other. We hadn't been inside Bruce and Laura's front door more than a couple of minutes when Mike started shaking hands with old acqaintances. He was on a first-name basis with far more people here than I'd ever been.

"Sally," Laura cried, coming forward and pecking me on the cheek, "you look great! How do you keep your figure like that? It isn't fair!"

"Don't talk to me about fair, Laura Placer, not when you live in a palace." I wasn't really joking. Not many Baltimore city schoolteachers preside over a mansion reminiscent of Tara. I cast an admiring glance toward the living room. Laura had furnished it in antiques from Maryland's classical period. Everything looked right, down to the antique-painted Greek Revival furniture and the chrome yellow color on the walls.

Her equally gussied-up guests added to the impression of festive affluence. Their polite chatter wafted up to the high ceilings and bounced off the Italian crystal-and-amber-colored chandelier adorning the big entry hall.

"I just married the right man." Laura winked. "But, hey, you're not doing so badly in the man department yourself, I see." Both of our gazes had found Mike. He lounged in front of the punch bowl in the dining room, deep in conversation with Laura's lawyer husband.

"Mike and I just met."

"Oh, really? Well, lucky you. Mike Theologus has to be one of the most eligible bachelors in Baltimore right now."

"Sounds as if you know him well."

"Not personally, I'm sorry to say. But he does business with Bruce's firm, so I've seen him around. I do know he has quite a reputation with the ladies." She winked again. "Think you can handle it?"

"I don't know," I answered seriously. "I haven't really dated much since Joe and I called it quits. This is sort of a new thing for me."

Laura sobered right up. "Oh, I can imagine, Sally." She touched my arm. "It was insensitive of me to talk like that. I'm so sorry about Joe."

"I know you are."

"Now this thing about Frank Leftwich. Have you heard?"

"Yes, I heard." Why tell her I'd been on the scene or that I stared into Frank's dead eyes minutes after he'd drowned?

"It's such a strange coincidence. I mean, first Joe falls off a bridge and then Frank tumbles into a shark pool. I mean, have you ever heard anything so bizarre?"

"It's pretty bizarre," I agreed glumly.

Pret-ty bi-zarre.

All the rest of that evening the phrase rattled around in my head. Partly because of Mike, who was either having a great time or was a great actor, I stayed longer than I'd expected to. At first it was hard talking to people I hadn't seen in so long and with whom I no longer had anything in common. After everyone had a few drinks, the conversation loosened up.

It was Marsha Zekorske, the plump wife of a C&G junior partner, who told me what I wanted to know. Marsha was ambitious and dissatisfied. As she talked about mutual acquaintances at C&G, that jealous dissatisfaction lay imbedded in her smooth young voice like a layer of salt. "I'm surprised the Pozeres aren't here," she said while playing idly with the stem of her champagne flute.

"Who are they?"

"Oh, don't you know? No, I guess you wouldn't since you've been out of the scene for so long. A year ago Al Pozere moved back to Baltimore from the Boston branch. I understand he's a home-grown product who went north to make a name for himself. Anyhow, he came in here on an equal footing with Jim," she said, referring to her baby-faced husband. "That didn't last long. From the minute he arrived he's been burning the track, impressing the hell out of everybody. It's not definite yet, but word is he'll be taking over Joe Winder's position."

If I'd been a Doberman pinscher, my ears would have pricked to attention. "Oh, really? I'd like to meet this guy. Are you sure he's not here?"

"I don't see him. Oh, wait, they must have come in when I wasn't looking. There he is in the corner, talking with Allan Pryce."

I swiveled. Following her direction, my eyes lit on the back of a tall man with close-cropped dark hair. He was in earnest conversation with someone I didn't know. He bent his head to the shorter man as if he were eager to suck up every word. Even before he turned so I saw him in profile and took in his heavy black eyebrows and bony nose, I recognized him. Al Pozere was the man with Frank that night in front of the aquarium. Now, as then, I felt a shiver walk up my spine.

"Here, let me introduce you."

"Oh, no, that's not necessary."

My protest came too late. Marsha took me by the arm and waved at Pozere. "Yoo hoo, Al." A minute later she'd made the introduction and left us alone.

"I'm delighted to meet you," Pozere said. "I've heard a lot about you." He gazed down at me with hard black eyes.

"You have? From who?"

"From Joe Winder, of course."

"He talked about me?"

"Only in the most complimentary terms, of course. Now I can see why." Pozere cast a comprehensive glance over me and smiled. I could see it was meant to be charming and I was reacting irrationally, but it made me angry. I try not to prejudge the kids that I deal with. Nevertheless, over time I've begun to put them in categories. This guy was a chess player, I thought. He was a man who looked at life as a game set up for him to manipulate, a man who played the game by using people as pawns for his advantage. Of course, that didn't mean he'd murdered Joe. Chess players can be criminals. But my snap personality profile suited an up-and-coming CEO just as well.

"We all miss Joe," he said.

"I miss him, too," I answered stiffly. Then I gave the first lame excuse I could think of and retreated to the other end of the room, as far away from Al Pozere as I could get.

"Enjoy yourself?"

It was cozy and plush in the dark interior of Mike's car. The leather passenger seat cradled me. "I don't know if 'enjoy' is quite the word."

At the red light where he'd pulled to a stop at an intersection, I caught his half smile. "Know exactly what you mean."

"Oh? Whenever I scoped you out you seemed to be having such a good time at the party that I quit feeling guilty for dragging you to it."

Mike chuckled. "I have just three things to say about that. First, guilt is a waste of energy. Second, nobody drags me. If I hadn't wanted to be your escort, we wouldn't be riding together along Falls Road. Third, it's always good business to have a good time when you're doing business."

"I gather that means you were doing business tonight? Men! What kind of business could you have been doing?"

Mike's laughter cracked. "Anytime you're in a roomful of power guys like that, everything you say and do—it's business."

"You mean guys like Al Pozere?"

Mike shot me a quick glance. "He's definitely a high kicker in the chorus line."

"Now, let me see if I can figure out the translation for that. Al Pozere is a very important man in this town."

"A real up and comer."

"Takes one to know one."

"Damn right." Mike flashed me a roguish wink.

"You amaze me. I'd hate having business on my mind every waking minute."

"Of course you would. You're a girl. What do little girls do? Dress dolls and jump rope together. What boys learn to do is to win." He shook his head. "Win, win, win, win. That's all I ever heard when I was a kid."

"You mean that's all you wanted to hear. Along the way someone must have pointed out there's more to life."

"Right, and for a while there I was willing to consider the possibility. Now, with a few more years experience and a divorce under my belt, I'm not so sure. There are times when I think maybe my dad and my football coach had the gospel all along. Winning is it. Any more questions?"

"Yes, where are we going? We're headed north, but I live downtown."

"I was wondering when you'd notice. Well, here's my thought. We didn't really spend much time together this evening. I figured I'd take you to my place. We'd have a drink together, talk a little and get to know each other."

"You might have consulted me about this agenda."

"No salesman worth his quotas turns his game plan over to a reluctant customer." He quirked an eyebrow. "Just how reluctant are you, by the way?"

"If by 'talk' you mean we're going to wind up in bed together, forget it."

He gave a long, mock sigh. "Very reluctant. Does that mean there's another guy?"

I thought of Duke and then, with an illogical twinge of guilt peppered with irritation, dismissed him. Duke and I were family, and despite his unsubtle maneuverings, I'd keep it that way, dammit. "No."

Mike grinned. "Just what I wanted to hear. Sally, don't worry that I'm going to try jumping your bones. Honest, I just want to get to know you better. Say no now and I'll turn the car around and take you right home."

Mike had pulled off onto a country lane and turned into a small circular drive. It had the rustic dishabille you have to pay a landscape architect a lot of money to achieve. Tufts of pampas grass nodded over stone planters. Somewhere close a fountain plashed musically and freshened the air with gentle moisture. A raked white gravel path led through artful mounds of greenery to a sprawling redwood house built low to the ground and festooned with decks.

Against my better judgment, I didn't say no. Instead, I allowed Mike to lead me inside. Okay, I was curious about the house. But I was also mightily attracted to him. His brashness didn't put me off. Quite the contrary, it energized and intrigued me. His boyishness, his outrageousness, and—yes, his obvious success disarmed me. He was nothing like Joe, yet I recognized many common denominators. The confidence, the swagger, the need to have his own way. What is it about men like this that bowls me over? Maybe it has something to with their being the opposite of the kind of losers my mother shacks up with.

After I admired the inside of Mike's house, I made use of his powder room. It amused me to find a stack of *Soldier of Fortune*-type magazines stacked next to the john. Apparently Mike's macho philosophy had more than one dimension. When I came out I remarked about this and he laughed.

"All I ever wanted to be was a high-school dropout marine storming beaches on foreign shores. My old man made me go to college and be a business exec. The magazines are my fantasy life. Sort of the male version of the fashion rags you women drool over."

He poured us each a drink. We went out onto one of the decks and talked. He told me about his divorce.

"How long has it been?"

"Just over a year. She's getting remarried next month."

"You're not over it yet, are you?"

"Maybe I'm not. But that doesn't mean I'm not willing to try." He drew me to him and we kissed. Though I liked his kisses and the musky scent of his aftershave, I held him off.

"What have you got against sex?" he asked as he finally saw me back outside to his car.

"Nothing. We just met, that's all. I don't jump into bed with a man when I barely know him."

"That's fine with me. I'd just like to be sure that's the only reason you're not interested." As he nosed the car onto the street, he shot me an inquiring look. "Guess I might as well tell you. I've been hearing some stories about why you and Joe Winder called it quits."

"Gossip certainly gets around. What have you heard?" I hated people talking about me behind my back. I especially hated knowing Joe had done it with Al Pozere. Now here was Mike, a stranger until a few days ago, telling me he'd been hearing stuff about me. It hardly seemed fair since I knew virtually nothing about him.

Mike looked uncomfortable. "Look, this is none of my business. I should have kept my big mouth shut."

"Yes, you should have. But now that you've opened it, what have you heard?"

"Only that you had a bad experience a while back and afterward you and Joe broke up."

"I suppose you're referring to my assault. Several months ago I was assaulted while I was out jogging. Yes, that did have something to do with why my relationship with Joe Winder went sour. If you're really asking if I'm now sexually dysfunctional, the answer is no."

Actually, I wasn't too sure about this. But I certainly wasn't going to admit a sexual problem to this man, or any other. "Why do guys decide there's something wrong with you if you're not panting to let them rip your clothes off after five minutes acquaintance?"

Mike laughed. "Isn't it obvious? We can't bear thinking we're not irresistible to the entire female gender."

"Why? Is it because all women are surrogate mothers?"

"Oh, yeah, I forgot. You're a psychologist. Well, maybe you've got something there. But when I look at you I'm certainly not thinking about my mother."

"I'm sorry about what happened to you," he said a few minutes later after he pulled up in front of my house. "If I could go back and change it for you I would. But I didn't know you then. I'm hoping you'll let me get to know you now. When can I see you again?"

"I don't know. At the moment, my life looks complicated."

"Not too complicated for the simple pleasures, I hope." He pulled me into his arms. I'd held back on the kissing at his place. This time, feeling safe in the car, I relaxed and enjoyed myself. Mike was a good kisser, and I suspected he'd be an exciting lover.

"You could invite me in," he whispered when we finally drew apart.

I shook my head. But I was tempted. I told myself being tempted was good. Like purple crocuses in March, a hopeful sign.

"Okay, I won't make a big obnoxious deal. But I'm not giving up, either. I'll call you, okay?"

"Okay," I said, and slipped out the passenger door. I stood on the curb and waved as he pulled off. Then, fumbling for the key in my purse, I turned toward my stoop.

"Well, well. Looks like you had a fun evening." Like a destroyer lying in wait for an enemy sub, Duke heaved out of the shadows.

9

"Duke! What are you doing here?" I dropped my keys. They clattered off the curb and into the gutter. "Damn!" Gingerly, I kicked at the mound of sodden leaves and other unappealing objects into which they'd sunk.

"Stay back. You didn't dress for alley picking." Duke switched on a flash and fished up my keys. "Want them? Or shall I play the gentleman and open your door?"

"Knock it off, Duke. Give them to me."

"No, I think I'll be suave and do the unlocking. That's what you like, isn't it? Real smooth gents with manners?"

As Duke followed me up my steps, his shadow swallowed me. The man had the shoulders of an ox. In his gray sweats he looked a lot like someone you wouldn't want to meet in a dark alley. Must be nice, I thought. A guy Duke's size could wander the streets at night without a qualm. "Duke, it's very late."

He turned the flash on his watch. "One-forty-nine, to be exact. When you pulled up with lover boy, it was one-thirty-six. That means, subtracting a couple of minutes for chatting, you were smooching in there for a good ten minutes."

"Did you set a timer? How come you were lurking around here in the dark spying on me?"

"Me spy? Lord-a-mercy, Miss Sally! I told you before, I'm an insomniac. I get restless at night and take walks."

"Why don't you walk in your own neighborhood?"

"It's not as interesting as this one."

"Hey, you've caught Jamal. Now I'm taking care of him. What makes this neighborhood so interesting?"

"Don't play dumb. You're in it." He turned the key and pushed the door open. Barking maniacally, Mopsy came flying through. Duke snagged her collar and held her back so her flailing paws and lolling tongue wouldn't ruin my dress.

While I reached to quiet her, I stared at Duke. "I left her out in the yard. How did she get inside?"

"I put her inside."

"What? You? How?"

"When I came by, she was barking, bothering the neighbors. So I put her inside."

"I locked the door and set the alarm. You're telling me you broke into my house?"

"Nothing's broken. Oh, yeah, I disarmed your alarm. When you go in, you'd better turn it back on."

I stood there gagging with outrage. "You, you . . ."

"Sally, you had me worried. It's not like you to be out so late. I had to make sure nothing was wrong."

"So you broke into my house to make sure I wasn't lying on the kitchen floor in a pool of blood?"

"You've gotta admit, some funny things have been happening."

"I'll say. You have some nerve, you know that?"

"The Baltimore PD will be glad to hear you think so. It doesn't usually recruit shrinking violets. Now, are you going to tell me where you were tonight? Who's that clown you were swapping spit with? I thought you said you wanted a friend, not a lover. You and that joker sure looked more than friendly playing anaconda in his car."

"I shouldn't even go on speaking to an obnoxious male chauvinist pig like you," I replied through gritted teeth. "And I wouldn't if there weren't something I want you to know."

"That's all right. Charm me with your womanly wiles. Don't hold back. We're pals, remember?"

I sputtered. Then, biting down on my anger, I described the party, Al Pozere, and his connection with Joe and Frank Leftwich.

Duke stood gazing down at me with no visible reaction. When I finished, he said, "You still haven't answered my question. What do you know about that schmo you were doing kissy-face with?"

"What does it matter what I know about him? Mike has nothing to do with all this."

"So, it's Mike is it?"

"Duke, you big lunkhead, I was telling you about a man named Al Pozere who's taking over Joe's job. I saw him threaten Frank. He's the one who should interest you."

"You wanted me for a big brother. Big brothers are protective of their little sisters. You should be more careful about who you date, Sally. There are a lot of creeps driving around in fancy cars out there. Another thing, you shouldn't wear such sexy dresses." He eyed my neckline and then my legs. My skirt had ridden up in the car. "That's just asking for trouble."

"Duke!"

"While we're on this subject, what's that guy got that I haven't? Besides the heavy-duty metal and the overpriced threads, that is? If we're such close family, how come we don't share the same values? Didn't Mama teach you that money isn't everything?"

I grabbed Mopsy's collar, brushed past him and slammed the door in his face. While he pounded on the knocker, I shot home the deadbolt.

"I'm not through talking to you, Sally."

"I'm through listening. If you break in here again, I'll swear out a warrant."

"Ha! That's a joke."

"You won't think it's so funny when they fire you for conduct unbecoming to an officer."

Ignoring Duke's hammy fist drumming on my door, I walked back to the kitchen and fixed myself a cup of tea. He went away after a while, but I was far too worked up to go to bed. I was just heading for the stairs and considering a hot bath when the doorbell rang.

Duke again, I thought. But when I peered out through my peephole, it was Jamal. He had his blond girlfriend with him.

"Miss Dunphy," he whispered when I cracked the door. "I'm not here because I mean harm, honest."

"It's two in the morning, Jamal. What do you want?" My gaze darted to the girl. She hung back in the shadows, only the glimmer of her pale hair visible in the moonlight.

When we made eye contact, she started to back off. Jamal grabbed her arm. "I know it's late Ms. Dunphy, but you've been straight with me, getting me that job and all. I can't go no place else with Chrissy, here. Can we talk to you?"

Mama would say that letting Jamal in wasn't the smartest move I've ever made. Sometimes in a job like mine you just have to operate on instinct.

"Okay, what's this all about, Jamal?" I'd switched on the overhead in the hall. Beneath its glare, my two visitors were an odd couple. Jamal was decked out in gold chains and a black nylon warmup suit decorated with violet, aqua, pink, and yellow chevrons. He looked tired but wholesome in his colorful fashion. Chrissy, his partner in crime, was another story.

In my previous sighting of her she'd worn jeans, and her face had been soap-and-water pale. Now, arrayed in poison green high-heeled platform sandals, a tight, crotch-high denim skirt studded with fake diamonds, and a pink stretch top sprayed with red glitter, she'd tricked herself out like a hooker. Her hair hung in lank blond strands and ended in half-inch brown roots. She'd carpeted her pinched features with cheap makeup.

Some of my reaction must have shown on my face. Her pale blue eyes, behind their narrowed gates of artificial lashes, gazed out at me with deep hostility.

She tried yanking away from Jamal. "This was a lousy idea. Let's get the hell out of here."

"You're stayin' Chrissy, so just be cool."

"I'm tired of you bossing me. Who do you think you are?"

"Your friend, that's who I think I am. The only friend you got, as a matter of fact."

"Friend, hah!"

"I'm a whole lot better friend than that shithead pimp you got yourself hooked up with."

I glanced from tight young face to tight young face and cleared my throat. "Would you two like a drink and something to eat?"

You don't get raised by Mama Spikowski and not turn to food as the universal cure-all. Of course, she would have offered reheated stew and homemade cookies, or a selection of heavenly just-baked pastries. The best I could do was chips and Cokes.

Five minutes later Jamal and Chrissy sat at my kitchen table. Though he no longer had a lock on her wrist, she looked ready to bolt. On the other hand, she was clawing her way through the bowl of chips I'd set between them as if they were ambrosia. Judging from her coat-hanger frame and the pasty skin beneath her clownish makeup, her nutrition hadn't been up to Julia Child's standards of late.

While I opened a couple cans of tuna and added mayo for sandwiches, Jamal and Chrissy exchanged insults. "Why can't you just let me alone?"

"If I let you alone, you'd be dead, baby. I told you, I'm the only friend you got."

"I'm doin' okay without you."

"You call spreadin' your legs down on the Block, okay? You probably already got a disease. Half the dicks down there are getting ready to fall off."

In bits and pieces, the story came out. Chrissy was a runaway. Two months ago she'd arrived on a bus from God knows where. After Jamal rescued her from a night on a bench in Druid Hill Park, they teamed up. They'd talked each other into becoming the Black and White gang. Yes, that's actually what they called themselves.

By day, Chrissy had set up housekeeping in one of the many derelict row houses in Jamal's neighborhood. Sunday nights the two had sallied forth to Federal Hill to rip off yuppies. "Things were going pretty good until we broke into your place," Chrissy declared sullenly.

"It wasn't her who nailed us, it was that big white cop."

"Then how come you don't hate his guts?"

"I do. That cop's no friend of mind."

"Yeah, well, then how come you're doing just what him and this lady tell you to do?"

"I told you why. I like workin' with the seals and building the boats. Besides, my mother's on my case all the time now. I don't want to go to no jail. Time I wised up. Time you wised up, too."

Clearly Jamal's new attitude was a major letdown for Chrissy, who'd relied on the income their robberies had brought in. Unfortunately, her solution was a pimp who set her up for business on Baltimore's sin strip, the Block.

"I thought you had more smarts than to get hooked up with that creep show." Jamal crushed the empty can of Coke he held and gazed at it in disgust.

Chrissy pretended unconcern. "I gotta' eat. Besides, Jimmy takes care of me."

"Yeah? Tonight that greaseball rat couldn't run away from you fast enough."

"Only because you pulled a gun and said you'd blow off his balls. Just who do you think you are, anyway? Some kind of skinny black Arnold Schwarzenegger?"

I rose up out of my chair. "Jamal, are you carrying a gun?"

His mouth clamped tight and his gaze glued itself to the salt shaker.

Chrissy snorted. "He's got a live piece in his underpants."

My eyes stayed fixed on Jamal. "Is that true?"

He nodded. His underlip shot forward. Underneath the gold chains and neon threads and muscles popping out from nature's freshly brewed testosterone cocktail fizzing through his veins, he looked like a guilty little boy.

"Jamal, why?"

"For protection."

"Let me see it."

Still not meeting my eyes, he reached into his waistband, fished, and withdrew a small revolver. He slapped it on the table, barrel pointed carelessly at the stove. Gingerly, I hefted it. The barrel was still warm from his body. I checked the cylinder. It was fully loaded.

"Jamal, one of the reasons the judge let you off the hook is that when you were caught you weren't armed."

"Sure he was," said Chrissy.

Jamal pitched her a glare. "I was clean when that moose detective grabbed me and nearly twisted my arm off."

"Only because you passed the gun to me and I ran for it," sneered the determined-to-be-unhelpful Chrissy.

"I'm not robbing no Federal Hill townhouse with nothin' but my pocket watch in case of trouble," Jamal defended himself. "One of those rich white honkies with no sense might pop up shooting wild."

"You didn't have a gun when you broke into my place."

"He did," sneered Chrissy. "He was just too chick-enshit to use it."

This gave me quite a little shock. Jamal employed his melting smile on me. "I didn't want to shoot at you, Miss Dunphy. Besides, you looked too fine in that nightie to get messed up with no bullets."

While Chrissy snorted, I gazed at him in despair. "Jamal, why are you walking around with a gun in your pants? Don't you realize how dangerous this is?"

"Ms. Dunphy, you don't know the meaning of dangerous if you don't live in my neighborhood. Man, when I was nine I learned to hit the deck when I saw a black car come speeding around my corner with its windows rolled down. When a drug dealer told me and my friends to get inside because lead was going to fly, we did double time. My grandma used to cry every time I went outside because she thought I'd come back shot. You know what? She was right. It could of happened easy. Just a couple months back my cousin Rich got shot because of a beef with a kid who wanted his jacket. Maybe if he'd a' had a gun, he could've protected himself. He didn't and now he's crippled in the arm."

Unfortunately, I knew that all of what Jamal said was true. In neighborhoods like Jamal's, children as young as nine ran errands for drug dealers and played cops and robbers with Tec-9s. At that age they couldn't even begin to grasp the danger, didn't fully understand the notion of death.

"I'm not giving this back to you."

He shrugged and favored me with another limpid smile. "Okay, I won't carry anymore."

"You mean that?"

"Sure I mean that. You helped me. Will you help Chrissy?"

"What if I don't want no help from her?" Chrissy declared mutinously.

Jamal turned to the girl. "Sure you want it. You don't want to cuddle with some pervert tonight. Drooling all over you, giving you AIDS. Think about it. A guy like that might screw you, then slit your throat. That Jimmy, he isn't going to come save you. All that guy wants is most of the take."

I asked, "Do you have a decent place to sleep tonight, Chrissy?"

"Sure."

"No, she don't," countered Jamal. "The house where she was camping, it isn't safe now. A gang's using it to stash. I'd let her stay with me, but my mom won't have her around. Says she's white trash."

To be honest, I could see Carrie Bassett's point of view. Chrissy was damaged goods. On the other hand, sometimes damage will heal if it gets the right medicine. I felt sorry for the girl. And I was impressed at how Jamal had charged the Block like a knight in shining armor to rescue her from a life of sin. Even if it weren't my job, I would have wanted to give him a hand.

"Chrissy can stay here tonight," I said. "Tomorrow I'll see what I can do to help her out. Now you go home and get some sleep, Jamal. I happen to know you're scheduled to work at the aquarium tomorrow."

As the door closed behind him, Chrissy and I sat staring at each other. "Now what?" She gave Mopsy an idle pat and then slumped back and cocked her haystack head.

"Bed," I said. "I have an extra bedroom upstairs. Come with me. I'll give you towels, a clean nightgown, and whatever else you need."

"No way can you give me what I need," Chrissy grumbled. Nevertheless, she followed me. She accepted the knee-length sleep shirt I offered with no more protest than the curl of her lip. Then she disappeared into the bathroom and spent the next half hour presumably scrubbing off the deposits of garish makeup layering her face. When I finally got a chance at the bathroom myself, the place looked like a paint factory after a strike by Hurricane Gilbert.

That night I lay in bed, too uneasy to sleep soundly. Sometime close to dawn, I woke up and heard creaks and faint clicks on the ground floor. I slipped on my robe and padded barefoot down the stairs.

"The TV and VCR are too old to be worth much," I said from the entry to the living room. "The CDs cost me plenty, but used CDs don't bring much on the street."

I'd surprised Chrissy kneeling in front of the cabinet where I kept my stereo. Next to her, the couch pillows lay at odd angles on the floor and the small antique blanket chest I use for a coffee table hung open. Old magazines and a couple of afghans filled it. She'd tossed one of the knitted throws at the wall.

Chrissy's wildly mussed head jerked around, and she glared at me. Watery gray light leaked through the shuttered windows. In it, her face, still streaked around the eyes with runny mascara, made me think of starving children in Somalia. She'd propped her pathetically bony rump up on her skinny heels. "I was just lookin' for some decent music to play," she declared defiantly.

"At six-thirty in the morning? Sure." I walked over and closed the cabinet. "Chrissy, I'm just a poor working girl. There's nothing valuable enough in this house to make it worth your while carting to a hock shop or a fence." Actually, this wasn't quite true. Besides the art over the mantel, I had some jewelry Joe had given me that was worth real money. I made a mental note to hide it.

"You're right," she retorted shrilly. "This is just a bunch of crap."

"Well, now that we've had a meeting of the minds, why don't we get ourselves a cup of coffee? Who knows, maybe we'll find something else to agree on."

Out in the kitchen, I scrambled eggs and nuked a carton of frozen Sara Lee goodies. One thing about microwaving, it's great for aroma. The kitchen started smelling like a bakery on a Monday-morning, and the tension between Chrissy and me eased up. After she wolfed two Danish and a plate of eggs and inhaled two cups of fresh-brewed coffee heavy on the cream and sugar, her hateful manner thawed even more.

"Why'd you run away from home, Chrissy?" I asked after I drained my own cup and refilled it.

"The bunny didn't leave enough chocolate eggs in my Easter basket this spring." She pulled a packet of Virginia Slims out of the breast pocket of the sleep shirt I'd given her and lit up. I watched her go through the ritual. As she drew smoke into her lungs, I reached for a saucer she could use for an ashtray.

"Do you have brothers, sisters?"

"Nope."

"Do you live with your parents?"

"Nope."

"Are you an orphan?"

"You might say that."

"Were you in a foster home?"

"I'm not answering any more of your questions."

"I think you were in a foster home, Chrissy. Why did you run away from it? Didn't you get along with your foster parents?"

When Chrissy didn't answer, I sighed. I'd placed a lot of children in foster homes myself. Most worked out well. But I'd seen some horrifying instances when they didn't. "You know, Chrissy even when you're in a good home it's hard to be a teenager. When you're not, it's really rough. I know because I was a runaway myself."

"Oh, yeah? Then how'd you get to be a probation officer?"

"Juvenile counselor is the title. I was lucky, Chrissy. The foster family that took me in were fine people.

They helped me get an education. Of course, I did my part, too. Stayed in school, got decent grades."

"Very uplifting. Sounds like the 'CBS Afternoon Special.'"

"Maybe, but it could be your story, too. If your foster home isn't working out, you can be placed in another. What's your last name, Chrissy?"

She inhaled deeply and then blew a smoke ring. We watched it sail lazily up to the ceiling and float apart. "Why should I tell you?"

"I promised Jamal I'd help you. I can't do that if I don't know your name."

"Right, well, I'm not tellin' you my name or where I come from. Maybe Jamal thinks you're Miss Santa Claus. To me you're just another busybody. You know what I think? I think if you know my name you'll try and make me go back and I won't be able to get away. I'm not doing that. Nobody pushes Chrissy around anymore."

Despite her declaration, Chrissy didn't walk out. She lounged on the couch all morning, watching cartoons on TV, playing my loudest CDs, eating and drinking whatever she could find in the refrigerator and filling my ashtrays with cigarette butts.

Since it was Sunday, there wasn't a lot I could do in a professional capacity. Nevertheless, I called a contact in Missing Persons and asked him to search on a fifteen-year-old runaway matching Chrissy's description. When he got back he told me there was no record on the computer. So, either she was lying about her first name or whoever she'd been living with had not reported her missing. In the parental concern department, this did not get a gold star.

"Jamal's at the aquarium," I said after Chrissy and I had each downed burgers and chips for lunch. "How about going over there and saying hello?"

"He's no friend of mine."

"Sure he is, Chrissy. A lot better than this Jimmy I heard about."

"You don't know shit about Jimmy."

"Maybe, but I do know that Jamal is your friend and that he cares about you."

She shrugged. "Okay, as long as it don't smell too fishy, sure. Why not? I've never seen the inside of that place."

I loaned Chrissy jeans, some fresh underwear, and a T-shirt. Dressed in them, she looked almost like an ordinary teenager. "You know, your clothes aren't too drab," she acknowledged as we headed out the door. "That blue beaded number I saw in your closet looks okay."

She was referring to a showy evening outfit I'd worn when I was playing hostess for Joe. I doubted I'd ever wear it again, but it had been so expensive that I couldn't bring myself to toss it. "Thanks for the compliment. After we're through at the aquarium, we can stop in at the Gallery. I'll buy you some jeans and underwear so you won't have to borrow mine."

No thank-yous, but I thought she looked pleased. She even admired my car as we walked past it and gave its red fender an admiring pat. I began to feel hopeful. Maybe I really could help her. When I'd run away from home, I'd been younger than Chrissy. Still, with all that anger and rebellion boiling inside, she reminded me of myself during that episode. I didn't find her particularly likable. But I hadn't liked myself much in those days, either.

The afternoon was warm and perfect. Cherry blossoms still fringed the kwanzans. Like velvety pale pink snow, their petals floated on the spring-scented air and piled up in drifts at the water's edge.

Multicultural knots of tourists kicked the drifts aside. The tourists hurried, ambled, gawked along the brick promenade. They snapped pictures of the paddle boats or munched treats from the vendors in the Light Street Pavilion. With edgy amusement, I observed a covey of eraser-headed black youths carrying rap-blaring boom boxes. They stalked through a pair of white stroller-pushing couples from the suburbs. As was usual in these encounters, each group pretended not to see the other.

I paused to admire a cloud of gulls. They wheeled and squawked over a skinny little black kid tossing crusts of a stale hot-dog roll. The ornithologist at the aquarium calls gulls "flying rats," but I can't think of them like that. Obviously, neither did the youngster. When he threw a scrap of bread high over his head, a gull wheeled and snatched it out of the air. The boy gave a joyful shout and I recognized him.

"Hi, Tyrone."

Tyrone saw me and looked uncertain. Then his face split into a grin and he came over. Behind him the gulls shrieked in protest. But they'd already eaten the last of Tyrone's hot-dog bun, anyway.

"How you, Miss Dunphy?"

"I'm fine. How are you? Where's your sister?"

"Keesha? She's home with my mama."

After I introduced Tyrone to Chrissy, I asked what he was up to.

"Nothin'," he admitted. He scuffed a sneakered toe on a piling and smiled shyly. "Just hangin' out. I found some bread somebody threw away in that trash can over there, so I been feeding the gulls. They're real hungry."

Despite their raucous screams, I doubted that. Baltimore's Inner Harbor has the fattest, sassiest, most obnoxious sea gulls on the eastern seaboard.

"Well, I'm glad you're not out trying to wash wind-shields at stoplights. That's so dangerous."

"I'd be there, only some bigger dudes chased me off."

"You know what you need to occupy your time when you're not in school, Tyrone? You need a regular job."

He sulked. "Nobody's going to hire a little kid like me."

I considered him. "You like dogs, Tyrone?"

"Sure. Long as they don't bite me, I like 'em fine."

"I've got a dog named Mopsy and she never bites. On nice days I leave her out in the yard. Even so, she gets pretty lonely all by herself while I'm away at work. If I paid you, would you be willing to go to my house after school and take her for a walk in Federal Hill Park?"

Tyrone's face lit. "Sure would. You live close by?"

"Just around the other side of the harbor. If you want, you can come over tonight and meet her. Hey, do you have to go back home soon?"

"No, ma'am."

"Then, would you like to go with us to the aquarium and meet a friend who works there? I'll buy you a ticket."

Tyrone beamed. "Sure. I never been there, 'cept once on a school trip."

"Great. If we hurry we might be in time for the dol-phin show."

"Dolphins are fine," Tyrone volunteered, happily falling into step with us. "But you know what I like to see best?"

"What?"

"The sharks. I heard they ate a guy last week."

Frank's image popped out of its hidey-hole. I saw his blank drowned face gazing at me, the frenzied shark tails thrashing around him. Though I shoved the violent image back into its mental file drawer, it never retreated altogether. During the rest of that afternoon it lurked in the shadowy corners, threatening to jump out at me like a horrifying jack-in-the-box.

That night as I lay in bed, I listened for sounds from Chrissy's room. There were none and that reassured me. She had seemed to enjoy the aquarium. She, Tyrone, and Jamal had laughed and joked together like the children they really were. Later, when I had shopped for her, she had been almost pleasant. Maybe there was hope.

Yet, despite my exhaustion I was uneasy. I was aware of every little sound in the house, every creak and shudder.

Again, Frank's image crept into my mind. I fought the pictures that reeled through my head, the dead eyes, the helpless floating arms and legs. The images were too strong for me. They wouldn't go away. Even in sleep they haunted me. I dreamed of a drowned man in the shark tank. But my dream wasn't of Frank. The face I saw in the water surrounded by predators with slashing teeth and cruel, soulless eyes was Joe's.

The next morning I woke up late. Apparently, I'd slept like the dead and hadn't heard Chrissy come into my room. Now she was gone. So were her new clothes, my purse, my beaded blue dress, and all the jewelry Joe had given me.

10

"*See anybody who* looks familiar?"

"Nope."

Duke guided his unmarked Cavalier down Baltimore Street. Music thumped from the open doors of storefronts. Their gaudy marquees advertised peep shows and a variety of other entertainments. "Beautiful live girls." "Adult books." Guys with pony tails sauntered in and out, sometimes gathering on the sidewalk in little knots of red and yellow neon light.

Girls in miniskirts and short leather jackets promenaded past in twos and threes. Loners stood hipshot on the curb, eyeing passing cars. One of them, spotting Duke and Pete and me cruising along, gave us the finger.

"You're a popular guy around here," Pete teased his brother.

"All the regulars know a Cavalier with an antennae is a cop car." Duke turned to me. "Still don't see any sign of this Chrissy?"

"No. But I'm sure she'll show up here eventually."

Duke and Pete had appeared at my door around eight that night. "My big brother says you're mad at him," Pete had cajoled while Duke hung back looking sulky. "Any chance we can sweeten you up by buying you an ice cream at Ben and Jerry's?"

They'd arrived just as I'd been nerving myself to go looking for Chrissy. I hadn't exactly been thrilled about invading the Block on my own. One look at Duke's broad shoulders and Pete's ex-football-tackle build and I'd decided it was worth sacrificing my pride and using my womanly wiles to get their help.

"This is awfully nice of you guys," I told them now.

"Oh, listen to that." Pete reached around me and slapped Duke's back. "She's your slave for life."

"I don't need a slave. That doesn't mean I like the idea of her coming down here at night on her own." He shot a scowl at me.

"I'm not made of glass, Duke. And I have to find this girl. She's only a kid."

"She could have left town by now," Pete suggested.

"I don't think so. She'd found herself a pimp, a guy named Jimmy."

Duke cocked his head. "Jimmy Geese, or Jimmy-the-Cushion Slyburn?"

"I don't know his last name or his nickname. Jamal described him as a shithead."

"That fits them all. Okay, if you haven't seen her maybe we should go farther afield." Duke gunned the motor at the light and sped past the gold dome of city hall and the jagged black hulk of the Holocaust memorial.

He turned right on Calvert. "What's down here?"

"A couple of informants I used to do business with."

"My brother is on a first-name basis with every slimeball in this city," Pete commented. He slumped down and crossed his arms over his chest. I wondered why he wasn't home in Columbia trying to make peace with Joyce. Didn't he care at all about preserving his marriage?

"Between the two of us, that might be true," Duke shot back. "Of course, the slimeballs you hang out with all carry briefcases and gold credit cards."

Pete shot me a sly wink. "Speaking of my friends, I hear you went out with Mike Theologus last weekend. How'd you two get along?"

"She hated him," Duke said. "She's never wants to see his smirking face again."

Pete lifted his eyebrows. "No kidding? That really true, Sal?"

"None of your beeswax." I stared out the window. "My God," I exclaimed a couple of minutes later. I'd spotted a gaggle of girls gathered around a bus stop. "Are they waiting for a bus?"

Duke shot me a derisive look. "Since when are you that naive? They're waiting for someone to pick them up."

I stared wide-eyed at the outrageous assemblage. Though the night had begun to turn cool, they wore microminis or short shorts. Flirty gold purses dangled from their wrists. They were all tall, too tall. One, despite his mesh stockings, was obviously a guy. "Are they for real?"

"Cross-dressed for success," Pete commented.

"Calvert from Fayette to Mount Royal is the strutting ground of transvestite prostitutes," Duke explained.

"I guess I'd heard that, but I never took it seriously."

Just then a white Honda Accord slowed at the curb. Wearing a leopard-print jacket over a black sequined miniskirt, spike heels, and glossy lipstick, one of the "girls" ran around to the driver's side and leaned his/her head through the open window. A moment later he/she was gone and the Accord was roaring off into the night.

"Seeing is believing," Pete chirped.

"Glad you're in such an antic frame of mind, bro." Duke drove another block and then pulled the car over to the left and unrolled the window. "Hi, Candy. How's it going?"

A thin creature in thigh-high boots and what looked like a purple leotard and ballet skirt was leaning provocatively against a lamppost. She'd wound a scarf around her head. I thought I spotted five o'clock shadow on her cheeks. She was definitely older than the other "girls" we'd seen. Somewhere in her thirties, I'd guess, and well past her prime. "Peachy," she answered Duke's question with a wary sneer. She sounded convincing. No bobbing Adam's apple, no baritone voice.

"Working tonight?"

"Mercy me. Of course not. Just enjoying the night air." Her gaze assessed Pete and me.

"Then you won't mind taking a little ride around the block with us."

"What's this going to be? Twenty questions?"

"Easy money on a slow night." Duke flashed a twenty-dollar bill out the open window. As Candy snatched at it, I made a mental note to repay Duke. Candy slid into the back, and Duke pulled away from the curb.

"What's this about?"

I sniffed. The scent of Elizabeth Taylor's White Diamonds saturated the car.

"We're looking for a young girl named Chrissy. She hasn't been in town more than a couple months and she just started doing business. You want to tell what you know about her, Sally?"

After I described Chrissy, Candy sat tapping her nails and frowning. "I've seen her around, but not in the last couple days. We don't have the same territory."

"What about her pimp? It's probably either Jimmy Geese or Jimmy Slyburn."

"Geese left town. Moved to Florida from what I hear. Slyburn?" Candy shrugged slightly too muscular shoulders. "I saw him yesterday, as a matter of fact. At the Flower Mart."

I choked back a laugh. The Flower Mart is an annual event at Mount Vernon Square. Society ladies in big straw hats set up booths for charity. They sell lemons with peppermint sticks, and handcrafts and potted plants. The event brings out the whole spectrum of our fair city's inhabitants. Mount Vernon, of course, besides being Baltimore's most beautiful historic district, is also a hangout for gays. We were within a block of it right now. In fact, even as we spoke, Duke turned left and cruised past the Gothic Methodist church that graced one of its corners.

"Sorry I can't be more help," Candy told him as we rolled past the lighted shaft of the Washington Monument, surely one of the most gorgeous night sights in Baltimore.

"You've helped some. At least I've got the Jimmys narrowed down."

"This girl, she's a runaway?"

"She's only fifteen," I said.

Candy clucked. "Kids these days. I'll tell you." Now that our business had been transacted, Candy's wary manner receded and she became breezily talkative. "This is not a trade I would advise any young person to get into. Tricking ain't no easy thing, and it's not even lucrative anymore. You know why it's so dead out here? I'll tell you why. It's not just the recession like everyone says. It's because there are children in the alleys doing it for free."

"Unfair competition," Pete murmured. His voice shook slightly. Surreptitiously, I thumped his shoulder.

Candy's mascara-laden gaze had taken on a far-away look. "I'll tell you, when I first came out it was so different. Being in this life made you think you were a star. Dressing up in women's clothes, getting men. It was glamorous, a jubilee thing. I'll tell you, there ain't no glamour in it anymore."

After we'd dropped Candy back on her Calvert Street corner, I said, "Glamour, jubilee? Is she serious?"

"When it comes to number one, everyone's serious," Duke said.

Next to me, Pete sat grinning and shaking his head. "That's the old cynic talking again. I'll tell you, brother mine, you've really got quite a wide range of acquaintances in that little black book of yours."

"You get to meet a lot of interesting people in my line of work. Candy's got a record from here to China for prostitution and loitering."

"I can imagine. When did this person start dressing up in pantyhose and high heels?"

"He told me once it was when he was about twelve. He just did it in the house. He never expected to do it when he was grown. Then, when he was twenty-one he tried on a dress of his sister's and that was it."

"What kind of a life is it?" I asked.

"Not an easy one. Most of their business is conducted in cars parked in alleys. Johns pull weapons and take their money. Sometimes they're beat up and left on lonely country roads. In summer jerks from the suburbs will drive into the city in trucks. Beating up guys like Candy with a baseball bat is a night's good clean fun. I happen to know that a girlfriend of Candy's got killed recently."

That sobered me up and even Pete stopped with the wisecracks. In fact, as I sat between Duke and Pete, a gray mist of depression seeped over me. This was the world that Chrissy and a lot of other youngsters like her were caught up in. I felt responsible because I'd lost the chance to help her.

None of us wanted ice cream anymore and Pete had an early breakfast meeting with his campaign committee. After Duke dropped his brother off at his townhouse, he drove back along Eastern Avenue.

"Pete seemed to be in sort of a weird mood," I commented.

"He goes into class-clown mode when he's got something eating at him."

"It's about time he eased up on this election and worried about his marriage. Why isn't Pete trying to make it up with Joyce? Doesn't he care?"

"Of course he cares about his wife and kids. No man wants to lose his family."

"You wouldn't know that from the way he's behaving. He's acting as if he's auditioning for David Letterman."

"'Acting' is the operative word. I was like that too when Young Hee left. I pretended I didn't care. It wasn't true. I cared a lot."

I eyed him. This was forbidden territory, but I was curious. "Why do you think she left? I mean, really?"

Duke put on the turn signal. "What you said to me was right. She didn't like being married to me. Let's drop it, okay?"

"Okay."

For a long time both of us were silent.

"Still mad at me for breaking into your house?" Duke finally said.

"No. I haven't got the energy to be mad. I'm just worried about this girl."

"I'll speak to someone in Vice. We'll find her."

"How?"

"If she's still in town, she'll surface. I'll put the word out on her pimp. If I hear anything tomorrow, will I be able to get you in the office?"

"No, I'll be out in the field all day."

"How about I drop by your place after work?" Duke caught my hesitation right away. "What's wrong? You said you weren't still mad. Have you got a date with Pete's pal, Mike?"

"No. I do have some plans, though."

"What are they?"

I hadn't said anything to Duke about the strange mailing I'd received from Frank the day after he died. The omission had been nagging at me. I described the letter.

"Why didn't you tell me this before?"

"Somehow the opportunity just never came up."

"You mean you were too busy arguing with me. You know, you could be cited for withholding information."

"C'mon, Duke, I just told you about the letter, so the information isn't withheld. Besides, I never received it. So far as I know, neither has his sister."

"Have you spoken with her about this recently?"

"Not exactly. I've been calling, but all I've been getting is her answering machine and she never phones back. Tomorrow after work I thought I'd drive up there and knock on her door."

Duke didn't reply. He pulled up and let me off at my curb with only a terse good-bye. Yet, to tell the truth, when I got back from work the next day and found him parked in front of my house, I wasn't all that surprised.

"I arranged my schedule so I could drive you up to

Frederick," he said when I peered in through his half-open window.

"I didn't ask you to."

"I know you didn't. Don't fall over backward thanking me for my sensitive and caring attitude."

"You could have mentioned this last night."

"Knowing you, if I did you'd probably figure some way of leaving without me."

"Duke," I said, unable to suppress the big smile I felt spreading across my face, "I don't mind if you drive me up to Frederick. Really, I'm grateful. I've had a long day and I'm tired, so it'll be a treat to have a big strong handsome man chauffeur me around."

While Duke waited outside, I took care of Mopsy and put her outside in the yard so Tyrone could play with her. I changed into sneakers, faded jeans, and a lightweight pink cotton blazer. Back in Duke's car, I stretched my legs until my toes touched metal and let out a lengthy sigh.

"Long day?"

"Endless."

"What'd you do?"

"Oh, ran around trying to track down a fourteen-year-old who'd skipped his Friday appointment with me. Turned out he'd been arrested for shooting another kid over an insult to his girlfriend."

Duke grimaced. "This city is in real trouble with kids and guns."

We both nodded. A moment later, Duke said, "You're better, aren't you?"

"What do you mean?"

"A few months back you wouldn't have been playing kissy-face in that guy's fancy humpmobile."

"Are we once more on the subject of my date with Mike Theologus?"

"Are you going out with him again?"

"Now that you ask so politely, he's taking me to a ball game."

Duke's profile turned wooden. We'd come off the beltway and onto Route 40 now. Strip malls and car dealerships rolled past our windows as if they were on a conveyor belt. "If you'll go out with him, why won't you go out with me?"

"You know why. I explained it."

"Oh, yeah, that's right. You want to be my friend, and it would be incest for us to engage body parts because I'm your brother. Sally, we both know that's garbage."

"It's not garbage that I want you to be my friend."

"Friends can be lovers."

"I've never seen it work out that way. Whenever I've had a lover, something's gone sour."

"Are you saying you like me too much to take a chance on losing my goodwill?"

"Maybe. I do like you. And I admire you. Actually, I think you're a hell of a guy. I always have."

"Sally—"

"Duke, have a heart and leave me alone. Not long ago I was in love with Joe. I still have a lot of unresolved issues about his death."

"You won't be able to move on until you find some answers, is that it?"

When I didn't reply, Duke sighed gustily. We were past the strip malls now, heading out into the rolling green country. Cows grazed in a field. On a hill in the distance, I saw a red-and-white barn that looked as if it belonged in a Norman Rockwell painting. I asked, "Did you find out anything about Chrissy?"

"I ran down her pimp. He claimed he hadn't seen her, but I wouldn't believe anything that troll said. I'll keep an eye on him."

"Detective Perski questioned me about Frank Leftwich's death."

"How'd he treat you?"

"Very politely."

"Yeah, well I told him he'd better."

"He was a perfect gentleman, but he wouldn't tell me much. Is there anything new?"

"No one's come forward and admitted to pushing Leftwich into the shark tank. Homicide's interviewed all the aquarium's employees and every visitor they could track down who might have seen something. No one remembered anything suspicious. Seems when you're visiting an aquarium, you're looking at fish, not people."

I nodded. The entrance to the catwalk is in an unobtrusive alcove off the winding passage between the two tanks. The low-lit, blue-black painted passage tries to mimic the effect of diving deep into the ocean. To add to the drama, highlighted black cutouts of sharks catch the eye at strategic spots. People walking down that ramp are usually too anxious to keep up with their kids and get to the live sharks to be looking anywhere but where they're going. "Tell me, does Homicide really think it was an accident?"

Duke looked uncomfortable. "At this point, there's no solid reason to call it anything else. Apparently, Leftwich liked to watch the sharks gobble their fish. For someone in the know, the keys wouldn't have been impossible to get hold of long enough to get a wax impression. Maybe Leftwich had copies made, then sneaked out there with the idea of feeding the beasties himself and just lost his balance."

"Oh, Duke, can't you feel in your gut that's not true?"

"I'm not the investigating officer, so my gut doesn't have a lot to do with it. Sally, you live and work in this city, so you know the score. Last year Homicide clocked over three hundred murders in Baltimore. There wasn't anything doubtful about these killings. They were teenagers riddled with bullets, old ladies chopped up in their bedrooms with axes. They were storekeepers shot down in their place of business for a five-dollar bill in the register. Homicide has only forty overworked, overburdened investigators."

"In another words, it's more convenient to call what happened to Frank and to Joe accidents."

"As long as there's no evidence to the contrary, that's probably what they'll be called."

I sat seething. I could feel Duke watching me, but I refused to look back.

"There's something else that might interest you," he said.

"Oh?"

"You mentioned meeting a guy named Al Pozere at a C and G party recently?"

I sat up straighter. "He took over Joe's job. For a certain type of person, moving into the kind of salary Joe pulled down would be a more than sufficient motivation for murder. Also, Pozere is a cold-blooded manipulator. All you have to do is talk to him to see that."

"Maybe, but Al Pozere isn't a suspect, Sally. He's been interviewed and his story checked out. The night Joe fell off that bridge, Pozere wasn't even in Baltimore. He was attending a conference in Washington, D.C. on privatization in the former Soviet Union. There are corroborating statements from a half dozen people who saw him on the spot at the time Joe died."

"Washington isn't all that far from Baltimore."

"He was a speaker at a banquet. The man was

nailed to a table with people on both sides of him all evening."

Well, it was just an idea, I thought. Yet I felt unreasonably upset to have my fledgling theory blown away.

A few minutes later we rolled into Frederick. It's a historic old town with a quaint business district, charmingly restored.

"I could use some dinner. What about stopping at a restaurant first?" Duke suggested.

I shook my head. Now that we were this close, I was anxious to talk to Frank's sister about the letter. It might well be tangible proof that Frank's death shouldn't be dismissed as an accident and that it was connected with Joe's fall from the Chase Street Bridge.

After I consulted the map, we headed to an older neighborhood of three-bedroom bungalows with fenced yards. Duke rolled his car slowly down the wide, sparsely planted street, while I squinted at house numbers.

"It's seven thirty-two so it should be in the next block."

Seconds later we eased up in front of 732 and sat staring.

"Looks like lightning struck it," Duke said.

I gawked at the remains of Mona Leftwich's house. It had once been a brick cottage with a chain link fence surrounding the treeless, neatly clipped front yard. Now, it was a shell. Someone had nailed pieces of raw plywood across the doors and windows to keep out looters. Sooty blotches ringed the broken windows and blackened the roof. "You really think lightning did that?"

"Don't be dumb. Wait here."

While I stayed in the car, still too stunned to move,

Duke used a hand to lever himself over the fence and peered through a boarded-up front window. When he came back he shook his head. "Whatever happened, the place's inside is pretty well trashed. If there was a letter in there when hell broke loose, it's ashes now."

I sat shivering, my mind racing. Then I got out of the car and hurried up the narrow cement ribbon of a neighbor's front walk. With every step I could smell the odor of Mona's scorched house befouling the humid breeze.

"I'm a friend of Miss Leftwich," I told the plump middle-aged lady who answered when I knocked. She wore a pink-striped seersucker zip-front housecoat. "I wonder if you could tell me what happened to her and where I can locate her?"

The woman described a fire that she said broke out the day before yesterday, but didn't know Mona Leftwich's whereabouts. I had better luck at the white frame cottage on the other side of Mona's. There an older man and his gray-haired wife gave me an address and a number to call.

"Want to find a phone booth?" Duke asked when I returned to the car.

I shook my head. "Mona hasn't returned my other phone calls. I'd rather just go to this address and knock on the door."

"Fine, but first we eat."

"I'm not . . ."

"Maybe you don't need food, but I do."

Duke's tone of voice told me it would be useless to argue, so I sat back and wrapped my arms protectively across my chest. He drove us into the main part of town and stopped at a picturesque little sandwich shop. All this time we didn't say much. The burnt house and all it might imply was on both our minds, but neither of us seemed to want to put the fact into words.

While I picked at my salad, Duke wolfed down two burgers and a glass of chocolate milk.

"Aren't you going to say what you think really happened to Mona's house?" I finally asked.

"Why waste breath? Until we have some facts, all we can do is speculate. Hey, it's better for your digestion if you make your mealtime pleasant. Let's talk about something else, okay?"

"Whatever you say."

"I'm a little low on conversational gambits right at the moment, so you start."

"Very well. Your wish is my command. Isn't it a little unusual for a man your age to still drink that stuff?" I commented as I watched him drain his glass of chocolate milk.

"Good for my bones."

"Looking at you, I'd guess your bones are thick as an elephant's."

"I take that as a compliment. Elephants are an appealing endangered species. Mama tells me it will be the same with me if I don't find myself a mate." While his eyes teased me, he licked the chocolate moustache off his lip.

Watching him and half laughing despite my down mood, I flashed on the first time I'd ever seen Duke. It was just after I'd been placed with the Spikowskis. He'd came home on leave for a few days before going overseas to be stationed in Korea. Vividly, I remembered how big and solid Duke had looked in his uniform.

While Mama paced up and down warning him about all the dangers she imagined he'd encounter when he left home, he'd sat at the kitchen table downing glasses of milk and forking up her stews and strudels. Though he'd been polite to me, I hadn't really seemed to make much impression on him. Since I was just at the age when girls get concerned about their power over the opposite sex, I was insulted. Pete with his teasing ways always paid attention to me, so I'd decided that I liked him much better.

Yet Pete had hero-worshipped his older brother. He still did. "I'll never be the man that Duke is," he'd once confided to me.

"But Pete," I'd objected, "you must make five times what Duke does. You're better educated and better looking."

Pete had just shaken his golden head. "Maybe that's all true, but it doesn't change a thing. Duke is tempered steel and I'm not and we both know it."

Now I leaned across the table and said, "Here's another conversational gambit. Do you ever feel jealous of your younger brother?"

"You mean because he's a lawyer with a six-digit bank account? Once or twice I've wished I could trade cars with him."

"And that's all?"

"Sometimes I've envied the way he gets along with you."

I guess my expression showed how much that surprised me.

"You two have always been so easy with each other," Duke explained. "Sometimes when I'm with you I feel like a fifth wheel."

"We're easy because we saw so much of each other when we were still kids. Our memories go back a lot of years."

"It's the opposite with you and me, isn't it? By the time I got out of the service and came home, you were at college. While you were building your career, I was watching my marriage fall apart. Then I was licking my wounds. After that, you were always tied up with some guy."

"Like Joe?"

"Yeah. Like Joe." He pushed his plate away. "Tell me the truth, Sally. What was it about Joe that really made you fall for him?"

"That's a personal question. Why should I answer it?"

"No reason I can think of, except that maybe now we're finally getting to know each other better. Oh, yeah, and I'm about to pay for your dinner."

"You expect a lot in exchange for a cup of coffee and a five-dollar salad." I shrugged. "Okay, what was there not to like? Joe was good-looking, smart, successful, charming. You've already given me your cockamamie notion that he was a father figure. Well, I don't buy it."

"I don't buy it either, at least not completely. I think it's more complicated than that."

"Oh, Lord, what next? Don't you have anything better to do than sit around cooking up theories about my tortured psyche?"

"Sally, if I haven't told you this before, I'm telling you now. I like and admire you, too. Not just because you're a sexy, good-looking woman. That's not what I mean."

Flabbergasted, I stared at him.

"Mama used to write me about what a tough kid you were. She'd brag about how you held your own against a lot of odds and got grades good enough to earn you a college scholarship."

"She did?"

"Oh, yeah. She still talks about you all the time.

You're the apple of her eye. Even of you weren't, I'd admire the way you've helped kids in this city. With your brains and education you could have gone anywhere you wanted. Instead, you came back to Baltimore, to a low-paying job with a lot of headaches and a lot of heartache, too."

I found my voice. "You should know. You see the same things I do."

"Right, so I understand what's involved. You know what it is to be a kid with a lot of bad breaks. You got a hand up and overcame that, so you want to pay your dues by helping some other kids in the same situation."

"I'm getting uncomfortable. You're making me sound too nice."

"You're no goody two-shoes, but you're a good person, Sally. Anyone who knows you can see that. You're human, too. I think part of you is afraid of getting stuck in a life where you see too much pain, too much suffering. Part of you wants to know you can always get out. I think Joe gave you that assurance. As long as you were with Joe, you could get out any time you wanted."

"Joe tried persuading me to quit my job, but I wouldn't."

"Of course you wouldn't. Your job is too much a part of you. But you liked knowing you could retreat to that big country mansion of his and pull up the drawbridge. Who wouldn't like having a velvet-lined safety net like that in the background? Hell, I wouldn't mind it myself." He rubbed the back of his neck. "There are days when I see too much that makes me sick at heart and I'd like nothing better than to row myself out to a well-appointed desert island and just stay there."

"What's the point? What are you getting at?"

"Just this. Somewhere deep inside, you know what I'm saying is true. Joe, with all his money and his fancy friends, came from a different world than you and me. Maybe you're afraid that you somehow dragged him down and got him into trouble. Maybe you're afraid that somehow his death is connected with you."

"That's crazy. Why would I think a thing like that? It doesn't make any sense."

"Neither does the way you're behaving now, playing girl detective. For one, if there's anything to your idea that Joe's and Frank's deaths were not accidents, poking around like this could put you in danger."

"I suppose next you're going to say I should leave it to the professionals, like you."

"Yes, you should."

"Even when the professionals, you included, don't think it's worth their time or trouble?"

Duke looked at me steadily. "I'm here, aren't I? In answer to your other question, I don't envy my brother and I wouldn't trade lives with him. Strange though it may seem, I'm satisfied the way things are. At least, I thought I was."

"Thought you were?"

"Lately, I've been thinking I'd like to make some changes." Duke's gaze stayed focused on my face, I felt the area around my neckline get warm. The waitress brought the bill and he reached for his wallet.

My fingers fumbled to unzip my shoulder bag. "Oh, no you don't. I owe you twenty from last night."

"Forget it." Duke had already laid a twenty on the table.

I replaced it with one of mine and stuffed his in his pocket. "Now we've both had our five dollars' worth. Let's go talk to this Leftwich lady before she hits the sack."

*   *   *

Mona Leftwich's temporary housing was in an old brick apartment building close to Frederick's center city. Maybe because of the rundown area, maybe because of what had just happened to her, she wouldn't open the door to us until we had explained who we were. Then we had to prove our claims by passing our police identification and driver's licenses through the crack at the bottom of the door.

Even then, she opened up with obvious reluctance and gazed at us suspiciously out of her round spectacles. Like her brother, she was short and thin. She wore jeans, a flannel shirt, and bedroom slippers.

As Duke and I followed her into her living room, I caught more ways in which she resembled Frank. Same build, same bony nose and nearsighted hazel eyes. However, she had more steel in her backbone than her brother. A lot of women in Mona's predicament would have been weepy. Not Mona. Though she'd obviously just been through hell, her manner was brisk.

"Don't blame me for the way this apartment looks," she said. "It came furnished. As you can see, the interior decorator liked garage-sale rejects."

Looking around, I sympathized. With its matted green shag rug, chipped Formica coffee table, and stained beige couch, the place resembled a down-at-heels motel.

"As I mentioned out in the hall," Duke said, "we already stopped by your house. Looks as if you lost everything."

"Everything. One minute I owned a nice three-bedroom cottage filled with good antiques. The next minute I had the deed to a pile of cinders." Her eyes blinked rapidly behind her glasses.

"Does that include Frank's letter? The one I called you about?"

She shook her head. "No, can't help you with that. I never got a letter from poor Frank. I would have phoned you if I had. I meant to anyway, but it's been a busy time." She gave her head a rueful shake. "Who would believe that last week my brother would fall into a shark tank and this week my house would explode? Some months nothing goes right."

I was too stunned to appreciate the humor. "Your house exploded?"

She smiled bitterly. "I was just getting out of my car when it went up." She raised her arms and let her hands flutter slowly down, imitating either a fireworks display or a mushroom cloud.

"Let me get this straight. Are you saying that the place was deliberately bombed?" Duke demanded.

"Oh, I don't know about that." She looked shocked at the suggestion. "The man from the fire department thought I might have had a gas leak. He won't know what caused the explosion until he completes his investigation. Why would anyone want to bomb my house? It was just bad luck, that's all."

"Good luck that you weren't in it," I said weakly.

"Oh, yes, good luck about that. As for Frank's letter, who knows? If he ever wrote you a letter in care of me, I never got it."

"Well," Duke said a half hour later, "what's going through your head?"

I stared out the window. We were on a lonely stretch of Route 40, so there wasn't much to see. In the distance a sliver of moon rode atop a mass of furred trees. Through the open window I caught the drone of crickets. A truck roared past and drowned them out.

"Mona was right. It's a pretty big coincidence that she'd lose her brother and her house so close to each other."

"Big enough so you've decided that maybe it's not a coincidence?"

"Well, what if it isn't?" I shot him a defiant glare. What if Mona's house exploded because someone made it explode? That suggestion didn't come from me first, you know. It came from you."

"I wish I'd kept my big mouth shut. Listen, Sally, there are ways of determining the cause of an explosion. When the report on Mona's fire comes in, we'll know better what to make of this."

"You asked me what I thought."

"I did, and as long as we're on the subject, why would anyone deliberately sabotage Mona Leftwich's house?"

"Since I don't know anything about her, I can't say."

"You don't think it has anything to do with her, do you? You think it's connected with Frank and ultimately with Joe."

"Okay, what if someone fixed it so her house would blow up because they thought Frank's letter might be inside it?"

"Frank's letter? The one he wrote to you just before he died?"

"Exactly."

A muscle in Duke's jaw gave a little tick. "Who did you tell about this letter?"

"Except for you, no one."

"Then how would this supposed mystery bomber have found out about it?"

"How should I know? Maybe I'm not the only person Frank sent a card to. Maybe my phone is tapped."

Duke gave me a hard look. "There's not much I can do about your first idea. The second one I can check out tonight."

"Oh, Duke, c'mon. . . ."

"You're the one who brought the idea up. Let's find out."

It was just after ten when we parked a couple of cars down from my house and went inside. While I fed Mopsy, Duke started playing with my phones.

"Hey, I hope you can put what you take apart back together again," I said. He'd opened up a Swiss Army knife and unscrewed the receiver.

"Don't worry. I'm a master handyman."

"Yeah, sure." Followed by Mopsy, I walked back out to the living room and plopped down on my couch. Mopsy took up a position between my outstretched legs so I could pat her silky head. While my fingers stroked her, I leaned back against the cushions and stared up at the ceiling. I felt drained. My muscles buzzed I was so tired. After a while I became aware of a strange silence in the house. Duke was spending an unwarranted amount of time fooling with my kitchen phone.

"Duke," I yelled. "What are you doing in there?"

As he walked in, the floorboards under my feet shivered slightly. He held something small and black in his hand. "You guessed right," he said. "Your phone was bugged."

11

That tiny scrap of metal nested in Duke's big palm like a scorpion. Okay, Duke had warned me that by asking too many questions I might also be asking for trouble. Locked in my private doubts and guilts, I hadn't taken him seriously. Now, all that changed.

"Who's been in here lately?"

"Nobody."

"No repairmen, no guests?"

"Nobody. I haven't been in the mood to entertain."

"Not even this Mike applehead that my brother so kindly introduced you to?"

"Not him, either. The only appleheads who've been inside this house since I moved broke into it."

"Right. That would be Jamal, Chrissy, and me. If I could get past your locks and disarm your alarm system without you being the wiser, then someone else could, too, you know."

I sat frozen, thinking of a stranger, a malevolent faceless intruder sneaking around, touching my things, planting a listening device in my phone. I shot Mopsy an accusing look. "Betrayer."

Her tongue lolled out and she put her paw on my knee. I pushed it off. Doubtless, she'd followed the intruder around with that same idiotic love-me-I'm-yours expression in her big brown eyes. "I should have rescued the German shepherd instead," I muttered.

Duke stood there, his shoulders and barrel chest blocking the light from the kitchen. "It's not hard to kill a dog, Sally. Anyone wanting into your place seriously enough to bug your phone wouldn't have been stopped by a German shepherd. Probably the reason Mopsy hasn't got ground glass in her belly is because she's so gentle and friendly."

Cold and abruptly queasy, I grabbed Mopsy's head and shoulders and hugged her. She surged toward me. Her warm, wet tongue mopped my cheek frantically. "I'm sorry," I whispered into her floppy ear. "I didn't mean it." Still caressing her quivering back, I peered up at Duke. "I've had about all I can take today. Thanks for the ride to Frederick and for checking the phone. Maybe you should go home now."

"I don't like leaving you alone."

"That's silly. I'm in no danger. If someone bugged my phone to find out if Mona called me about Frank's letter, now they know she didn't."

"There are no ifs, Sally. Someone has been listening in on your phone conversations."

"Please go, Duke. I can hardly see straight I'm so tired."

He searched my face, then nodded curtly. "Lock up after me and turn on that alarm system of yours."

"For all the good it does me. Listen, don't start prowling around my house in the middle of the night," I warned as I saw him to the door.

"What if I get insomnia?"

"Get insomnia someplace else."

"Anything you say, captain." To my surprise, he curled his hand around my chin and planted a swift, hard kiss on my lips. Then he strode to his car without a backward look.

Several times that night I got up and looked out my bedroom window. I half expected to see Duke lurking in the shadows. There was nothing, only a light breeze riffling through the trees lining the block, and the mournful wail of a police siren in the distance.

The next afternoon Maggie and I went out for lunch. While we sat forking up divine food at Amici's in Little Italy, I told her Duke's latest theory about my attraction to Joe.

For once Maggie didn't agree. "Nothing wrong in my book with liking a man who can help you out in a pinch. I thank the Lord my Arnold makes good money. Sometimes I do believe it's knowing I can quit this job that gives me the strength to go on. In a profession like ours it's only natural to want to bail out sometimes."

"Yes, but I'm beginning to think that what happened to Joe and to Frank Leftwich wasn't natural in the least."

"More reason why you should pay attention to what Duke has to say about not sticking your nose into what don't concern you. That man has been around and seen a lot. Just maybe he knows what he's talking about."

I looked up from the green bean I'd been playing miniature hockey with in my bowl of minestrone. "I have to know what really happened to Joe."

"No, you don't. Stop feeling guilty about Joe. What happened to him has nothing to do with you."

"Maggie, Duke's theory is all wrong. It's the possibility that Joe committed suicide that makes me feel guilty. We broke up over the way I behaved after I was beat up."

"That assault was not your fault. You were not responsible for it."

"No, but I was responsible for the way I made him miserable afterward. It horrifies me to think of Joe being so depressed he'd take his own life."

Maggie glared at me. "You'd better pray that's how he died. If it wasn't, if the man really was murdered, then you could be getting yourself into a whole mess of trouble by poking around under rocks the way you're doing."

"Now you sound exactly like Duke."

Across the table, Maggie sat frowning. She put her fork down and folded her napkin. "Sally, I wasn't going to tell you this because I saw no reason to upset you. But maybe you need to be warned."

"Warned?"

"A few days ago I got a call from Personnel in Annapolis. They wanted copies of all the documents in your file sent down there."

"Why?"

"Because with the budget crunch, the governor's ordered them to review all state employees—you know, weed out those who are unqualified or close to retirement."

"Well, I'm only thirty and they can't say I'm unqualified."

"That's not what the call was about. They wanted our records because your file down there was missing."

That afternoon Jamal stopped by the office after school. He wanted to hear about Chrissy. It didn't improve my already rotten mood to tell him that I'd lost her and had no idea what had happened to her. He'd just left when the phone rang. It was Duke.

"Just thought you'd like to know what I learned about your bug."

"Okay, what?"

"It's a mail-order item, standard in several catalogs. The serial number had been scratched off it, which makes it virtually untraceable."

"You're always just loaded with such good news."

"There's no good news in this, except maybe that you're going to get what you wanted."

"What's that?"

"I went down to Homicide and talked to Perski yesterday. He said he'd have a second look at the Winder business and coordinate with the Mona Leftwich arson investigation in Frederick."

"Does that mean he thinks Frank and Joe were murdered?"

"At this point, he won't come down one way or the other. But he's willing to keep an open mind."

"What was that about Mona Leftwich's fire? Was it really arson?"

"No final conclusions they're willing to put out yet, but apparently it looks suspicious."

Time out to try and catch up with my breathing. I'd been trying not to think about my bugged phone and missing personnel file. Now I pictured the same mystery figure responsible for those events making Mona Leftwich's house burst into flames.

With an effort, I cleared the constriction from my throat and relayed Maggie's bulletin about my file. "Do you think it might be something sinister?" I asked.

"Does the governor shit in the statehouse?" Duke sounded angry and my back went up.

"It doesn't have to be something diabolic, for crying out loud. The file could just be misplaced. Those things happen all the time in a big bureaucracy."

"So does graft, bribery, and blackmail. Now, I'll tell you what I think. You've caught someone's eye. Someone wants to find out about you. The scuzz seems to be good at getting what he or she wants. Sally, be careful."

"I am careful, Duke."

"The hell you are. You ask for trouble. Then, when you get it, you want to pretend it's not there. Go straight home from work tonight and stay put."

"If you think I'm going to sit behind my locked door quaking in my shoes, you're crazy."

I could hear Duke trying to control his breathing. "I gather you have some other dazzling plan?"

"Mike Theologus is taking me to a ballgame."

The silence on the other end of the line was made eloquent by its length. "Have fun," Duke finally said.

"Thanks a bunch. I will."

The rest of that afternoon was no fun at all. My date with Mike was a godsend. I felt threatened and need-ed to take action, even if it was only a fast trek through the harbor and over the skywalk to the new ballpark.

By now everyone who watches television or reads newspapers has heard about Oriole Park at Camden Yards. City planners could have torn down the historic railroad station from which the Union shipped troops south during the Civil War. Instead, they restored it and incorporated it into our gorgeous new ballpark.

Camden Yards is only a stroll from my house, so you'd think I'd go there all the time. Uh-uh. From the day the park opened, tickets for every game were sold out weeks in advance. So I was doubly glad Mike had invited me.

Since our date at the Placers', he'd called with

other invitations. But they'd been so obviously romantic in intent that I'd found excuses to say no.

"Okay," he finally said with an exasperated sigh. "You don't get anyplace in life by lacking persistence. I refuse to let all this rejection wound me. How's a nice safe box seat watching the Orioles tangle with Cleveland sound?"

"Sounds great, Mike. Count me in."

When I arrived at the box office, Mike was waiting for me. I'd forgotten what a great-looking guy he was. With faded jeans molding his lean hips, an Orioles cap perched rakishly atop his thick black curls, and a roguish grin curling his mouth, he made a tasty sight for female eyes. In fact, as I hurried up to him, I noticed several other passing females seconding my opinion.

He hadn't been kidding about the box seats. We had a prime spot with a direct line of sight over the batter's plate. A blast of heat from the south warmed the evening, and strings of people in shorts strolled up and down the aisles. Their faces looked relaxed and happy. Even the kids in striped shirts doing mountain-climbing acts up and down the stairs while they hawked beer and popcorn wore smiles. Death and hate belonged to another world. Gladly, I sank into the fantasy.

By the sixth inning the Orioles were losing. "Think I'll go check out the ladies'," I told Mike as I got up to maneuever past him. Lost in the game, he waved me away. He megaphoned his hands and shouted, "What's the hell's wrong with you wimps down there? Hit the damned ball!"

In the ladies' room I used the facilities and then came out and peered into the mirror above a washbasin. I noted bluish shadows around my eyes. The stress of the past weeks was taking its toll, I thought. I have pale gray eyes, black lashes, and eyebrows. My hair is several shades of dirty blond. When I was with Joe I made Mama's day and let her lighten it to a champagne shade. Now it waved around my ears in its normal streaky disarray.

I finished washing my hands. As the water tinkled down the drain, I noticed the quiet. When I had come in, there had been three other women occupying stalls and a mother and daughter washing up. Now they were gone and I was alone.

I remembered reading how public bathrooms are getting to be dangerous places. I threw my paper towel in the waste bin, grabbed up my purse, and hurried through the exit. Just outside a message in grease pencil scrawled on the shiny aluminum swing door of a trash can caught my eye. "Troublemakers have accidents." I stared and then read it again. They keep Oriole Park squeaky clean, so I knew it couldn't have been there from before the game. Had it been on the trash can when I'd come in? Did someone write it for me? Of course not, I told myself. Stop being so paranoid.

Out in the promenade area, I forced myself to slow down. Of course that message hadn't been intended for me, I told myself again. The flat of my hand went to my breast and I felt my heart banging away. What's wrong with you, Sally? I thought. There's nothing to be scared of here.

Maybe not, but I'd lost my earlier relaxed feeling. Not wanting to go back to my seat just yet, I looked around for a beer stand. I'd just paid an outrageous three bucks for a paper cup of brew when I felt a tap on my shoulder. I jumped, splashing beer on my sweatshirt.

"Thought that was you."

"Pete, what are you doing here?" He looked rumpled

and out of place in his suit pants and formal shirt. Shadows smudged his lower eyelids.

"Watching the game, sort of. There is a baseball game going on, isn't there? Or am I wrong about that, too?" He rubbed the small of his back. "I'm in bleacher seats so high and far away from the action that it's hard to tell."

"Bleacher seats? You? I thought your firm had a box on home plate."

"We do, but I didn't plan on coming tonight, so I gave away my tickets."

"Then why are you here?"

"Humoring my big brother." Pete grinned.

I eyed his loosened tie and the patches of sweat under his armpits. "You look as if you were just yanked out of your office."

"You got it, babe. There I was, settled in for a long summer's night of paperwork when Duke showed up. He flashed a couple of last-minute trash tickets he was able to scrounge from the box office and demanded I offer him moral support. Hence our bleacher seats six miles from the action."

I stood blinking, not sure what this was about or why Pete had started to look so amused.

He patted my shoulder. "Duke said it was the game he wanted to see, but I don't buy that, kiddo. All night the guy's been hunched next to me with binoculars. They aren't aimed at the diamond. They're aimed at the box you and Mike are sharing." Pete let out a raucous laugh and then hummed an off-key rendition of "Jealousy."

"'I sometimes wonder if this spell that I'm under . . .'" he yodeled as he strode off to the men's room.

"What's that big smile on your face about?" Mike asked a few minutes later.

I slid past him and into my seat. "Oh, nothing." I took a sip of my beer. "How's the game going?"

"A little better. The O's just scored two runs."

"Hooray."

"At least we won't leave the park disgraced." He touched my knee with the tip of his forefinger. "Can I talk you into a snack at Bohager's or some other spot of your choice?"

"Not tonight. It's been a long day."

"Then how about lunch, Sunday? Spike and Charlie's does a great brunch."

"Thanks, but I already have a lunch date for Sunday."

Mike scowled. "Anybody I need to worry about?"

"It's just a kid, the son of a friend." Actually, it was Joe's son, Scott. He'd called to collect the lunch date I'd promised when he'd delivered the fish tank.

"How about next weekend, then? I'm thinking about throwing a little dinner party at my place. Just a few close friends."

"That sounds nice."

A roar from the fans cut off our conversation, which was good as I was starting to get that crowded feeling.

"Alll riight!" Mike glued his binoculars to his face. Ripkin had slammed a homer into the bleachers and people were going crazy.

It didn't save the day. The O's went down four to three. Despite the loss, the elation from the homer put everyone in a mellow mood.

"Want to stay for the fireworks?" Mike asked.

"Of course. I love fireworks."

"Here. Be my guest." He handed over his binoculars.

I accepted them automatically, not really intending to use them. The first skyrocket went up and burst into a shower of green sparkles. While the audience around us oohed and aahed, I sat grinning, loving the spectacle. A handful of white pinwheels exploded against the sky. Behind them a yellow starburst defied the night.

Suddenly I got an itchy feeling at the back of my neck. I was being watched. Duke, I thought, and lifted the binoculars. Scanning the bleachers opposite, I found him right off. He wasn't looking my way, as I'd half expected. He and Pete were arguing, exchanging heated words, their faces contorted by the red and yellow lights flaring overhead.

Keeping the binoculars trained, I observed them get up and join the stream of fans straggling out. I followed them until they were gone. Still, I felt unfriendly eyes on me. The sensation was so strong that I swung the binoculars around the eerily lit stadium. A familiar face came into focus. Fixedly, it stared at me. Another red rocket burst, bathing the face in a shifting wash of crimson. As if he'd realized I'd spotted him, he turned and disappeared into the milling crowd. But I'd recognized the man. It was Al Pozere.

"Great day." Scott Winder and I sat on the outside balcony at Uno's. He was having a pizza. I'd ordered soup and salad.

"Yeah, gorgeous weather." Below us, the Sunday afternoon crowd swirled around the harbor. In the amphitheater to our right, an African-American a cappella quartet called Regency was performing "My Girl." While the tenor wailed, the bass, a skinny little guy, boomed like a full orchestra. Passersby stopped to listen. Some flipped money into a cardboard box.

"Those guys sound great," Scott commented.

"They're my favorites. I come down to hear them whenever I can."

Scott gazed at his half-eaten pizza and then settled it on his plate. So far our conversation had been strained. We'd talked about the weather, school, sports, and why I hadn't got around to setting up Joe's tank yet. That covered just about everything except what Joe's son really wanted to discuss.

"Scott," I said gently, "how are you and your mom doing?"

"Mom's doing okay. She's started dating a guy, a psychologist."

"Oh?"

"She met him from a dating service. Weird, huh?"

I didn't know what to say. A dating service was the last place I'd expect a classy lady like Janet Winder to patronize. "How do you like him?"

"He's okay. I mean, I wouldn't go out with him. After being married to a man like my dad, I don't see how Mom can, either." Scott sat twiddling his fork. Except for his morose expression, he'd pass as an idealized version of the All-American boy—glove-leather moccasins, sand-washed jeans, a Polo shirt faded to just the right shade of bleached jade.

"I think I understand how you feel. You thought the world of your dad."

"Yeah. Well, I admired him from afar, you might say. I never really saw that much of him up close. He was too busy."

"Joe had an important job with a lot of responsibilities."

"Right. I understand that. But, you know something that really bothers me, now that he's gone, I mean?"

"What's that?"

Scott rubbed at the back of his neck and cast a nervous glance around, as if he were afraid someone might be listening in. "Last year a couple of guys at school had their fathers die. One went of a heart attack. Another, my best friend's dad, flamed out in a car crash. He was driving along in his Jag when the brakes went on him. Colin was right there in the passenger seat."

"My God, how awful. He was lucky he wasn't killed, too."

"Yeah, well, he was thrown clear. When it happened I wondered how I'd feel if my dad died. I thought maybe it wouldn't be so bad. I thought maybe it would be a relief in a way, because he always expected so much of me." Scott sat staring at me with tortured eyes, his cheeks pale, his throat working.

"So now you're feeling guilty."

He nodded. "It wouldn't be so bad if he hadn't committed suicide. That's what's really getting to me."

"Oh, Scott, don't blame yourself! Everyone thinks about their parents dying. You had nothing to do with what happened to Joe."

"How can I know that? I mean, how can I ever know that?"

Scott and I sat looking at each other, both of us trapped in a cycle of guilt. I acknowledged to myself that it could never be broken until I knew what had really happened to Joe that night on the Chase Street Bridge.

After Scott left, I walked along the water's edge. Lost in thought, I felt alone despite the people all around me. Then I looked up and stopped dead. Fifty yards away, standing in the shadow of the excursion boat tied to the dock, stood Duke and Al Pozere. Their heads were bent toward each other. They were deep in conversation.

12

"I *saw you down at* the harbor early this after-noon."

Duke answered warily. "Oh? I didn't see you."

"That's because you were busy schmoozing with Al Pozere."

Long pause. "Oh, I get it. I wondered why you were breaking your vow of silence and doing me the honor of calling me at home. It's because you saw me with Al Pozere?"

"That's right. I haven't been able to get it out of my mind all day."

Duke laughed, but he didn't sound amused. "Now, why is that? Is it because you're imagining that Pozere and I are a team? You think we were coordinating our next ax murder?"

"Of course not. What were you doing with the guy? I didn't even know you knew him."

"Then you have a short memory. I interviewed him about Joe's death."

"Oh. I remember now."

"Well, I ran into Mr. Pozere at the harbor and we exchanged a few words."

"What about?"

"You really are suspicious, aren't you? About last night's game, okay?"

"Oh. Okay."

"Okay? That's all you wanted to know?"

"That's all. Thanks." I hung up before Duke could say anything more and when he called back, I didn't answer. I felt embarrassed for what I'd been thinking. The minute I'd seen Duke with Pozere, all kinds of odd ideas had popped into my head. I'd thought about how Duke was big enough and strong enough to throw Joe off a bridge. Since he was coming onto me so hot and heavy, maybe he'd had a motive to want Joe out of the way. I'd thought about how hard Duke had been trying to discourage me from questioning the suicide verdict on Joe. I'd even asked myself if he'd been down at the harbor spying on me.

It sickened me to entertain such ideas about Duke. Duke might be maddening. But he was also a rock, one of the few in my life. If I couldn't trust him, what was there left to count on?

So I believed what he said about running into Pozere. Still, the coincidence nagged at me. Why had Pozere just happened to be at the harbor when I was there? Had he been the one spying on me? Suppose he'd tapped my phone. If he'd been listening in on my phone calls, he would have known I'd attend the game Saturday night and he'd have known I was lunching with Scott on Sunday. Maybe he had a good reason for staring at me during the fireworks. Maybe he was the one who'd scrawled that threat on the trash can at Camden Yards.

Part of me considered all this to be sheer paranoid craziness. Another part was seriously scared. Since I had to do something, I decided to spend what was left of the afternoon at the Enoch Pratt Library.

During the nineteenth-century Baltimore had wealth. Enoch Pratt was a Scotsman who came here from New England and made a fortune selling hardware. Though he wasn't much of a reader himself, he set up the free library system. Now, unfortunately, the main library he bequeathed is gutted by budget cuts. People have to run a gauntlet of aggressive panhandlers to get to it. And if they're fastidious, they avoid the bathroom in the basement below the lobby.

Once past the lobby, however, the imposing stone building is a palace of hushed voices and high-ceilinged splendor. I settled down at a long oak table with back issues of the *Washington Post*.

I wanted to know more about the meeting Pozere had attended the night Joe died. Oh, I didn't doubt that he'd been there. But wasn't there something too neat about his having such a splendid alibi? I found a notice about it in the calendar of the *Post*'s Monday business supplement. It was an International Monetary Fund conference on privatization in former Soviet countries, and it had been tailored for financial officers of area business and banking institutions. While I read and reread the listing, I sat tapping my forefinger in frustration. I'd learned exactly nothing.

On impulse, I used a pay phone in the lobby to call the hotel where the conference had been booked. They confirmed what the paper said and estimated that some one hundred and fifty people had attended the meeting. A small conference, but apparently perfectly respectable. More frustration.

I went back to my newspapers and started reading

through section by section. It had been a so-so week in Washington. Aside from the national tale of woe, city police had cited a senator for drunk driving. A four-year-old fell out of a window in a low-cost high-rise. A housewife had been carjacked. A college professor had been caught making obscene phone calls. A romance author on a promotional tour had been given a juicy write-up in the style section.

The papers published on the days preceding the conference I merely scanned. When I got to the dates of the conference, I read more carefully. Except a brief notice in the business pages in the back of the sports section, there was no write-up.

Disappointed, I started leafing through the following Monday's paper. I guess I was looking for something about Joe. Nothing. Apparently, the death of a Baltimore businessman wasn't newsworthy in D.C.

Then a small local news item jumped out at me.

PROMINENT BANKER DIES MYSTERIOUSLY
IN SUBWAY ACCIDENT.
A few minutes before midnight Roger R. McCahan, 59, a chief official at Lincoln Bankcorp was crushed to death by a southbound train in the Dupont Circle subway station.

As I read the article, the back of my neck prickled. I was remembering the plot of a Hitchcock movie I'd caught on the late show a couple of nights earlier. It was about strangers meeting on a train and plotting to commit murder for each other, thereby giving themselves perfect alibis. There was no obvious reason to connect McCahan's death with Joe's. Yet it had certain features in common. McCahan either jumped, fell, or was pushed onto the tracks in front of an

oncoming train. The station at that late hour was all
but deserted, so no one saw it happen. McCahan was
a successful older man in a position of power. The two
deaths had occurred on the same night, McCahan's
approximately an hour after Joe's.

I made a copy of the article and walked back home.
In the dusk the streets of downtown Baltimore were
empty. Twice scruffy panhandlers with downcast
expressions approached me. Too preoccupied to resist
being an enabler, I dug change out of my pocket.

"Oh, thank you, honey. I can see from your pretty
face you got a good heart."

Since when did doling out a couple of quarters I
wouldn't miss mean I had a good heart?

As I pondered this question, an unkempt head of
bleached blond hair caught my eye. The skinny,
miniskirted girl wearing it was strutting down the
street in white leather cowboy boots. Her arm was
linked with a guy whose head had been shaved in a
pattern of fanciful patches and curlicues. He wore
tight black jeans, and a muscle shirt that showed off
forearms purpled with tattoos.

"Chrissy!"

One look over her shoulder and she pulled free of
her companion and started running. I took off after
her, but Mr. Tattoos blocked me. "Who do you think
you're chasing, lady?"

As I stared up into his pinpoint eyes, I wished it
weren't so late and that there were more people
around. He looked strung out and mean. Judging from
the condition of his nose, he either used cocaine or had
a bad cold. Was this the pimp Jamal had mentioned?

"Is your name Jimmy?"

"What's it to you?"

"That girl you were with is an underage runaway."

His dark eyes narrowed from pinpoints to pin-pricks. "So?"

"So the police are looking for her. She's jailbait." I glanced past his shoulder, but Chrissy was long gone.

Jimmy's bad expression darkened. "Mind your own business, bitch."

"Yeah, sure. Hey, just thought I'd let you know the score. Wouldn't want you to get in trouble or anything. 'Bye now." I sauntered off with as much aplomb as I could manage. Three blocks down Charles I could still feel Jimmy's poisonous gaze drilling into the small of my back, passing judgment on the shape of my behind and generally projecting a very bad attitude.

That night Pete knocked on my door. "Am I bother-ing you? Is this a bad time?"

His appearance shocked me. Above the collar of his shirt, his face looked flabby, like a day-old balloon puckering from a slow leak. His eyes were faintly bloodshot, as if he were holding back tears.

I grabbed his wrist. "Not at all. Come on in."

"I was just in Columbia trying to straighten things out with Joyce."

"How did that go?"

"Not good. She's determined to get out of the mar-riage. She won't admit it, but I think she's met some-one else."

"I'm sorry, Pete. Want to talk about it?"

"Yeah, well, I guess that's why I'm here. I was driv-ing around feeling lower than spit and I saw your light."

Halfway into my living room he stopped and stared at the new addition in the corner. "What's that?"

"Joe's aquarium. He willed it to me, in a manner of

speaking. So I thought I'd set it up. It was saltwater when he had it, but that's so hard to maintain. I decided to settle for freshwater. I just bought those fish and put them in. What do you think?"

Pete gazed at the four angels, half dozen neon tetras, and one scarlet Siamese fighter swimming around. "Very pretty." He gave his head a shake. "What is it with you and fish, anyway?"

I stood next to him with my hands jammed into the back pockets of my jeans. "They're beautiful and exotic and they live in a different world. I just like them."

"Oh, yeah. I remember the goldfish you used to keep when you were a kid. You sure did get mad when I emptied a can of Pop's beer into their bowl."

"That was cruel, Pete."

"Just a dumb joke." Still looking at my setup, he cocked his head. "That has to be a twenty-gallon tank you've got there. It must weigh a shitload. You sure this old floor is going to support it?"

I surveyed the softly lit glass container. For the last hour I'd been sitting in my living room with the lights off admiring its beauty. The angels, two black and two white, had long trailing fins that made them into goassamer creatures of fantasy. The Siamese fighter darted between them like a flamboyant devil. He flitted behind what I considered to be a very artful arrangement of ferns and gravel. "You really think the whole shebang might go crashing through to the basement?"

"Something to consider."

"Pete, I don't want to consider it."

"You always did like to live dangerously."

"Hah! People in glass houses. You're the one who's always had a thing for walking the edge, not me."

"Yeah, well, this time I may have fallen off."

"You're talking about your marriage?"

"That and every other damn feature of my life lately." He slouched over to the couch. Like a man carrying an unbearable weight, he sagged onto it and let his head drop into his hands.

I asked, "Didn't you realize that if you ran for city council and spent half your nights here instead of out in Columbia, Joyce might lose patience and walk out?"

Pete groaned. "I honestly didn't think about it. I just felt running for council was something I needed to do to make a difference, to make something meaningful out of my life. After I won, I figured she'd come around and we'd work it out. But that just ain't gonna play." He rubbed a palm across the lower part of his face as if trying to massage it back to life. "Joyce is going to take my kids away, Sal. She'll get the house and God knows what else. If I lose the election, too, I'll have lost everything."

I stood gazing down at him, brimming with sympathy but helpless.

"Oh, Pete, I'm so sorry." I patted his shoulder. "Want a beer?"

"Sure. Why not? The twentieth-century universal cure-all."

Pete stayed for a couple of hours. While he kept putting his troubles into different sets of words, I sat gazing at the fish in my tank. Compared to our world, theirs appeared so beautiful, so free of care. I knew that wasn't true. Fish have problems that probably seem a whole lot more serious to them than ours. It's a bloody and violent world in the deeps. But the illusion in my tank was of loveliness and perfection. Sometimes a healing illusion is preferable to reality.

"The floor hasn't caved in yet," I pointed out when I finally saw Pete to the door.

"Just you wait."

"Sweet of you to reassure me so I'll be certain to get a good night's sleep."

Pete's red-rimmed eyes smiled wearily down at me. "You're the sweet one, Sal. Only a real pal would listen to me moan and groan like this."

"You're my friend, Pete. You're the closest thing I'll ever have to a brother. I care about you."

"I care about you, too." He frowned. "Hey, Duke's told me some of your troubles. I don't like what I'm hearing. Be careful, Sally."

"Sure."

"I'm not just saying that. I really mean it. Except Mama and my brother, you're the best pal I've got, or am ever likely to have the way things are going. I don't want to lose you. Watch your step."

Despite Pete's teasing about my floor caving in, I slept soundly most of that night. Close to dawn, I had a dream about Joe. We were at the beach, lying on the sand in our bathing suits soaking up the hot summer sun. Joe rolled over and kissed me. I could taste the salt on his lips, feel the warmth of his skin. I opened my eyes and looked into his. As always, their clear blue brimmed with the confidence that had been his essence.

He laughed at me and got to his feet. He tried pulling me to mine, but I resisted. I was still heavy with sleep, too drowsy in the warm sun to want to move. Beckoning me to follow him, my lover ran into the surf and struck out strongly for the open ocean. The water was clear and blue, a match for the cloudless sky and Joe's fearless eyes. Propped up on my elbows, I watched proudly as he drove himself through the waves. His boyish exuberance made me smile.

Then, in the distance, I spotted a dark shadow

beneath the water. In that split second I knew it was evil. With horrible speed, it homed in on Joe. I opened my mouth to call out a warning, but my throat wouldn't work. I stumbled to my feet and tried to run, but the hot sand sucked me down. Then the shadow merged with Joe and he was gone.

With my heart pounding, I jerked up in bed. My whole body felt clammy. My heart drummed in my ears and I struggled for air. Gradually, I became aware of my surroundings and of a strange noise in the room. Mopsy, who always slept with me now, was sitting in front of the closed bedroom door whimpering softly.

The cold sweat bedewing my body seemed to congeal into a thin coat of ice. I sat up very straight. Though I listened with all my might, I didn't hear a thing. Still, as I'd known the shadow in my dream was evil, I knew something was wrong downstairs.

"What is it, girl?" I whispered.

I checked the clock. Four-thirteen A.M. Taking a deep breath, I swung my feet onto the floor and padded to the window. All the while I kept listening and testing the air as if I were a rabbit stalked in a forest overpopulated with hungry foxes and owls. I got to the window in time to hear a car's motor roar to life. Before I could identify the make or model, headlights swung out of sight around the corner.

For a long time I stood there staring out at the dark street. Should I go down and check the first floor? I wrapped my arms around my chest. It felt safe in the bedroom. I didn't want to leave it. Compromising, I got my gun out of the closet, loaded it, and placed it on the night table. Then I petted Mopsy until she quieted down. She followed me back onto the bed and settled herself so I could lay my hand on her warm back. Five minutes later she put her head on her paw and closed her eyes. I listened to hear breathing steady and slow. Miraculously, I went back to sleep and didn't wake up until my alarm went off.

Downstairs, the morning sun streamed through the tops of my shuttered living room windows. Mercilessly, it picked out the dead fish scattered on the floor in a semicircle around Joe's tank.

In the kitchen, I downed two cups of coffee. Strengthened by the caffeine, I made a circuit of the house. Nothing appeared disturbed. After flushing the tiny corpses of my fish, I dressed in a gray linen suit and spent more time than usual with my makeup. I left a message for Maggie that I wouldn't be coming to work but could be reached at the Mayflower Hotel in Washington, D.C. in case of emergency. Then I called Tyrone's mother and asked if Tyrone could come over after school and play with Mopsy in the backyard. A half hour later, I stepped aboard the train to Washington.

As I sat watching urban sprawl flash past, I considered last night. Someone had come into my house without tripping my alarm and deliberately killed a dozen helpless tropical fish. Why? As a warning? As the second warning I'd received—the first one possibly being the scrawled message at Camden Yards?

Who? Who even knew that I had the tank and had set it up? Pete, of course. But I didn't believe he'd do such a thing. Scott and Janet Winder? I dismissed Scott and considered Janet. She knew of my fondness for tropical fish, and she hated me. Scott could have admitted to her that he'd given me the tank and that might well have put her in a rage. But I just couldn't feature her sneaking into my house at three in the morning to sabotage my tank. How would she know how to get past the burglar alarm? That took someone with special skills.

Duke had proved he owned those skills. Pete might have told him that I'd set up the aquarium. And, of course, he'd know about my sentimental attachment to it. From the first Duke had warned me not to ask questions about Joe's death. Duke had the skill to bug a phone and the presence of mind to divert suspicion from himself by being the one to find the bug. Duke was big enough and strong enough to throw Joe off a bridge. If he was as keen on getting together with me as he pretended, he had a motive. Duke had been down at the harbor talking to Al Pozere.

"You're turning into a nut case, Sally Dunphy," I muttered under my breath. "Duke's not going to kill somebody because he has the hots for you. He's not involved in any of this." But that didn't mean Al Pozere wasn't.

Since I'd spotted Pozere talking to Frank Leftwich that night in front of the aquarium, I'd had a bad feeling about the man. I pictured his hawk features and cold black eyes and Frank's terrified body language during their encounter. Pozere had the look of a man who might know how to break into a house and plant a bug. He also came across as a man who knew how to get what he wanted—like my personnel file, for instance. I sensed he was a man who might enjoy threatening a woman in twisted ways. It wouldn't take high powers of logic to deduce from my volunteering at the National Aquarium that I liked fish. And if he'd been aware of Joe's hobby . . . Added to that, Pozere had stepped into Joe's job, so he'd had a good reason for weeping crocodile tears over Joe's death. Trouble was, Pozere also had an alibi.

MANTRAP 201 ◇

Forty-five minutes later in downtown Washington, I checked into the Mayflower. The hotel where Pozere's meeting had been held is one of D.C.'s oldest and grandest. A single night there was all I could afford. After I dumped my bag, I looked up the conference rooms used during the meeting and engaged a bellboy in what I hoped was subtle questioning. I also talked to the manager and a clerk at the desk.

There could be no doubt that the conference was legitimate and had taken place. The bit of information I gleaned from a waiter who'd served at the banquet sealed Pozere's alibi. The affair hadn't broken up until eleven o'clock. Joe's body had been discovered in Baltimore around ten.

Time to change tacks, I told myself. Back in my room, I got out the phone book and looked up Lincoln Bankcorp. Twenty minutes and four phone calls later, I'd tracked down Robert McCahan's office and title. He'd been chief currency exchange officer in the International Finance Division—a very classy title, indeed. And judging from the prestigious Dupont Circle condominium building listed in the phone book for his private residence, he wasn't undersalaried.

After pausing briefly at the hotel's coffee shop to fuel up on a bagel and cream cheese, I headed down Wisconsin Avenue. Robert McCahan had been a big wheel in a shimmery blue glass office tower. Before stepping into its center revolving door, I bought a small notebook at a drugstore and stuffed it into a side pocket in my briefcase.

Inside the marble-floored building, I studied the directory next to the phalanx of brass elevators, then pressed seventeen. The ride up was smooth and fast. I walked out of the elevator onto a sea of burgundy carpet.

The walls had been papered in a tasteful gray herring-bone and decorated with art prints in narrow gold frames. Beneath the muted clicks of computers and the occasional jangle of a phone, a cathedral hush reigned. Only the symbol for deity in this temple was the dollar sign, I mused.

A pretty young woman presided over McCahan's headquarters. She was sleekly groomed and wore a green linen suit cut along what the fashion mavens like to call "deceptively simple lines." A brass name-plate said that she was Miss Cleep. Miss Cleep sat enthroned behind a semicircular polished rosewood desk mounted on an eight-inch platform. Thus, as she replaced the phone on her console, she gazed at me almost at eye level.

"May I help you?"

"I hope so. I'm a financial reporter with the *Washington Post*. I'm here to get some questions answered about the recent accidental death of Mr. Robert McCahan."

She paled and then moistened her glossy pink lips. Part of me admired the way she had her chestnut hair pulled back from her face. I wondered about letting my hair grow so I could try that style. Would Mama throw a fit if I stopped going to her for haircuts?

"Do you have an appointment?" Ms. Cleep asked.

"My editor called. I'm supposed to interview the gentleman who's taking over Mr. McCahan's duties. Let's see—" I pretended to check my notebook. "It's a Mr., hm . . ." I shook my head. "I'm afraid I jotted this down in an awful hurry. I can't quite make out my handwriting."

"That would be Mr. Hoyt Coffman. At the moment he's in conference and can't be disturbed." She stud-ied the open page of a large leather-bound calendar.

"I'm afraid I don't find an appointment in the schedule for you. What did you say your name was?"

"Thompson, Sara Thompson. My editor made the appointment before he gave me the assignment, so it may not be under my name. Look, I only have a few simple questions, just to give my article about Mr. McCahan some detail. Would you be able to spare me a minute or two?"

"I'm sorry, but I'm not at liberty—"

"Surely you can say if he was a nice guy. You want the article to be positive. It's going to be sort of a posthumous appreciation."

She brightened. "Oh, Mr. McCahan was a wonderful man. Here at the office we're all devastated. It's so hard to believe that a vital person like he was is gone. I cried when I heard the news."

From the expression on Miss Cleep's nice face, I thought she probably meant that. "Was he an energetic man?"

"Oh, very. He was almost sixty, but you'd never know it to look at him. I mean, he could have passed for forty-five easily. He was extremely active. He belonged to the Sierra Club and took forty-mile hikes with them. He was an environmentalist. Whenever he could he walked or used the subway instead of driving his car."

"Hmmm." I scribbled a note. "Is that why he was in the subway at that late hour?"

She nodded sadly. "He belonged to a Gilbert and Sullivan Society. All that week they were having late rehearsals."

I clucked and scribbled some more. Meanwhile, I was thinking that a lot of people could have known about those rehearsals and known that he'd be using the subway late at night. "Sounds like quite a man. I guess he's going to be tough to replace."

She hesitated and then answered in official tones. "Of course, no one can ever replace Mr. McCahan in a personal sense. But I'm sure his official duties will be transferred smoothly. On that score, our customers have nothing to fear."

"You're talking about this Mr. Coffman who's handling Mr. McCahan's duties now. Just what was his relationship to Mr. McCahan before?"

Miss Cleep shot a glance at a closed door to the right of the reception area. I guessed that must be where Coffman was in a meeting. "Mr. Coffman was Mr. McCahan's associate currency exchange officer. He worked very closely with Mr. McCahan."

"Does that mean he will probably take over the job on a permanent basis?"

Miss Cleep began to look alarmed. "That I couldn't say. No official announcement has been made yet."

But it sounded to me as if he was slated to take over McCahan's job and she knew it. "Would you happen to have a company publication which identifies the officers and describes their duties?"

She thought a minute. "Nothing like that, but we do have a newsletter that goes out to stockholders with the annual report. I'll get it for you."

She dug around in a drawer and fished out a folder printed on heavy textured cream stock. It had the company name and logo embossed on the front in gold lettering. After I stuffed it into my briefcase and thanked her, I left. But I didn't go far.

Out in the hall, I studied the folder. The annual report with its facts and figures didn't interest me, though I wondered if it should. What caught my attention was a brochure that included a rogue's gallery of the International Finance Division's leading officers. McCahan's photo showed a thinnish, good-humored-looking man with neatly combed white hair. To the right of him was a photo of Hoyt Coffman.

Coffman looked like a young, corporate Mr. Clean. He was bald, with a broad face carved into planes by Slavic cheekbones and small, pale-colored eyes. His smile showed large, perfect white teeth. They were square, not pointed. So why did his smile make me think of the sharks in the Open Ocean display back in Baltimore?

I heard a door open behind my back and whirled around. A man came out. Recognizing him, I sucked in my breath. From his picture, I'd suspected that he might be tall. But I was unprepared for the giant in a gray business suit who stared at me with calculating stockbroker eyes. Coffman had to be at least six foot four and 275 pounds. He was built like a linebacker, with massive shoulders and hamlike hands. As he shot one of those hands toward me, I pictured them heaving Joe's limp body up and over the barrier on the Chase Street Bridge.

"Ms. Thompson?"

I nodded dumbly and wished that instead of lingering in the hall to study the brochure I'd made a beeline for the elevator. By now I'd be safely headed back to my hotel.

His voice, unlike his unsettling physical presence, was smooth, a controlled, well-educated baritone. "I'm delighted that I've caught you in time. I just got out of a meeting. My receptionist told me you wanted to speak with me."

"Uh, she gave me most of the information I wanted."

"I can't say I'm pleased to hear you say that. Sheryl isn't authorized to give out information to the press. Please come with me. My office is just around the corner."

He opened the door and stood aside so I could precede him. What could I do? Make a dash for the elevator? I'd thought Duke was physically overwhelming. Just looking at this man made me feel as if I'd been shot with a paralyzer dart.

Nevertheless, I made it across the thick expanse of corporate carpet and through the mahogany door he indicated. Coffman ushered me into an office decorated in shades of rich green and burgundy. A polished rosewood desk flanked by leather wing chairs dominated it. An Oriental carpet on the floor and gilt-framed English hunting prints on either side of the damask drapes added a touch of decorator-inspired class. Coffman didn't go with the decor. His build was too massive and his head was too square for understated elegance. Everything about him suggested boxiness, sharp corners, and unyielding bulk. I thought of a sociopathic Joe Palooka. I recalled bloodless archvillains in James Bond flicks.

"Was this Mr. McCahan's office?"

Coffman, who had been motioning me into a chair, missed half a beat. "Yes, as a matter of fact. I moved in just yesterday. If my desk looks a bit messy, that's the reason."

His desk didn't look messy. To my eyes, it looked unnaturally spartan. I was about to babble something about my desk at Juvenile Services when I realized what a stupid giveaway that would be. It just went to show how far knocked off-center I felt. What had given me the idea I could pull off a stunt like this? I sat down and cleared my throat. "I guess that means you'll be taking over Mr. McCahan's position, then."

"Quite possibly. Before his tragic accident, I was his closest associate here." Coffman had walked around behind his desk and lowered himself into a wing chair on a swivel base. He leaned forward, placed the pads of his fingers together and regarded me without blinking. Calm down, I told myself. He's not going to throw you out the window.

He asked, "Is that what your article is about, the succession here in our division?"

"Sort of. Naturally," I improvised, "a change of leadership in an important banking department like this would be of interest to our readers."

"You surprise me. The *Post* doesn't usually show much interest in our dealings. I'm curious. What is your background, Ms. Thompson? How did you happen to become a business reporter? Do you have a degree in business?"

"Yes."

"From where?"

"The University of Maryland."

"Oh, really? That was my alma mater, too. Perhaps we can compare notes."

"Sounds like fun, but I didn't come here to talk about college."

"What exactly did you come here to talk about?"

I dragged my notebook out of my briefcase and consulted it. "There are a few things you could clear up for me about Mr. McCahan's death. Is there any information about how he actually had his accident?"

"No, since no one saw it."

"You mean he was alone on the platform when it happened?"

"So it seems. It was quite late, you understand."

"Surely there must be some theories. Could he have had a heart attack?"

"That's a good likelihood. But since he fell into the path of an oncoming train, there was no possibility of an autopsy."

"No, of course not." His body had probably been even more messed up than Joe's. What could have made an athletic man capable of walking forty miles fall in front of a train? Could he have been pushed? Drugged?

A light began to flash on Coffman's phone. He picked up the receiver. "Put him on," he said after a second.

There are moments when I really believe in women's intuition. In that split second I knew Coffman had instructed his receptionist to contact the business editor at the *Post* so he could check out my credentials. Unfortunately, I was right.

After he had introduced himself to the party on the other end of the line, Coffman said, "I have a Ms. Thompson sitting here with me who claims you sent her. Could you verify that, please?"

I got up and walked out of the office. Coffman called after me. Ignoring that and Ms. Cleep's open mouth, I quickened my step. Once outside the suite door, I ran down the hall to the elevator. Thankfully, it opened immediately. In the lobby, I shoved through the revolving door to the noise and heat of the street. Then, despite my high heels, I sprinted three city blocks before I finally slowed down to catch my breath.

For a full minute I stood with my hands pressed to my breast, chest heaving, heart jumping. Then I headed for a pay phone and dialed a number I'd jotted in my notebook.

"Lincoln Bankcorp, International Finance Division."

"Miss Cleep?"

"Yes?" Wary.

"This is Ms. Thompson. I was there just a few minutes ago saying I was a reporter."

"You were lying to me." She had lowered her voice, so I knew Coffman wasn't standing next to her. If he'd been in hearing range, she wouldn't have talked at all.

"Yes, but it was in a good cause. Please believe that."

"The nerve. I should hang up on you."

"Please don't. Please, it's important. I'm just going to ask you one question. You can answer it yes or no. Mr. Coffman was attending a conference in Baltimore the night when Mr. McCahan died, wasn't he?"

"Yes," she whispered. *Click.*

13

I *slammed down the* phone. Five minutes later I eased my shaken body into a fast-food booth. For several minutes I sat sipping from a paper cup of coffee and not thinking.

I couldn't hold onto the blessed void for long. Just what was going on here? What did it mean that Hoyt Coffman had been in Baltimore the night Joe died? Did I really think he might have some connection with Joe's plunge from that bridge? That he might even have engineered the plunge?

I did or I wouldn't have put the question to Ms. Cleep. But judging from experience, no one else was about to agree with me.

Yet I couldn't stop myself from asking what if. What if Coffman and Pozere were conspirators? Now that I thought about them together, they were the perfect match made in hell. Pozere's slim, satanic, grand inquisitorial darkness was the ideal foil for Coffman's Teutonic death-camp commandant look.

So, what if they'd plotted to commit the perfect crime by killing each others' bosses? What if Frank Leftwich had found out somehow? What if that's why he'd become shark bait?

Another hot possibility came to mind—what if Ms. Cleep spilled my Baltimore question to her boss? I thought she probably wouldn't, but you never know. If Coffman really were conspiring with Pozere, it wouldn't take either of them long to come up with my name. In fact, the only positive thing about this whole scenario was that it made my earlier suspicions of Duke seem absurd.

I drained the last of my coffee and headed back to the Mayflower. In my room I stood by the window gazing down on the snarled skein of five-o'clock traffic. Horns blared. Tires screeched. Bureaucrats desperate to escape the city stampeded down the street like cattle through Dodge City on the way to the stock pens. It had been smart of me to take the MARC and use the subway. However, getting back to Baltimore in time for work meant I was going to have to catch a very early train. Or, I could return tonight.

I pulled the drapes, kicked off my shoes, and flopped down on the bed to think it over. My growling stomach woke me up. I flipped on the light and checked my watch. It was after eight.

A shrimp dinner and a glass of chardonnay in one of the hotel's fancy restaurants seemed the least I could do to reward myself for the day's difficulties. While I lingered sipping the wine, I mulled over the prospect of checking out and heading back to Baltimore.

I had picked up the information I'd come here for rather more easily than I'd expected. There was no reason to stay. What's more, though I had penned

Mopsy in the yard with plenty of food and water, and presumably Tyrone had walked and played with her, I didn't like leaving her alone overnight.

On the other hand, my new facts meant there were a lot of other questions I wanted answers to. Could Pozere have got out of his banquet in time to work McCahan's accident? Was the timing right for Coffman to have orchestrated Joe's fall from the Chase Street Bridge? What was the connection between Pozere and Coffman? To have cooked up a scheme like the one I suspected, they had to have known each other from somewhere, and known each other pretty darn well.

When I went back upstairs, I had decided to stay on until morning. Coping with subways and railroad timetables held no appeal. All I wanted was a hot bath and oblivion.

The blinking light on my telephone made both impossible. The desk had a message from one of my neighbors. Mopsy had got out of the yard and been hit by a car. The message didn't say if she was dead or just injured.

Panicked, I tossed my toothbrush into my briefcase and flew out. It was after ten, but people still filled the sidewalk. Traffic was thick in the street. Preoccupied with worries about Mopsy, I didn't notice much else until I took the escalator into the subway.

Washington has some subway exits and entrances that look like a science-fiction freak's worst nightmare. They are giant escalators that sink you deep into the bowels of the earth. As you stand on them heading hellward, you feel like a figure in an Escher drawing. I was on one of these conveyances when it occurred to me that none of my neighbors knew I was here in Washington. So how would they have known to leave a message at the Mayflower? It was then that I got the feeling I was being followed.

I told myself that I was imagining things, that I was upset about Mopsy and the theories I'd concocted after my interview with Ms. Cleep made me hypersensitive. Maybe one of my neighbors had called my office and Maggie had told them where I could be reached. Maybe so, but I wished there were more people around.

During the day, D.C. subways are busy. At rush hour they're jammed. Now, however, it seemed I was their only patron.

Carrying me along like a component on a conveyor belt, the escalator burrowed into its concrete hole. Embedded in the slick gray walls above my head, round lamps gleamed like the blank eyes of subterranean worms.

When I stepped free of the moving steel snake, my heels drummed against the hard floor. The noise disappeared in the honeycombed hollows of the cavernous ceilings. Ticket machines lined a wall. A small metal booth sat in front of half a dozen turnstiles. Inside the booth a man in a uniform kept his eyes glued to a magazine. I saw no one suspicious, yet I couldn't shake the feeling of danger.

Once through the turnstiles, I took another escalator down to the level where the trains ran. Only four people waited on the other side of the track. My nerves twitched and jumped. I looked down the blank hole of the tunnel and thought of the deserted passages I'd have to negotiate to get to Union Station. I hadn't checked a schedule. Who knew how long I'd have to wait for a train? I thought of how it would be when I pulled into Camden Yards. The walk from there to my house is short. But at this hour, the trip would be lonely and dark, not a taxicab in sight.

On impulse, I went back up, around and down to the other side of the track. As I arrived, the white lights on the lip next to it started pulsing, signaling a train was on its way. I looked around at the other passengers awaiting it. There were five. I felt safer.

That feeling didn't last long. The car I chose held a dozen people. But with each stop, the numbers thinned. Apparently, not many Washingtonians traveled to the northern suburbs at this hour. At the Fort Totten stop, a pair of black teenagers got off. Leaving me alone with a man in jeans and an AU sweatshirt. He had sandy hair and wore rimless glasses. Mr. Glasses sat three seats behind me reading a newspaper. He was one of the five other people who'd got onto the train with me. Had he been behind me? Had he been following me?

As I twisted around and shot him a quick glance, nervous flutters rippled inside my gut. It was either diarrhea or terror. Calling myself a fool, I got a compact out of my briefcase. My cold fingers worked unwillingly. Managing, I opened and then palmed the mirror so I could study his reflection unobtrusively. I didn't want to see anything suspicious. But as I observed, I convinced myself Mr. Glasses was only pretending to read. Despite his studious posture, the muscles of his forearms were tense. His knuckles showed white. Periodically, he shot me quick glances. The greenish glow from the fluorescents overhead reflected off his lenses so I couldn't see the expression in his eyes. My heart went into overdrive.

The train rattled along toward Tacoma Park. I knew what that stop was like, a lonely open-air platform. An excellent place to make an unfortunate accident happen.

A bump on the head, a quick slice with a knife, a push. No one would see a body lying beneath that platform until next morning's rush hour.

"Tacoma Park." As the conductor's voice wafted through the loudspeaker, the man in the sweatshirt got up. Through the pinkish powder frosting my tiny mirror, I saw he'd left his newspaper on the seat. He walked toward me carrying a white silk scarf between his hands. His gaze lit on the back of my neck. I felt the hair at the base of my skull lift.

The train slowed its brakes screeching beneath my feet. My knees flexed. He was very close now. I thought I could smell his breath. Yet I felt disconnected from myself and what was about to occur. Part of me just wanted to sit and wait to see what would happen next. I snapped the mirror closed. I seized the handle of my briefcase, ready to whirl and use it as a weapon.

I was halfway out of my seat when the door opened. A gust of warm spring air blew in with a burst of high-pitched laughter. Two young women and a boy, all decked out in punk hairdos and black leather regalia, tumbled in. They were drunk and loud and none too clean. I could have kissed them on their pierced noses. For a split second the man and I stared into each other's eyes, knowledge passing between us. Then he walked on past me and took a seat at the front of the car. I collapsed back down, my heart thumping so hard it threatened to jump out of my rib cage.

When the train got into Silver Spring, I dashed out and scuttled down the escalator as if pursued by a gang of motorcycle vampires. Never looking back, I stuffed my ticket in the turnstile and sprinted for the front door. When I spotted a single taxi pulled up across the street, I hurled myself at it.

"Baltimore, please. The Inner Harbor."

"That's a long way from my territory, lady." The cabbie looked as if he'd been asleep and was none too happy to be jolted out of a pleasant dream. Since I was in the middle of a nightmare, I didn't give a damn.

"I'll give you an extra twenty. And I'll show you where you can probably pick up another fare."

"Are you kidding? I wouldn't pick up the tooth fairy in downtown Baltimore at this hour. You look all right, though. Hop in."

All the way back to Federal Hill, I kept asking myself if there was any reality to what had just happened. Had I truly been in danger on that metro car? Or was I turning into a paranoid hysteric?

What about Mopsy? What was I going to find when I got back? I spent thirty miles in the back of the cab biting my lip.

"It's right on Conway and then right again on Light."

"Okay, lady. It's a while since I been up here." We cruised past the Science Center with its slash of red neon tube. Across the water the Domino sugar sign was even redder. As I fixed my gaze on it, it beckoned like a scarlet beacon of safety.

"Harbor looks real pretty lit up at night."

"It does, doesn't it."

I corkscrewed my neck toward Pratt and the aquarium. Its blue neon tube light mimicked a wave. Nested inside its azure squiggle were the ring tanks where the sharks circled in endless silent menace. I thought of Frank floating in their midst and shivered.

"Left here. It's the third townhouse from the end, on the right."

As the cab stopped at my curb, I stared at my front stoop. Jamal and Chrissy sat there waiting for me.

Mopsy, looking perfectly healthy, crouched between their feet.

I shoved money into the cabbie's hand and hurried over to them. "Where've you been all this time?" Jamal demanded as if we'd had an appointment. "We been waiting more than an hour."

I was too busy zeroing in on Mopsy to pay attention. Barking wildly, her tongue lolling out at an obtuse angle, she leapt at me. Shimmying like a vacumn cleaner gone berserk, she scrubbed my cheeks and forehead clean of any makeup that might still linger.

Instead of flinching, I leaned into the slobbery kiss. "Mopsy! You're all right!" Throwing down my brief-case, I squatted, wrapped my arms around her quiver-ing, wriggling torso and gave her a big smooch right back. All the while Jamal and Chrissy regarded the scene with raised eyebrows.

When Mopsy and I finally calmed down, I turned to the kids. "I got a message that a car hit Mopsy. I thought she might be dead."

They stared back quizzically. "Dog started barking her head off in the backyard when I came along," Jamal said. "But there wasn't nothin' wrong with her. She's okay, as you can see."

She did indeed appear to be perfectly fine. To be sure, I checked her head for injuries, ran my hands along her back and belly and legs. Everything appeared in tiptop shape. I sat back on my heels and stroked one of her floppy ears. "Well, that's a relief."

But was it? "While I was staying at a hotel in Washington, I got a message from one of my neigh-bors that Mopsy had been in an accident."

"Which neighbor?" Jamal asked.

"I don't know. They didn't leave a name."

"Maybe someone just wanted to play a trick on you," Chrissy spoke up in a jeering tone.

"Could be." I gazed at her hostile face and thought, or could be someone wanted me out on the streets of Washington at night where I'd be a lot more vulnerable to an accident.

With a last pat for Mopsy, I stood. After taking a shaky breath, I said, "Well, this is a nice surprise. Long time no see. Chrissy. To what do I owe the honor?"

Her mouth shaped into an upside down horseshoe. "Don't kid yourself I come back here because I wanted to. This is Jamal's dumb idea."

"I found her on the Block again," Jamal said. I noticed he had his hand locked around Chrissy's skinny wrist. "She was standing on a corner trying to thumb a ride for you know what. Selling herself. Man, just scan her over. You ever see anything so trashy looking?"

Since she was wearing my blue beaded cocktail dress, matching dyed satin pumps and a pair of dangly diamond earrings that had been an engagement gift from Joe, I held my tongue.

"Hey, you want this stupid dress back? You can have it." With her free arm, Chrissy reached around her neck to unzip the gown, but I stayed her hand.

"You can keep the outfit. It's yours."

"Yeah? Well, guess what? I don't want it." Yanking free of Jamal, she unscrewed the diamond earrings from her ears and hurled them at me. Somehow, I managed to snag them out of the air before they struck the sidewalk.

I glanced down at my palm where the gewgaws lay winking in the steetlight and then rubbed them between my fingers. "As long as you're returning jewelry," I said, "what happened to the other stuff you took?"

"You want that crap back, you'll have to get it from the hock shop I used."

"You stole Ms. Dunphy's things and hocked 'em?" Jamal's voice rose in outrage. Through my own irritation I was amused and gratified. Lately, every time I saw him he came across more like a model citizen.

"I had to get some money," Chrissy spat. "What choice did I have? After she stuck her nose in and scared Jimmy off, I didn't have enough money to eat."

"Listen, the best thing ever happened to you was losing that Jimmy scum."

Ignoring Jamal's remark, Chrissy glared at me. "Jimmy wouldn't have nothin' to do with me after you talked to him. Said I was going to get him in trouble."

"Well, he was right. You're an underage runaway, Chrissy. The last place you belong is on the street with a character like Jimmy." I checked my watch. "Listen, it's after eleven. We can't stand out here talking like this. Come on in. I could use a Coke. How about you?"

After I opened my door, Jamal and Chrissy stood for thirty seconds glaring at each other. Then he walked past me, dragging Chrissy behind him. As I followed the two down the hall and into the kitchen, I gazed sadly at the girl's mutinous backside. Plainly, she hadn't had a bathtub available to her recently. The low cut of my beaded dress showed a ring of gray around her neck. When I'd worn the dress I'd been ten pounds heavier. Chrissy didn't come anywhere close to filling it out. The way it hung on her made her look like a grimy little girl playing a pathetic game of dress-up. No wonder she hadn't had much success on the Block without Jimmy to lure customers and hawk her charms.

"Like a sandwich with that?" I asked after I poured them each a soft drink and got myself a beer.

"Not me," said Jamal.

Chrissy shot him a bitter look. "Yeah, I could use one."

Actually, she was ravenous. When I put a ham sandwich in front of her, she attacked it as if she hadn't eaten in days. Which maybe she hadn't. Watching her scarf down the food, I considered what I should say to her. I'd already blown it once and didn't want to make any more mistakes. But I was tired and discouraged after all my failed efforts to get between her and her attitude.

"Chrissy," I began in what I hoped was a gentle and understanding tone. "You can't go on living like this. It's not healthy, and it's a dead end. You need to get your life straightened out."

"I'm as straight as I'm ever going to be."

Jamal snorted. "You got to be kidding. You're one fuckin' mess. Just look at you. You live like this much longer, you're going to wind up dead."

"Chrissy, he's right. You need a decent place to live, decent food."

She sneered. "Aren't you going to say I need to finish my education so I can go onto college and become a rocket scientist?"

"First things first. Before anything else, you have to have a home that's safe and healthy. I'd like to help."

Chrissy leaned back in her chair and crossed her arms over her chest. From beneath the load of runny mascara weighing down her eyelids, she challenged me. "Go ahead, help. As a matter of fact, I could use a bed for tonight. You going to let me sleep in that room upstairs?"

"If you're dumb enough to say yes, she'll probably just rip you off again," Jamal muttered darkly.

If he thought that, I wondered why he'd brought her over. Poor kid couldn't think of anything else to do with her, I suppose. "Chrissy, before I can do anything for you, I need to know who you are. If you truly come from an unhealthy home situation, that can be dealt with."

"Not a chance." Chrissy jumped out of her chair. It fell over backward. Kicking it out of her path, she ran for the hall. My high-heeled satin pumps, a half size too big, made her no match for Jamal who sprinted after her. He caught her halfway to the front door. They stood snarling at each other, Chrissy yelling obscenities that made even my well-seasoned ears glow and Jamal returning them in good measure. As I was going to his aid, the phone rang.

"That's okay, Ms. Dunphy. You take your call. I got her. She ain't going nowhere."

"Fuck you!"

"Fuck you right back, girl!"

I stood undecided for a second, then hurried back to the kitchen. Glancing at the wall clock over the refrigerator, I saw it was almost midnight. Who could be calling at this hour?

Immediately, I flashed back on the scary scene on the Metro. As I picked up the receiver, my jaw tightened with fear. I was half expecting to hear a whispery voice mutter a threat.

"Sally, hon, I didn't wake you, did I?"

"Mom?"

"Oh, it's me, all right. Your ever-lovin mama." She giggled.

Even without the giggle, my mother sounded eerily chipper. I wondered if she was high on something. Whenever I'd received late-night calls from her in the past they'd been a bad sign. The last time was when I had to call 911 and have her committed to Taylor Manor. "Are you okay?"

"I'm so okay, sweetheart, it's like a big fat miracle." Coyly. "Now, I know what you're thinkin'. No, I am not soused, in case that's what you got on your mind."

"Well, it is almost midnight. You don't usually phone so late."

"I know, sweetie, and I'm sorry. But I just had to call my little girl and tell her. It's going to be July eighteenth."

"July eighteenth?"

"That's the date Jeffie and I just set. Lover man is sitting here next to me just beaming, aren't you, honeybunch?" Smacking sounds. Loud into the receiver again. "Isn't it perfect?"

As her question trilled in my ear, my brain churned sluggishly. "A July wedding? That sounds very warm." Baltimore is an oven in July.

"Oh, doesn't it? And guess what? Mama Spikowski said she'd give us a reception at her place."

"She did? How did that happen?"

"Now, listen, honey, don't get that tone in your voice. I didn't ask her, if that's what you're wondering. A couple days ago I dropped by The HairStop to buy shampoo. She's the one who offered all of her own free will."

As I rubbed my forehead with the heel of my hand, I pictured the scene. Vivian would have come in like a cocker spaniel wanting approval. Big-hearted Mama would have made the offer because she thought she'd be doing me a favor.

Even during the worst of times, Mama has always encouraged me to stay in touch with my mother. That hasn't always been easy. When I first went to live with the Spikowskis I wanted nothing more to do with her. But Mama always came riding in to her defense. "Whatever she does, no matter how low she sinks, she's still your mom. Blood is thicker than water. You'll always have a loving home with the Spikowski family, honey. But that doesn't mean you can ever walk away from the woman who gave you life."

"What color dress do you think I should wear?" Mom was asking now. "Jeffie don't think I should go with the white. I thought maybe a pale green. You know, for rebirth. And you could be pink or rose. Together we'd be like a summer garden."

"That sounds very pretty, Mom, but—"

A yell and a crash from the hall cut me off. I heard running feet. The door slammed. "Listen, Mom, can I call you back tomorrow? I've got company here, and—"

"Oh, I get you." Conspiratorial laugh. "Far be it from me to mess up your love life just because mine is so great. I want the whole world to be happy like I am. Sure, you can call me back."

I said "'Bye" and was down the hall. Jamal sprawled on the floor. He was holding himself between the legs and rocking back and forth. "That fuckin' bitch kicked me in the balls," he screamed.

I looked at the door, which still seemed to rock on its hinges. "She's gone, huh?"

"Oh, yeah. And that ain't all." His head gestured at the small wooden rack on the wall next to the staircase. "I think maybe she grabbed your car keys."

At a glance, I saw he was right. The keys to the Mustang are easy to recognize because they have a leather tab with the dealer's red insignia. I pictured Chrissy taking off in my beloved red car. Wondering if she could even drive, I made a dash for the door. By the time I was outside, Chrissy had unlocked the Mustang and slid behind the wheel.

"Chrissy! Don't!"

Too late. I heard the ignition grind. Still, I kept

running. It seemed Chrissy was not expert with a manual transmission. She tried to start off in third and killed the engine. As I got to the car, however, it sprang back to life. I pulled open the passenger side and jumped in.

"Chrissy . . ."

Staring down at the map on the stick, she shoved it into first and popped the clutch. The car leapt out into the street.

"Chrissy, for God's sake!"

"Leave me alone, just leave me alone!"

I tried to grab the wheel from her, but she elbowed me aside. I was lunging to take the keys out of the ignition when we went racing into the intersection. Something made me look up. I saw the truck. "Chrissy!"

"Oh, shit!" She floored the brake. But the Mustang kept rolling forward. I heard the crash and felt the metal tear and the glass shatter. Then I was lying on the pavement. Flames shot up and a blast of heat rolled over me, melting me into the earth. That's all I remember until I woke up in the hospital with Duke Spikowski staring down into my face.

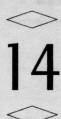

14

"What happened?" My voice sounded as if it belonged to someone else.

"You were in an accident," Duke answered. "You're going to be okay. You're just in the hospital for observation."

I turned my head and saw a pale green curtain hanging around one side of my bed. I tried to raise my head to look at myself, but my face and neck hurt. From what I could see of my arms and shoulders, however, someone had tucked me under a white sheet and I wore a hospital gown.

"Don't get all excited, Sally. You need to rest."

I stared up at him. "Chrissy was driving my Mustang."

"Yes."

"A truck crashed into us."

"That's right."

"What happened to Chrissy?"

When he didn't answer immediately, I searched his

face. Terrible knowledge fast-forwarded inside me. "She's not . . ."

"The girl is dead, Sally."

"Oh, God. She was just—"

"You don't have to explain any of it now. Jamal gave us the story, so we know what happened. Just rest."

And that's all I remember until I woke up again and there was bright sunshine burning a hole in my forehead.

"Sally, sweetie?"

A vision appeared above my face. My mother, her hair fluffed and teased to an ebony halo, her face aglow in full warpaint. A flowered dress with puffy sleeves framed her skinny neck. "Mom?"

"Now, don't say a word. I can see you're not feeling so well. Oh, my goodness, your pretty face, it's all red."

"It is?"

"I hope there's no scarring. But I'm sure there won't be. The doctor says you'll be fine. Now, don't talk. I just wanted to see you and introduce you to Jeffie. Jeffie, come on over here and say hello to my beautiful daughter."

A man's upper body swam up next to my mother's. He had limp white hair that hung around his shoulders and basset-hound jowls. I saw the top of a tattoo in the open V of his collar. He smiled weakly, obviously embarrassed. "Hiya, Sal. Sorry you're having these troubles."

"Thanks."

He turned to my mother and stage whispered, "Better go now, Viv. Poor kid's not feelin' so good."

"Yes, well, maybe you're right." My mother bent down and kissed my forehead. I smelled her hairspray and looked into her cleavage. Then she and her boyfriend tiptoed off and I plunged back into the blessed well of unconsciousness. When I surfaced again long shadows draped my bed.

"Well, it's about time."

I turned my neck and saw Maggie sitting there with a bouquet. "Daisies!" For reasons known only to my subconscious, the sight of the white flowers with their bright yellow centers brought tears to my eyes.

"So you can entertain yourself pulling off their petals. That's what I always do when I get a daisy, anyhow." Grinning, she pushed herself out of her chair and handed me one of the posies. "I asked the nurse to bring me a vase. They aren't big on quick service around here, are they?"

"I wouldn't know. I've been asleep ever since I arrived."

Her face sobered. She wore a beautiful sleeveless pink silk dress that made her skin glow. As she leaned toward me, I caught a whiff of her perfume and had a brief bittersweet thought of summer roses. "I know. My God, girl, what's going on in your life?"

"If I told you all of it, you wouldn't believe me."

"Is that so? Well, the little bit I got from Jamal here sounded bad."

Up until that moment, I hadn't even seen Jamal. He leaned against the wall opposite the foot of my bed. As I glanced his way, he stepped forward. "Hello, Ms. Dunphy." He didn't smile. "How're you doin'?"

"Jamal! I don't know how I'm doing. Okay, I guess. How about you?"

"I'm okay."

"This boy's pretty shook up," Maggie said. "But I gave him a talking to. I think you should know he went to school today. He got there late, but he went. He's not going to let the world's tragedies get between him and his goals."

"Jamal, I heard about Chrissy."

"She's dead. Ms. Dunphy, she never had a chance. After that truck plowed into her side of your car, it just blew up."

"I know. I was lucky. I guess when I jumped in I didn't shut the door securely. It must have come open on the impact, so I was thrown clear. Oh, Jamal, I feel terrible."

He shook his head. "Not your fault. It's me who's got to hold the blame. Guess I should never have made her leave that street corner. Should have just left her there."

Straightening, Maggie slapped her hands on her pink silk hips. "Young man, what am I hearing out of your mouth? If I understand this story, you were trying to help that poor child."

"Yes, he was, Maggie. And so was I."

"Well, now, sometimes even when you do the best you can, things just don't work out. It's nobody's fault she tried to steal your car, Sally, or that she didn't know how to drive."

"Chrissy knew how to drive," Jamal said. "We stole a car once and took it all around town."

Maggie muttered something under her breath that I didn't try to interpret. "A stick shift?" I asked.

"Yeah, I think it was. She was probably just too excited like to look where she was going. That's why she didn't see that truck."

As Jamal spoke, the scene in the car flashed before me. At first I'd thought Chrissy didn't know how to use a stick. Then she had shifted to first and let out the clutch. So she at least had the principle right. She had definitely known how to brake. In the seconds before the truck hit us, I had seen her press both pedals to the floor. Only three weeks earlier I'd had my brakes adjusted. They were in good working order. Why hadn't the Mustang stopped?

The question was on my mind through the string of visitors I saw after Jamal and Maggie left. An investigator from the police department took my statement about the accident. When I asked him if there could have been something wrong with my brakes, he shook his head. "I'll check it out. But tell you the truth, ma'am, I doubt there's any way of knowing. Car was pretty mangled up when it was towed off."

"I bet it was." I remembered the explosion and the sheet of flame. My hand went up to my cheek and touched it gingerly.

Before she'd left, Maggie had shown me a mirror. My face looked badly sunburned and my eyebrows had been singed off. It gave me a permanently surprised expression.

"I'm not sure this is a look I really want to cultivate," I said.

"Your skin will heal and your eyebrows will grow back," she assured me. "Couple weeks and you'll be gorgeous as ever."

When the doctor came in, he seconded that. "You're a very lucky lady," he declared as he scribbled on his clipboard. "Except for a few scrapes and bruises and those eyebrows, you're fine."

"Then why am I in a hospital?"

"Shock. With a traumatic event like this, it's always a possibility. We were also worried about a head injury. But you're coming out in good shape. All you need is plenty of rest and some TLC. You're free to go any time you wish."

"You mean, like now?"

"Now is fine."

"There's just one little problem. I don't have any

clothes or money. And I definitely don't have a car."

The doctor chuckled. "If I'm not mistaken, there are two gentlemen waiting out in the hall who are prepared to take care of that situation." He opened the door and Pete and Duke came slouching in.

It struck me that neither of them looked any too hot. Duke was gray with obvious exhaustion and Pete still had the deflated-balloon demeanor I'd noticed the night before I went to Washington. The glance he cast at me was dark with worry. Red lines crisscrossed his eyeballs.

"It's good to see you sitting up, Sal. Doctor says you're up to going home, but that's hard to believe. You feeling okay?"

"Peachy. Can't you tell by my suntan?" I tried to smile, but I guess I wasn't too convincing. Pete, who can usually manage to joke even at a funeral, didn't smile back.

My attention got distracted by Duke. The detective suit he wore looked even more shapeless than usual. I received the feeling that beneath the jacket sweat streaked his shirt. His arms hung down at his sides, one dragged low by a big canvas bag that belonged to me. "What have you got in there?"

"Clothes. Thought you might want to walk out of here wearing something." He set the bag on the floor at the foot of the bed.

"Does that mean you broke into my house again?"

"Didn't need to break into it. Place was hanging wide open when I got there. Half the neighborhood had taken a self-guided tour. Mrs. Fregelt next door likes your pewter candlesticks."

"Oh, lovely."

"It's okay, Sally." He ran a hand through his thatch of curls. "I rescued the candlesticks and checked through all the rooms. Everything seemed okay. Now it's locked up tight."

"What about Mopsy?"

"She's fine. I ran into that kid, Tyrone. He said he'll feed her and take her for a walk."

"Thanks. You, too, Pete. Thanks."

Pete was standing to the left of Duke. He had his hands jammed into his pockets. "Nothing to thank me for. I just lent my bachelor brother moral support while he picked through your bras and panties."

"That's very reassuring."

"Listen, if it hadn't been for me you'd be walking out of here in a peach silk peignoir. Duke thought it was a dress."

My gaze swept over to Duke. A faint red flush girdled his thick neck. He was smiling. I smiled back, and for the first time since the accident I felt a little better.

"I guess maybe you'd like us to get out while you change," he said.

"Sounds reasonable."

"Okay, we'll be in the hall."

When I unzipped the bag I found sandals, a pair of my most comfortable jeans and a blue cotton knit top. I also found several sets of underwear, toothbrush and toothpaste, a makeup kit, a pair of shorts, a sundress and a skirt, and the peach silk nightgown and matching peignoir Pete had spoken of.

"No wonder you looked as if you were dragging around a bag full of bowling balls," I said when I finished dressing and went into the hall. "You packed half my closet."

"Not quite." Duke finished a can of Coke from the machine and tossed it into a gray plastic garbage can. "You've got more clothes than I've ever seen."

"That's because you only own three suits and a pair of sweat pants. Where's Pete?"

"His beeper summoned and he took off. Some big meeting at his office."

"Oh."

We stood awkwardly. "Well, ready to hit the road?" Duke said.

"Sure."

"You need to get a prescription filled or anything?"

I shook my head. "The doctor left me some samples. I'm all set."

Out in the parking lot I settled back in Duke's car and closed my eyes.

"Tired?" he asked as he started up the engine.

"Maybe a little. Were you able to find out where Chrissy came from?"

"No. We're checking dental records, though. Something may turn up."

"Oh." Poor child, I thought. There was nothing left of her identity now but her teeth. Worse, except Jamal and maybe me, no one who knew she was dead would mourn. My eyes started to burn, so I squeezed them closed.

After a while I became conscious of Duke shooting me glances. "You've had quite an ordeal."

"You don't know the half of it."

"I don't?"

"No." I breathed deeply and told him about my trip to Washington.

"Hey, wait a minute. Why didn't you let me know this about your fish being killed?"

That made me laugh. "I figured, given your attitude to everything else, you wouldn't be impressed. Murdering tropical fish isn't exactly a federal offense."

"Christ, Sally, this is the third time some clown has broken into your place."

"Exactly right, and I'm not amused. That's why I decided to go to Washington. Are you going to let me finish telling you about what happened there?"

He hung a right so sharp the tires squealed. "I can't say I follow your logic, but sure. Go ahead."

I finished the story. When I got to the part about the subway, he exploded. "I can't believe you. Where are all those big brains you're supposed to have weighing you down? You go off on this wild goose chase completely half-cocked, with no plan in case things go wrong. What would you have done on that subway? What if those kids hadn't got on and the guy really had wanted to bash your brains out?"

"Does that mean you believe I could be onto something, that Coffman and Pozere might be in a plot together?"

"It doesn't. First off, the way you glommed onto this McCahan thing is loony. So what if he fell off a subway platform the same night Joe fell off a bridge?"

"Call it woman's intuition if it makes you happy, Duke. The minute I read about it in the *Post* I knew the two events were connected."

"You didn't know it then and you don't know it now."

"Duke, I'm positive the man in that subway car meant me harm. Every time I remember the look he gave me, my skin crawls. He wasn't an ordinary mugger. He was well dressed, in fact yuppieish looking. Coffman must have sent him after me."

"Sally . . ."

"Then there's what happened to Chrissy."

"I don't follow. Chrissy pulled your car in front of a truck."

"Before the truck hit us, she floored the brake. I saw her do it. But the car didn't respond. It just kept shooting forward."

"You certain?"

"Positive. I've been thinking about it, reviewing every detail of what happened over and over. Duke, someone must have fooled with my brakes. It could have happened any time I was gone. Unfortunately, the cop I talked to this afternoon said the car was too far gone to check the brakes, so I can't prove it."

Duke was silent for several minutes, his jaw working. "Okay, let's see if I've got this straight. You believe this guy Coffman and Al Pozere were a team. Pozere killed Coffman's boss and Coffman knocked off Joe. Sort of an I'll-put-your-early-retirement-plan-into-effect-if-you'll-do-mine conspiracy?"

Put baldly, it did sound farfetched. I held my tongue and waited.

"How do you think Coffman killed Joe? You think they were taking a little midnight constitutional down past the Chase Street Bridge and Coffman just picked Joe up and tossed him over a ten-foot barrier?"

"If you'd seen Coffman you'd know that's not so impossible. He's the opposite of puny."

"I don't care if he's King Kong and Arnold Schwarzenegger rolled into one. If a man Joe's size was struggling, no one could force him over a barrier that height."

"What if he was unconscious? He could have been drugged, hit on the head, injected with something. For crying out loud, you were in the military. A trained killer like you ought to know lots of ways to put a man out of action. I bet if the medical examiner hadn't been too busy to autopsy Joe, he would have found evidence of foul play."

Again, Duke was silent. Finally he said, "All right, Sally."

"All right what?"

"Tomorrow I'll set up an appointment for you with Perski. You'll tell him everything you've told me and we'll see what he has to say."

"Why do we have to put it off until tomorrow?"

"Because it's late. I'm tired and you're a basket case. It'll keep until morning. Any more questions?"

"Yes, what are we doing parked in front of your place?" I'd been so hot into my argument that I hadn't noticed until that minute. Duke had pulled up in front of one of the fine old Victorian townhouses that line the Charles Village section of St. Paul. I'd never been inside Duke's apartment, but I recognized the place. One night Pete had dropped Duke off there after we'd all gone out for a beer together after dinner at Mama's.

"You don't think I'm going to let you go back to your house after all this, do you? You'll be safer with me."

"You mean spend the night?"

"Don't look so shocked. Why did you think I'd packed all that stuff?"

"I figured you were just insecure about women's clothes."

"I wanted to make sure you'd have enough stuff to be comfortable."

"Duke, I can't be comfortable staying with you. Where will you sleep?"

"On the couch. Don't fret. I'm not going to threaten your virtue. With your face the shade of a cooked lobster and your eyebrows off, you're resistable, Sally."

"Aw, why did you have to ruin my day? Listen, if you don't think I'll be safe home alone, take me over to Mama's. She'll take good care of me."

"No doubt, but she happens to be in the middle of the ocean with Peg Rigowski at the moment."

It took me a minute to process that. "Oh, the cruise to Bermuda."

"Right, courtesy of my little brother, Mr. Moneybags. Where did you think she was all this time? You must know that if Mama were home she'd be swarming all over that hospital like a cheap suit the minute she heard you were hurt."

"I'm sorry. Guess my elevator isn't making it all the way to the penthouse. Okay, then why not let me stay with Pete?"

"Why Pete and not me?"

"I think you know why, Duke."

"Oh, yeah, the brother thing. Listen, if he's your brother then it's got to follow that I am, too."

"Stop playing games with me, Duke."

"Stop playing games with me, Sally. Pete's in the process of a divorce and a political campaign. It's possible Joyce may be having him watched by a private detective. The last thing he needs is a female spending the night who isn't related by blood—even if she has deluded herself into thinking she's his sister. Now, are you going to come in with me, or are you going to sit out here and wait for my brakes to fail?"

15

"I *didn't know you* were an art collector, Duke."

"How did you think I spent my spare time? Studying fingerprints under a magnifying glass?"

"Yes, come to think of it." I stared around Duke's apartment in amazement. His living room had once been the front parlor of a fine Victorian brick row house. The high-ceilinged room had been painted a pale gray. Solid white wood shutters were folded across the bottom half of floor-to-ceiling bow windows with top panels of leaded diamond panes. Duke's hardwood floors had been refinished a beautiful honey gold. A darker strip of reddish mahogany inlay ran around their perimeter.

My gaze strayed across the walls. Oriental prints and paintings covered them. The evening light that filtered through the window picked out a beautiful embroidered screen decorated with eye-fooling three-dimensional renditions of objects from a desk. It sat behind a couch at right angles to a white marble fireplace richly carved with fruit and, in the center bow, a cherub's face. Shelves on either side of the fireplace displayed ceramic ware.

I walked over to the shelves and stood in front of a pale green pot shaped like a closed lotus. It looked so delicate I could hardly picture it in Duke's big hands. It seemed far too fragile even to be in the same room with him. "This is very pretty."

"It's celadon, and quite old."

"How old?"

"Chosun Dynasty, sixteenth century."

Over my shoulder, I shot Duke a look. "That's old." He had set my bag on the floor, but he still stood in the entry. He looked rumpled and ill at ease, as if this weren't really his home. I asked, "How did you happen to start collecting oriental art?"

"It's Korean."

"Oh, of course. Did Young Hee get you interested?"

"I was interested long before I met her. As soon as the army stationed me in Korea, I found the art fascinated me."

"What was it that you liked?"

"The delicacy, the vivid colors, the stylized tigers and birds. While other guys were hitting sin strips on their three-day passes, I was going to museums in Seoul."

"Really?"

Duke laughed at the scepticism in my voice. He walked forward until he stood in the middle of the room. His size dwarfed it, bringing out the ethereal lines of the paintings by contrast. "Get that look out of your eye, Sally. Mama didn't raise her boys to be low on morality."

"She didn't raise them to prefer crocheting doilies to guzzling a six-pack, either."

"You think it's sissy to collect art?"

"No, of course not. You've just surprised me, that's all. This doesn't fit with my picture of you."

"What is your picture?"

"That you're a tough guy from East Baltimore," I answered in exasperation.

"Maybe a little rough around the edges?"

"Maybe. But with a heart of gold."

"Yeah, well, it was the rough edges Young Hee saw. And she saw too damn many of them."

I wanted to ask what he meant by that, but Duke didn't give me the chance. "Time to get some food into you," he said. "Sit down, take a load off your feet. I'll get us some chow."

I didn't argue. Just walking from Duke's car into his living room had exhausted me. He went into the kitchen and I sank onto his couch. While he stirred around at the back of the apartment, clanking pots and humming, I watched shadows gather in the corners.

A deep, numbing tiredness filled me. But was I really tired? Wasn't I just unwilling to think about the last forty-eight hours?

"Need any help in there?" I called.

"None, Sally. Just relax." Duke was always telling me that, I reflected. You'd think he'd know by now that it's dangerous to relax. In this jungle of a world, survival means staying alert.

Pleasant fragrances wafted to my nose. They nudged me from my torpor. I got to my feet and wandered out into the hall and then to the back of the apartment. Duke's kitchen was large and old-fashioned. Wedgewood blue paint covered its turn-of-the-century wooden cabinets. Copper pots with blackened bottoms hung from the rafters. An old oak library table set for two took up the center of the imitation brick tile floor.

"What's that you're cooking?"

"It's noodles mixed with vegetables, pork, and chicken."

"Looks wonderful. I didn't realize you were a gourmet chef."

Duke concentrated on the blue-and-white platter he was loading with noodles. "There's nothing to this kind of cooking. You have to be good with a knife, though. It takes a fair amount of chopping."

"Did Young Hee teach you this dish?"

"Yes, as a matter of fact. It was one of her favorites."

"She was a terrific cook. I remember how Mama and Pete and Pop and I came over and had dinner with you two over the Christmas holidays once."

"That must have been just after we were married."

"I think it was."

"That was a lot of years ago."

We sat down opposite each other and ate. As my stomach got filled, my curiosity sharpened. I hadn't thought about that dinner with Duke and his new young Korean wife for a long time. It had happened during my senior year in college. I'd been in the middle of a breakup with a guy I'd dated since sophomore year. When I wasn't fretting over him I was in a stew about job hunting. So my own problems had taken most of my time and energy.

Still, now that I thought about it, I remembered how impressed I'd been by Young Hee and by Duke's obvious happiness with her. He hadn't been able to take his eyes off her.

Young Hee had been very pretty, with porcelain skin, large brown eyes and a perpetually smiling mouth. She'd prepared the dinner for her new husband's family with the greatest care. Everything down to the green tea ceremoniously whisked and poured into thin cups had been meticulous. She'd worn a long loose black gown vividly embroidered. Her hair swinging around her delicate neck had been seamless and shiny as a raven's wing.

Despite all this, I'd thought she and Duke made an incongruous couple. I hadn't been terribly surprised when I'd heard the marriage had failed.

"Do you ever hear from Young Hee?" I asked

"Now and then she sends me a card."

"How's she doing?"

Duke took our plates to the sink, rinsed them, and returned with a teapot. "Doing fine so far as I can tell. She's remarried, a man of her parents' choosing this time. He manufactures tennis racquets for export. She says he's very successful."

"You sound bitter. In your way you're successful, Duke."

"My way was not one that Young Hee appreciated."

"You said you were too much of a tough guy for her. What did you mean by that?"

"Well, I didn't beat her if that's what you're wondering."

"Whoa! How much protein do you feed your attitude? Do you go looking for insults? Such a thing never crossed my mind."

"I don't know, Sally. You have one hell of an imagination. Sometimes you come up with some pretty wild stuff." Duke sipped his tea and then moved his head from side to side as if trying to work the kinks out of his neck. "I don't know if you remember, but when Young Hee and I split I'd been working Homicide."

"Now that you mention it, seems to me I do

remember Pop saying something about that. As I recall, he was very proud that you'd been put in that squad. Mama thought it was a promotion and that it would be safer than the burglary detail."

Duke laughed. "They were right on both counts. Ironic, isn't it? Solving murders is safer than robberies. Dead bodies pose no threat to life and limb. A cornered robber, on the other hand—"

"Is Homicide a promotion?" I asked, interrupting him.

"In this town it is. You need some political clout or at least a guardian angel. I was lucky to get the appointment at a young age. Pop's thirty years on the force may have had something to do with it. Maybe when he retired with a terminal illness, some of the higher-ups promoted his son as a back-assed tribute to him."

"If homicide detectives are higher up on the totem pole and it's safer, why did you go back to burglary? Didn't you like the job?"

"I loved the job. That was the problem. I became obsessed with it. I began to see myself as a white knight, charging around the mean streets, out there avenging the victims of this cruel world. It's hard to explain what happens when a murder case gets under your skin and you're the prime investigator. You dream about it, you think about it constantly, it starts coming out of your pores. That's what happened to me."

"You got hung up on a particular murder?"

"Yeah, a sixteen-year-old girl we found slashed up in a dumpster. She was Japanese, actually, visiting the city on an exchange program. I had to find who did it to her. For weeks I had no time for anything else. I got depressed, started drinking too much. The result was that Young Hee left me."

"Oh, Duke, I'm sorry. I know you were pretty broken up when it happened. Couldn't you talk to her about it, explain to her?"

"I tried, but she didn't want to understand. This was before there was such a large Korean community in Baltimore. Young Hee had no friends, no one she could really talk to. Mama tried to be nice to her, but they were just too different. Maybe the murdered girl being Oriental added to the horror of the situation for Young Hee. It was all over the papers. Anyhow, she packed up and went home."

"Wasn't there anything you could do?"

Duke grimaced. "I did the only thing I could think of. I quit Homicide, never touched hard liquor again, and went back to Burglary. But that was a stupid gesture, and it made no difference. I still lost my wife."

"That sounds as if you're sorry you gave up your promotion."

"Sure, I'm sorry. But once I turned in my resignation, I couldn't go back. The department wasn't going to roll over for that. I'd had my chance and I blew it. The Homicide guys tease me that I went back to Burglary because the bribes were better."

"You wouldn't take a bribe."

"What makes you so sure?"

"Mama didn't raise her boys to be dishonest."

"Most mothers don't. You'd be surprised how many boys I see out there who manage to get around what they were taught at mama's knee."

That made me think of Jamal and then of Chrissy. I guess my face fell because Duke immediately changed the subject.

"Hey, I've got some plum wine. Why don't I pour us each a glass? We can take it into the living room."

"Don't you want me to help you wash up?"

"Nah, I'll do that later. You're in no shape for housework. Come on."

Back in the front room, Duke switched on a floor lamp behind the couch. It shed a warm glow over the golden floor and burnished the yellow eyes of a big cat on the wall.

"Why do so many of your paintings show tigers?"

"Most of these are door-guardian paintings done by folk artists. The Koreans thought the tiger kept bad stuff out."

"You mean it protects them from evil?"

"Something like that."

"Maybe I should have a tiger picture on my door."

"Maybe you should."

Duke had dropped into the chair opposite the couch. We looked at each other. So far we hadn't talked about all the bad things that had happened. Now they crowded into the room, and I pictured Chrissy the way she'd looked in my beaded dress the last time I'd seen her. "God, that pathetic girl!"

"Sally, Chrissy died very quickly. She probably never knew what struck her."

"She knew we were going to be hit by a truck. I told you, I saw her try and put on the brake." I took a long sip of the wine. It was thick, sweet, and potent. "Duke, your pals in homicide aren't really going to go on pretending this is all accidents, are they?"

"Perski won't ignore what's been going on. He'll reopen their investigation and get to the bottom of all this. It's just a matter of time."

"Time? How much of that do I have before I'm next?"

"You're letting this get to you."

"Damn right I'm letting this get to me," I burst out. "I was just nearly killed. A young kid who made the mistake of sitting next to me wound up toasted like a marshmallow on a Girl Scout overnighter. I'm angry and upset, and—oh God!—I'm terrified!" I squeezed my eyes shut and smothered the lower part of my face with the inside of my hand. For a long moment I just sat there struggling to pull myself together. It horrified me how quickly I'd come apart at the seams. One minute I'd been together, sipping wine like a semicivilized human being. The next I'd dissolved into a shivering, babbling wreck.

The couch sagged as Duke sat down next to me. I felt his arm, warm and solid, go around my shoulder. "Sally, take it easy. It's going to be okay."

"Yeah, it's going to be just lovely. I don't even have a car, and now I'm afraid to go home."

"You'll stay here as long as you need to. I won't let anything happen to you."

"Mama will kill you if you do."

"That's right, she will."

I felt his chest heave as he laughed softly at my joke. His arm tightened on my shoulder. "I've kept you up too long. You should get some rest."

"I don't know where to go." I hiccupped. Tears had made a swamp of my face. I needed to blow my nose.

"That's dumb of me. I should have showed you the amenities straight off. Come on. The bedroom and bathroom are just down the hall."

Duke helped me to my feet and then steered me down the hall. He wrapped his arm around my waist and supported my weight as if I were an old lady who'd lost her walker. I'm not normally the dependent type. This time I was grateful I could lean on him.

"So this is your bedroom." It was a plain room with bare wood floors. The bed was nothing but a mattress on a platform. Like the living room, the lower half of the double-hung window was curtained with closed wooden shutters.

"Nothing fancy. Just a bed and a bureau. But it does the job."

"Thanks Duke."

"Don't thank me yet. I haven't changed the sheets."

"I'll do that."

"Uh-uh. By the time you get out of the bathroom the bed will be all ready for you." Duke opened a closet door and started poking around inside, his shoulders filling the door. Through the crook of his arm I caught a glimpse of three identical suits hanging on the wood rack and not much else.

I asked, "Where will you sleep?"

"The couch in the living room makes into a bed. I'll be fine." He came out with a towel and washcloth, presumably clean. "Bathroom's next door down the hall. The toilet's got a special trick. You have to pull the lever up after you flush or it runs until the planet turns into a dried prune."

A few minutes later I came out of the bathroom. I found Duke's bed freshly made, but he was nowhere in sight. I have to admit to a twinge of disappointment. Since my filmy peach nightgown and peignoir was the only nightwear Duke had packed, I'd put it on. I'd wanted him to see me in the outfit. Not that I looked particularly attractive with burn cream smeared all over my face and my eyebrows twin lines of singed stubble.

Telling myself I was losing my mind completely, I climbed under the brown cotton coverlet and switched off the bedside lamp. The last thing I saw before I fell into unconsciousness was the stone Buddha that gazed enigmatically at me from the top of Duke's battered bureau.

Maybe I should have taken the sedative and the pain medicine the doctor at the hospital had left with me. Sometime in the middle of the night, I woke up with my face burning and an achy feeling all through my body. I tried going back to sleep, but it was no soap. Finally, I sat up in bed and wrapped my arms around my knees. For several minutes I huddled there and tried not to think about Chrissy and Joe and Frank. But their faces haunted me. In my imagination they seemed to be standing in a row at the foot of the bed, reaching out to me, begging me to do something for them.

That's when I heard it. The soft creak of large feet plodding down the hall. They came closer. They stopped. While I held my breath and listened, it seemed as if the whole building were breathing around me. The noise had to be Duke walking down the corridor from the kitchen. Why had he paused in front of my door? What was he doing standing there not making a sound? While I stared at the closed barrier, I hugged my knees tighter and waited.

Finally the steps resumed. The sound of them faded, but Duke didn't stop moving around. I heard creaks, faint shuffling noises. Gingerly, I climbed off the bed. I pulled on the peignoir and tied it at the waist. Then, gently, so as not to make any noise, I opened my door and slipped out into the dark hall.

"Duke?" I whispered when I'd reached the living room.

Wearing sweatpants and nothing else, he stood by the window. The moon picked out the solid plains of his burly shoulders, the muscular slope of his flanks. I saw he held a glass in one hand. He turned his head. In the dark, I couldn't see the expression on his face. "Sally? What are you doing up?"

"What about you? Why are you up?"

"I told you before, I'm an insomniac. I spend a lot of time wandering around at night."

"Like a vampire?"

"This isn't blood I'm drinking." He lifted his glass. "It's another plum wine. Want some?"

"Yeah, I could use a glass."

"Stay right where you are. Back in a minute."

It had been more like five minutes when Duke finally put a glass into my hand. While we stood next to each other in front of the window, I sipped at it gingerly. It lit a warm glow in the pit of my stomach.

"I'm sorry if I woke you up," Duke said. "I tried to be quiet."

"I can't sleep either."

"Why not? Is your face hurting you?"

"A little bit."

He touched my cheek gingerly.

I said, "I know how I must look."

"Everything I see looks good to me. I wondered how that gown would be on you. I wish I could see it in the light."

As his gaze drifted below my neck, I resisted the urge to draw the peignoir closed over my breasts. Instead, I just stood there feeling his admiration warm me. I was admiring him, too. I couldn't take my eyes off his chest. There wasn't much hair on it and no sign of fat. The glow from the moon turned his skin into creamy velvet. With a rib cage that size, he must have amazing lung capacity. I wanted to touch him.

"Moonlight's better," I whispered.

"What?"

"It's better for us to look at each other in the moonlight now."

"Why? Is it because that makes it seem unreal for us to be standing here like this?"

"It doesn't seem unreal to me, Duke. Right now this is more real than all the things that have been going on in daylight. Why do you have insomnia?"

"I don't know."

"Have you had it for a long time?"

"Yes."

"Did it start when Young Hee left you?" I took a step toward him.

"Before that. It got worse after, though."

"I can't imagine not being able to sleep. It must drive you crazy."

"That and other things." His voice was dry.

"Is there anything I can do to help?"

"Yes, as a matter of fact. You could let me make love to you. That would help a lot."

"Okay."

"Okay?" His eyebrow lifted. "Did I hear you right?"

"You heard right. It's been a long time for me, though. I may not remember how."

"It's like riding a bicycle." He set his glass on the window sill and then took mine. When both our hands were free, he reached for me. As his palms cupped my shoulders, he said, "Why now, Sally?"

"What do you mean?"

"I know after the assault you and Joe had a hard time with the sex thing."

"How did you know?"

"Pete told me. You confided in him once. Are you okay with sex now?"

"Let's not talk about it, okay? Let's just find out."

"Action, not words?"

"You got it. Only, be careful of my face. It's tender."

"I'm going to treat all of you tenderly, Sally—every square inch of you."

Saying no more, Duke bent me back and kissed the V between my breasts. Then he led me back to his bedroom and stripped the peach gown away from my body. He hadn't been kidding around. He really did make love to every square inch of me—very tenderly and very, very thoroughly. And I was okay with the sex thing.

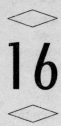

16

I *woke up the next* morning with a sore face. The rest of me, however, felt good. In fact, as I lay there and thought about the night before, I felt terrific. That Duke Spikowski had hidden depths.

Mine was the only body in the bed, so I figured Duke had thoughtfully gone to work without waking me. Judging from the angle of the sun seeping through the closed curtains, the hour was late.

I saw just how late when I glanced at the alarm. Eleven. I groaned. Then I rolled over on my back and lay gazing at the ceiling. I stayed ruminating in that position until almost noon. Was it a mistake what happened with Duke? Right now it didn't feel like a mistake. But I knew it wouldn't be long before this satisfied glow would evaporate and reality would set in.

Where would Duke and I go from here? Would having had sex ruin our friendship? Might it mess up my relationship with Mama? Even with Pete? Would Duke want to make love again? Of course he would. Be honest,

Sally, I thought, you're already imagining a repeat performance.

Finally I'd had enough of lying in Duke's bed stewing and running through erotic scenarios that made me blush. I got up and stopped feeling so good. My body ached, my face glowed too hotly.

Instead of retrieving the peach peignoir from the floor where Duke had tossed it, I rummaged through his barren closet. I found an old flannel bathrobe, the kind that looks like a cheap roadside Indian blanket. After wrapping it around my body, I slouched into the kitchen.

A note from Duke stuck to the refrigerator with a magnet shaped like a bowling ball greeted my eye.

Dear Sally,

Nobody expects you at work or anywhere else. Trust me to take care of what needs to be done and stay put in my place until I get back. By the way, Sis, last night was fun. How about a family reunion tonight, just you and me?

Your extremely affectionate nonbrother,

Duke.

I tore the note off the refrigerator and laughed at it. So Duke was going to take care of my problems. God, I hoped so. I certainly didn't feel up to dealing with them. Maybe this having-a-man-in-your-life again stuff wasn't such a bad idea.

After twenty minutes of dazed rummaging, I found the ingredients for coffee and toast. I must have lingered over breakfast for an hour, just sitting there at the table letting sunshine puddle around me and feeling dumbly and irrationally and stupidly pleased.

Finally, I roused myself to take a shower and wash

my hair. All my energy went down the drain with the tap water, so I went back to bed. If the phone rang, I didn't hear it. The clock read four-ten when I finally woke up. Maybe I should get dressed, I told myself as I sat on the edge of Duke's bed still comfortingly embraced by his robe. It smelled like him, soap and coffee and gun oil.

Though the closed shutters blocked much of the afternoon sun, the bedroom had turned hot and airless. I rummaged through the bag Duke had packed and retrieved shorts, sandals, and a sleeveless top. He'd probably be getting back soon. When he walked in the door, I wanted to look inviting. So much for any resolve I might have been entertaining to call the whole romance thing off. I knew enough about men and about myself to know there was no going back from something like this.

That's when I stuck my hand into the pocket of Duke's bathrobe. I wasn't snooping. I just felt so comfortable in his clothes I'd forgotten I wasn't wearing my own robe. My fingers touched a piece of slick, folded paper. When I pulled it out I was staring at Hoyt Coffman's face. It was on a copy of the same brochure I'd seen when I'd visited Coffman's office in D.C. What the hell was Duke doing with it?

You know that cliché, "my heart stopped"? Well, it wasn't just my heart. The whole world froze, the track of the sun, the sounds of cars passing in the street, even the breeze from the fan in the bathroom—dead halt. It was as if I were trapped like a ladybug under a glass jar. All I could hear was the roar of my pulse and the scurrying of my thoughts.

I'd told Duke about my scary meeting with Coffman. Why hadn't Duke mentioned that he knew the man? Of course, it was possible that his having the man's brochure in his bathrobe pocket was just a bizarre coincidence. Duke could have picked it up at a bank the same way I was always picking up odd bits of paper.

Much as I wanted to entertain that theory, I dismissed it. As Duke had proved last night, he was Mr. Methodical. He never did anything without a purpose. I remembered seeing him with Pozere down at the harbor and choked on a strangled scream. Was he in cahoots with those two somehow? There'd been a time when I'd wondered if Duke could have any connection with Joe's death. I'd dismissed such notions as pure superstitious fantasy. Had I made a very large and stupid mistake?

Like a roach when the kitchen light's just gone on, I panicked. All I knew was that I wanted out of Duke's apartment. I didn't want to see him. In ten minutes I'd dressed and wadded my belongings into the duffel. Halfway to the door I realized I had no money. Cursing under my breath and sweating with nerves that quivered like spider webs in a high wind, I did a pocket search on the clothes in Duke's closet. Lucky me, I found enough loose change to pay for a bus ride downtown.

This deep into rush hour teenagers and overweight ladies jammed the city buses. Wedged next to a sweating middle-aged woman with two overflowing shopping bags between dimpled-cantelope knees, I huddled on an orange plastic seat. As the bus lurched down the avenue filled with potholes and manhole covers belching a noxious-looking mist, I tried to think, tried to make some sense of what I'd found in Duke's pocket. I failed utterly. Somehow he was involved in this mess. All along, he'd been deceiving me. And last night he'd made a complete fool of me. Or rather, I'd made a fool of myself.

I had no place to go but back home. Besides, I had

Mopsy to worry about. How did I know that Tyrone was really taking care of her? Maybe Duke had lied to me about that, too.

Once off the bus, I hurried across the harbor. As I approached my street, my feet slowed. The days were long. Though it was well after six, the hot sun still beat down through the leaves. My street looked peaceful, but I didn't trust appearances. Was something waiting inside my house that I wasn't going to like? Of late, my homecomings hadn't exactly been joyful occasions.

Within yards of the front door frenzied barking broke the stillness. Mopsy had caught my scent on the evening breeze. Forgetting caution, I hurried to the gate at the back. Mopsy, her tongue a lavender-pink flag against her shiny black curls, was well into a welcome frenzy. Tears came to my eyes when I saw her. This was a being I could trust, a lover who wouldn't betray me.

"How ya doin', girl? Didja miss me? Hey, now, calm down, calm down." I grabbed her collar and let her in through the back. Inside, the house was close and still. I stood on the landing for a full two minutes, listening. Mopsy stared at me quizzically.

"I guess if there were anybody here I didn't want to meet, you'd tell me, wouldn't you girl?"

Mopsy panted and looked hard at her food dish. I laughed and came up all the way into the kitchen. "Okay, okay. Chow time."

I had just filled her dish when a tap on the back door jerked me around. Gingerly, I peered out through the small window. It was Tyrone.

"How're you, Miss Dunphy?"

"I'm fine, Tyrone. How're you?"

"I'm fine, too. I just come by to see to your dog. You got her inside?"

"Yes, I do. Thanks for all your help. You've obviously done a good job."

"I come every day, just like you and that police asked me." Tyrone tried peering around me. His bright, brown face looked concerned and anxious.

"I know you did. Mopsy's just fine. Would you like to come in and say hello to her? It's hot out today. How about a glass of lemonade?"

Tyrone hesitated for only a minute, then nodded and grinned. "That'd be fine."

While Mopsy greeted him with her customary immoderate enthusiasm, I mixed lemonade powder in a tall glass with ice cubes. Then I scrounged around until I found a box of Girl Scout cookies Maggie had blackmailed me into buying on behalf of her daughter.

"Have you been here every day?" I asked.

"Yes, ma'am," Tyrone said between gulps. "Every day since you called my mother. Wasn't a day went by I didn't spend a couple hours in your backyard, sometimes more."

"Then you need to be paid, don't you."

"If it wasn't for my mother knowing you offered money you wouldn't have to pay me nothing," Tyrone said shyly. "I liked coming here and playing with your dog. She's real nice and friendly. If I could I'd come here and play with her every day."

"Well, she obviously likes you, too. But I am going to pay you. Just wait, I'll be right back."

When I returned, Tyrone was down on the floor, giggling and rolling around with Mopsy. When he finally got up and sheepishly accepted the twenty dollars I extended, I asked casually, "Did you hear what happened to my car?"

"Yes, ma'am, I heard it blowed up. I heard somebody in it got killed."

"That's right."

"I'm glad you didn't get killed, too."

"Thanks."

"You look kinda funny without your eyebrows."

"Yes, I do, don't I. Tyrone, since you spent so much time here, I wonder if you saw anything unusual."

"Unusual?"

"For instance, that first afternoon when you came to tend to Mopsy, did you happen to notice anybody touch my car? You've seen my red Mustang before, haven't you?"

"Yes, ma'am. I cleaned its windshield a bunch of times." Tyrone stood frowning and thinking. "I didn't notice nobody touch it. But I did see a dude look at it."

"Who?"

"A white dude in a truck. I was standing inside your gate with Mopsy when he drove past real slow. He looked at your house, then he looked at your car. Then he gunned his motor and he was gone. You think maybe later on he did something to your Mustang?"

"I don't know, Tyrone. I don't know." Unconsciously, I'd crossed my arms over my chest. Despite the heat, I was hugging myself as if I were standing naked in a November wind.

When Tyrone left a few minutes later, I went upstairs to check the messages on my answering machine. Among my calls was one from Mike and one from Scott. I returned Mike's first.

"It's good to hear your voice," he exclaimed. "I didn't hear what happened to you until Pete told me yesterday. I've been worried sick. I went over to the hospital last night, but you were already gone. Then I drove by your place. It was all dark. Where'd you spend the night?"

"Uh, with a friend. I was pretty wacked out. You know, filled with sedatives and stuff." Why was I lying?

I wondered idly. It was none of Mike's business who I spent the night with. Still, the chicken-hearted diplomat in me wanted to give him the impression I'd been unconscious, not screwing like a rabbit. Or maybe that wasn't it at all. Maybe I was just distancing myself from Duke, refusing to think of how I'd let my guard down with someone who'd been lying to me.

"Well, if you're back home now you must not be in such bad shape."

"Missing an eyebrow or two and fried around the edges, but otherwise okay."

"Can I come over and see for myself?"

"I don't know, Mike. I'm still pretty tired."

"Promise, I won't be a pest. I just want to see you and make sure you really are in one piece and don't need anything. Besides, when I went to the hospital last night, I brought a carful of flowers. Now I don't know what to do with the damn things. They're stinking up my bachelor pad, making it smell like one of those pink-and-white gift shops where they sell sachet and bath beads."

I laughed, flattered and absurdly guilty that I hadn't been around to receive his offering. "Goodness, we can't have that. Okay, but just for a little while."

I replaced the receiver, thought for a minute, and then dialed Scott. While the phone rang, I hoped Janet wouldn't answer. If she did, I'd just hang up and try later.

"Hello."

"Hello, Scott. This is Sally Dunphy, returning your call."

"Oh, Sally, hi."

"Hi. Is it okay to talk?"

"You mean, is my mother listening in? No, she's out with her new boyfriend. Hey, I heard you were in an accident."

"Where did you hear it?"

"One of the guys at school has a father who's a surgeon. He's heard me talk about you, so he recognized your name. Are you okay?"

"I'm fine, Scott. Thanks for your concern." As I answered, I stood blinking, wondering at the chain linking people. They say you can get to anyone you want with three connections. It must be true.

"I'm really glad you're okay. I was worried. I even called the hospital."

"Scott, I'm touched." I was, too. A kid his age calling the hospital without being nagged, that was something.

"Sally, I like you. I understand why Dad wanted to marry you."

"Why, Scott—"

"No, really, I really do. It'd really freak me out if anything happened to you after . . ."

"You mean after what happened to your father?" I supplied gently.

"Yeah." Scott swallowed.

I thanked him again, but he wanted to go on talking. Maybe he was lonely, or maybe he really had been afraid for me. It warmed me. Hey, right then I needed every bit of niceness I could get.

"Jeez, seems like there's an awful lot of accidents lately," he said.

"Yes, I remember you saying something about a friend of yours at school losing his father in a car crash." The remark was more to hold up my end of the conversation than anything else.

"Yeah, Colin, Colin Frostburg that was."

"Colin's dad didn't work for the same company as yours, by any chance?" I asked on a sudden quixotic hunch.

"Colin's dad? Oh, no. Mr. Frostburg was a vice president, though. Made piles of money."

"Where was he a vice president?"

"At Alexander."

I felt as if I'd just been jolted with a cattle prod. "At Alexander?"

"You know, that company that builds all those shopping malls."

I knew all right. Alexander was Mike Theologus's company. And Mike had just come into the position of vice president.

I thanked Scott again and hung up in a dither. The pieces of a nasty puzzle were beginning to click into place. Yet it was so strange I still questioned my logic. I couldn't picture Mike involved in what I was imagining. On the other hand, I didn't want to be here when he arrived with his flowers. What if there were something in those posies not good for my health? I hurried to my closet and found the Ruger where I'd hidden it. I packed the gun and a full clip into my purse.

It was now almost nine. Late to go walking anywhere and I had no car. I could catch a taxi, but where would I have it take me? Mama was on vacation. Pete's? Maggie's? My mother's? I shied away from invading Jeffie's and her love nest as if I were afraid it might be filled with daughter-stinging scorpions.

All the while I rushed around, grabbing money, keys, my address book, a light jacket. By the time I'd snapped on Mopsy's leash I'd decided on my usual refuge, the harbor. Given the warm summer night, there would be people and life on its brick promenade for another two or three hours.

As I headed for the door, the phone rang. I hesitated, waiting to see who it was. When the answering machine clicked on upstairs, Duke's gravelly voice came wafting down the staircase. "Sally, where the hell are you?"

I hurried out. You have to trust your lover. When you don't, it's no good.

Mopsy dragged me toward Key Highway. We had just rounded a corner when a car with a familiar configuration swung past the corner opposite. Just in time, I stepped behind a tree and watched Mike's car disappear up the hill. Poor guy was going to be pissed, bringing all those stinky flowers over and finding me gone. But when you're so polite you stick around so as not to give offense, even when you fear the object of your graciousness might have murder on his mind, good manners are getting out of hand.

Tightening my grip on Mopsy's leash, I ran across the highway. Once past the carousel, I felt a little better. Legions of Baltimoreans were out promenading. A colorful sea of chattering humanity snaked along the water's edge.

"Let's head over to those phones." Reluctantly, Mopsy let me drag her to a public phone outside the information kiosk. I put a quarter in and dialed Maggie. No answer. I considered, then recycled the quarter and dialed Pete. His answering machine clicked in on the third ring. "Pete, it's nine-thirty. I'm down at the harbor. If you get in within the next hour, would you meet me in the Harborplace Amphitheater?"

"Well, girl, that's the best I could do." Mopsy wagged her tail. I gathered up her leash, shot an anxious look around, and headed back into the stream of foot traffic. Since I couldn't take a dog inside a pavilion, I sat down on one of the benches at the water's edge. It was close enough to the open-air amphitheater so I could watch a pair of jugglers performing for change and keep an eye out for Pete. I needed to talk to him. Right now he felt like my only friend in the world, and I badly needed to tell someone my doubts and fears. I needed someone to reassure me that all these evil thoughts I was having about Duke, and now Mike, were hogwash.

A couple of familiar figures emerged out of the crowd. "Jamal, Tyrone, what are you two doing down here?"

Jamal wore his aquarium uniform. Carrying a little cardboard tray filled with two white bags of fries and a bag of crispy onion rings, he walked toward me.

"Yo, Ms. Dunphy. I was just takin' a break when I run into Tyrone here." He came to a stop in front of me and stood shifting his weight uneasily. He looked tired. I knew he must be grieving for Chrissy. I wished I could think of something comforting to say to him.

"Jamal got me some fries," Tyrone chirped proudly. He shot his new friend a worshipful look. Like an indulgent big brother, Jamal handed a bag of fries to the younger boy who seized it eagerly.

"Want some?" Tyrone offered.

"No, thanks. That's sweet of you, Tyrone." I returned my attention to Jamal. It made me feel less lonely and frightened to have someone to talk to. "This is pretty late for you to be working, isn't it?"

"We got a sick seal they sent up from Virginia. I'm nursing her."

"Is she very sick?"

"She's pretty bad off. I'm takin' good care, though. I only got another ten minutes before I gotta' get back."

While Jamal answered, a bright idea flew into my head. "The aquarium is closed to the public now, isn't it?"

"Yes, ma'am. Late as this, it's just me and the husbandry staff down in the holding area behind the seal pool."

I considered. "Jamal, the last thing I want is to get you in trouble, but I need you to do me a favor."

"What's that?" Jamal's eyes narrowed.

"I'd like you to get me inside without anyone seeing me so I can check something on the computer in the staff library."

Jamal's throat bobbed as he swallowed the piece of onion ring he'd been chewing. "They got rules against that. Nobody supposed to get in the building this late without authority."

I wanted to explain that I was in fear of my life and that I was desperate. The words caught in my throat. I still couldn't quite believe them myself. It just all seemed so farfetched.

"I know. I wouldn't ask if it weren't important." For a split second my eye caught Tyrone's. While he chewed fries a mile a minute, his shiny gaze swiveled back and forth between Jamal and me. Avidly, he waited to see what his hero would decide.

"Jamal," I added, forcing myself to put the strangeness into words, "I think there might be something on that computer that would help explain what happened to Chrissy."

His expression darkened. "Don't need no explanation. She was run into."

"I think there might be more to it. You remember the man they found in the shark tank?"

Tyrone let out a gasp. In his excitement, bits of shredded fry flew out of his mouth.

"Sure I remember," Jamal answered guardedly. He handed Tyrone a napkin.

"The computer was Frank Leftwich's personal toy. I don't know why I didn't think of it before. I want to check and see if he left any files on it that might explain what happened."

"You mean like secret files?"

"Exactly."

Jamal cocked his head. "Didn't the police check none of that?"

"I don't know. If they did, I never heard about it." I suspected they hadn't. I also suspected no one else on the aquarium staff had touched Frank's computer. He'd always been very possessive about it. The thing sat in an inaccessible spot. No one spent time in the staff library unless they had to.

"Okay," Jamal said reluctantly. "You've been straight with me. I guess I owe you. But we got to be careful."

"I'll be extremely careful. Just give me a chance to make a quick phone call. Then I'll do whatever you say."

I left a message for Pete telling him I was on an errand at the aquarium and wouldn't be able to hook up with him for another hour. Then Jamal, Tyrone, and I started walking east.

"What about the dog?" Jamal asked as we skirted the World Trade Center.

"I'll take her," Tyrone volunteered. I shot him a grateful look. To tell the truth, I'd been so preoccupied thinking of what I might find on Frank's computer, I hadn't even given Mopsy a thought.

"You wait by the escalator," Jamal told Tyrone as I handed over the leash.

"I shouldn't be too long," I told him, though I really had no idea how much time this would take. I knew computers, but I wasn't exactly a disk-drive whiz kid.

"That's okay." Cheerfully, Tyrone settled on a bench.

"We're in luck," Jamal whispered a couple of minutes later. He'd used a passkey to unlock the doors of the members' entrance. No one had objected when we'd slid into the dark and deserted reception area. "Everybody's with the seal."

"Thanks," I whispered. "You go back to work. I'll take it from here."

"Don't set off no alarms."

"I won't. And I'll be as quick as possible."

"You do that, 'cause I can't leave you in here once we lock up. If you set off an alarm trying to get out, it'll be my ass."

"You really care about this job, don't you?"

"Yeah, I do. I like it and I don't want it to go bad on me. Too many things have gone bad. I cared about Chrissy, too. Don't ask me why, but I did. Look what happened to her."

I gave his shoulder a squeeze, then slipped away into the shadows. He watched me until I turned into the corridor to the volunteer area. After I found the key to the auditorium and library hanging on the hook in the lounge, I retraced my steps and took the stairs. Jamal was nowhere in sight.

Upstairs, the dim light from the bubble tubes cast an eerie glow around the lobby. Their bloop, bloop, bloop sounded vaguely threatening in the deserted space. Inside the auditorium, I had to turn on the overhead to find my way down to the steel door guarding the staff library. The concrete cubbyhole under the stage was, as always, dank. The computer in the back sat forlornly. Already, dust covered its screen. As I'd supposed, it hadn't been touched.

Like I said, I'm no computer whiz. Fortunately, this was an older model PC with disk drives and no hard drive. That meant checking the files available to it was just a matter of going through the five-and-a-quarter floppies lined up in the dusty plastic box on the shelf. This shouldn't be too hard, since there weren't more than a couple of dozen.

When I investigated, I found that the printer was a

dot matrix with a faded ribbon. The letter I'd received from Frank had been printed on a faded dot matrix. Why hadn't I noticed that earlier?

I began digging through the plastic bin. The word processor was an ancient version of Wordstar. No problem there. The floppies, however, didn't yield any immediate gold. Most were labeled things like "Volunteer Birthdays," or "Phone Number Update," or "New Volunteer Training Schedules."

It seemed unlikely that Frank would have put anything personal on diskettes like those. On the other hand, some had as many as thirty files. He could have buried a file with a coded heading knowing it wasn't likely to be disturbed.

Yet such carelessness wasn't like Frank. He hadn't been into risky behavior. If he'd written that letter on this computer, he would have made some effort to hide the file. Most likely, he'd just erased it. But I had to be sure.

Shivering, my legs goosebumped because I wore only shorts and the room was cold, I slipped on my jacket. I kept calling up files. As I checked them, I glanced back and forth between the computer screen and my watch. This was taking a lot of time, and I'd promised Jamal I'd be quick. Also, I felt very weird sitting here. Memories of Frank pummeled me, as if what remained of his earthly spirit were stronger in these surroundings. Maybe that wasn't my imagination. After all, he'd spent hours in this chair squinting at this screen. If his ghost was going to hang out anyplace, it might well hang out here.

On the other hand, maybe that was good. Supposing Frank had been murdered, wouldn't he want me to find any clues he might have left about his killer? "Come on, Frank," I whispered. "What did you do with the file on that letter you wrote me? Did you hide it someplace?"

I don't know if it was Frank answering my plea, but suddenly I remembered that the computer had been on when I'd gone looking for him only to find his body floating in the shark tank. He must have been working on something just before he died. What if it was the letter he'd promised to send me via his sister? What if he'd taken the disk out and hidden it someplace just before he walked away?

That made sense, actually. If I'd been working on a secret letter and been unexpectedly called away, wouldn't I hide it? But where?

Slowly, I rotated the typing chair's swivel base, my eyes scanning the shelves. Thousands of books and magazines were stored in this room. He could have stuck a floppy into any one of them. Probably, however, he'd been in a hurry so he'd put it into one that was in easy reach. I stretched up to the shelf above the computer and pulled out a thick tome on cartilaginous fishes. Nothing.

I sat back and studied the shelves nearest me all over again. "Come on, Frank," I whispered. "Give me a clue." I closed my eyes and pretended I was Frank writing my letter. If it was the kind of letter I imagined, I'd be anxious, nervy. Then someone would tap on that metal door and would stick his head in. "Hey Frank, you're wanted upstairs." I'd jump a foot.

Clang. "Miss Dunphy?"

I jumped a foot.

"Jamal, you scared me."

"Sorry, Miss Dunphy, but we gotta go. The mammology staff is all leaving for the night. They think I'm gone already. We gotta get out. They probably got a night watchman comes on duty soon. I don't want him catching me."

"I'll be out in just a minute, Jamal. Honest. Can you wait just a minute?"

At the sound of my name, I'd leapt to my feet. When I'd seen Jamal's face, I'd leaned forward in relief. One hand rested on the top of the computer. With the other I steadied myself on the third volume of an orangy red encyclopedia of fishes slightly pulled out from its companions. As I ran my finger along the top of its spine, I'd felt a smooth edge that wasn't congruent with the pages. Gingerly, I pulled the volume out and opened it. An unlabeled diskette lay wedged inside.

"Okay," Jamal was saying, "I'll wait out here in the auditorium, but you better hurry on up"

"I'll hurry. I promise, I'll hurry."

As the door clanged shut, I slipped the diskette into a drive and called up its directory. The only file on it was labeled "Sally." I opened it and had a mental conversation with a voice from the grave.

Dear Sally,

Even as I write this, I'm not sure I'll send it. Yet, I have to send it. I have to tell someone. For the last six months I've been living in a nightmare. I'm so sorry about what happened to Joe. But it's not my fault. I swear it's not my fault. You've got to believe that. I warned him. At first it was just an anonymous note. When he didn't pay attention, I went to his house one night and warned him personally. He only laughed. He wouldn't take me seriously.

It started at a fraternity reunion party. Surprised? Yes, I was in a fraternity at College Park, though how I was ever pledged by those guys I'll never know. Maybe it was because they got their kicks teasing me. Even so, I thought I was lucky to belong. Now I know I never really belonged and that belonging at all was a curse.

This party happened a little over a year ago. I went even though I knew I'd feel out of it. That's exactly what happened. No one had much to say to me, and I didn't have much to say to them. As a result, I drank too much and fell asleep on a couch in the library.

I woke up in time to hear a conversation. It was between four of the guys who'd been big men on campus. I was groggy and still half-asleep. So for a while I just lay there listening without making any noise. Then I realized what I was listening to.

They were complaining about not being able to get a promotion. For all of them there was an older man standing in the way who probably wouldn't retire for another decade or two. They started joking around, saying that maybe the way to step into his shoes was to form a secret club and call it the Departure Society.

The Departure Society. I thought of the scrap of paper I'd torn away from Frank that night at Joe's house. "Departure S," it had read. Duke had speculated it might be a schedule from a travel agent. Now I knew it had been part of a printed warning from Frank to Joe. Probably that was what I'd seen them arguing about through Joe's living-room window. Frank had retrieved it from Joe's house because he didn't want to be implicated in Joe's death. Why hadn't he gone to the police? Too scared?

Horrified, I refocused my gaze on the screen.

At first this Departure Society sounded innocent enough. They said they would just get together to brainstorm ways to encourage their bosses to opt for early retirement. Pretty soon, though, the jokes got morbid. They talked about bumping each other's bosses off. They said it would be the perfect crime. They said no one would ever guess because if you killed someone else's boss, then you didn't have a motive and the guy who did have the motive could provide himself with an airtight alibi.

Well, at that point I sat up and let them know I was there and that I didn't approve. They just laughed at me. They said it was all a joke. I wasn't so sure. The way they had been talking really gave me the creeps. When I went to bed that night I couldn't sleep for worrying about it. By morning I'd decided it really was a joke and that I'd overreacted. Then, six months later

The letter ended abruptly. At that point someone must have called Frank away from the computer. For some reason he'd gone upstairs to the catwalk over the shark tank. He'd never returned.

I sat staring at the unfinished sentence. My whole body had turned to pack ice. I couldn't move, couldn't take my eyes off the screen. Then I came to life. I printed out a copy of Frank's letter and stuck it in my jacket pocket. I turned off the machine and took the diskette out of its slot.

"Hey! What are you do—" It was Jamal's voice cut off in the middle of an exclamation. Shuffling sounds seeped through the door. Then I heard a crash and a thud. I jumped up, stuck the diskette back in its hiding place, and ran to the door. When I threw it open, Pete, Al Pozere, and Hoyt Coffman had just thrown Jamal on the floor. There was blood oozing out of his forehead.

17

Just *Coffman* and *Pozere* alone wouldn't have caught me so flat-footed. I would have had the presence of mind to slam the door on them and lock myself in the library. Then I would have got my gun and loaded the clip. There's a phone in the library. I would have called out for help.

None of that happened because Pete was with Pozere and Coffman. All I could do was stand there staring at him. "Pete?"

"Get her," Pozere snarled. Pete and Coffman were holding down Jamal. It was Pozere who came after me. By that time I had finally gathered enough wit to think of locking myself in the library. Too late. Pozere caught the door as I tried to slam it in his face. I never had a chance to get my gun.

After he'd wrestled me to the floor and rolled me over on my face, he straddled me and sat on my back. "This young lady carries an automatic in her purse," Pozere said. The flat of one of his hands crushed down on the back of my neck so hard it froze my spine. I couldn't see him going through my purse with his other hand.

I managed to look at Pete. I couldn't believe this was happening. I couldn't believe my eyes. "Pete?"

He didn't look at me. He and Coffman were still subduing Jamal. "Motherfuckers," the boy screamed. He bucked like a rodeo bull. "Get your motherfucking hands off me!"

Coffman slammed a fist into Jamal's jaw. His head rocked back so his cornrows flew and his eyes rolled up.

"Christ, Coffman, are you trying to kill him?" Pete asked.

"Just shut him up."

Coffman had a pair of handcuffs. As Pozere had done with me, Pete and Coffman rolled Jamal over on his stomach. As Coffman secured his hands, Pete asked, "You walk around with cuffs in your pocket, or what?"

"I like to be prepared. That should hold him until we figure what to do."

"It won't hold his mouth when he comes to again."

The last voice was Pozere's. I couldn't see anything. He had shifted his weight on my back, grinding my nose into the auditorium's dirty carpet.

"You know what we're going to have to do," he continued.

Several seconds of silence followed the remark. "Spit it out," Pete said. "Just what did you have in mind?"

"Oh, come off it, Spikowski," Coffman snapped. "You know we're going to have to shut them up permanently."

"What are you talking about? You're talking about murder?"

"I'm talking about doing what needs to be done. I'm talking about covering our asses, all our asses."

Pozere shifted his weight again, enough so I could get my face out of the carpet. "Pete! For God's sake, Pete!"

For the first time, his eyes met mine. They looked bloodshot and blind. Pozere's hand went around my mouth. Suddenly, I was gagging on a wad of cloth.

"You don't need to do that," Pete insisted. "Nobody can hear her in here. We won't have a night watchman in here for another two hours. Coffman took out the alarm."

"I don't want to have to listen to her, okay? Now let's get this straight. She's been making too damn much trouble. She has to go."

My head swam in pain. Tears blinded my eyes. Fear tightened through my body like coiled razor wire. I arched and struggled, but it did no good. Pozere kept me pinned to the floor.

"What about the kid?" Coffman's voice.

"Did you see the name on his badge? Jamal Bassett. We're in luck. He's a juvenile delinquent and she's his parole officer."

"How do you know?"

"I did some research on the young lady, with Pete's help. Isn't that right, Pete?"

"Yes." He muttered the answer.

"So?" This from Coffman.

"So, here's the story. She caught the black kid robbing her apartment. Against her supervisor's advice, she took his case. Big mistake, okay, because he's incorrigible. Tonight she catches him ripping off the aquarium. They struggle. She shoots him. We use her gun for that. He pushes her into the shark tank. It looks as if they've done each other. The shark tank is perfect because it connects her back to Frank. There was some question she might have been involved in Frank's thing. She would have been a serious suspect if there'd been any hard evidence. Maybe, if we're lucky, they'll think she killed him, after all. She was here when he bought it, so the theory might work."

"I can't believe what I'm hearing," Pete exclaimed.

Pozere's voice went steely. "We don't have time to fool around with your Hamlet act. Now help me get these two upstairs."

I'm not exactly sure what happened next. I remember Pozere grabbing my hair. I remember rough hands dragging me up the aisle. I remember the elevator, the darkness and faint fishy smell of the ring tanks. After that I have a hole in my memory big enough to drive a straitjacket through. Somewhere along the line terror just blanked me out.

My next recollection is the cold stamp of the gridded catwalk digging into my bare legs. Still unconscious, Jamal sprawled next to me. Below us the water in the tank gurgled and sloshed. The batwings of the aerator whirred. I opened my eyes and stared through the catwalk's mesh floor. Directly below me a leathery fin sliced past.

The sight shot me out of my fear-drugged stupor. I tried to get up, but Pozere pushed me down with his foot. A metal shard wedged into one of the interstices of the steel mesh bit into my cheek. I felt wetness. A drop of blood pooled on the metal. Another couple of minutes and there might be enough to trickle into the water. I knew enough about blood and sharks to season my spit with the taste of panic.

I worked my tongue against the wad of cloth gagging me and spit it out. "Pete," I yelled, "how can you do this?"

"I'm sorry, Sally. I didn't mean it to happen. I didn't mean any of it." He sounded near tears. Right at the moment I was low on sympathy and high on fright. I couldn't believe he would really allow them to kill me. This was my big brother whom I worshiped and adored. "Pete, please!"

"Why wouldn't you keep your nose out, Sally? Why are you always poking around where you're not supposed to? I know Duke warned you."

Was Duke in this, too? A wail of despair blew a windy place through my mind.

"Don't talk to her," Pozere ordered. "It's not going to do either of you any good."

"God, Pos, you're a hard man," Coffman said from somewhere behind me. He sounded favorably impressed.

"What now?"

"Shoot the kid and push her in with the gun."

"No." This from Pete in an anguished growl. "You can't do this. I won't let you."

The catwalk shuddered. Heavy thuds rattled it more. I heard curses, felt feet moving around, heard someone land a punch. Pete had waded into Pozere and Coffman. As the three men standing over me fought with each other, I struggled to get to my feet. I had the crazy idea I could help Pete. But I was still dizzy from the blows Pozere had dealt me. The three-foot-wide strip of suspended metal creaked and swayed like a crane in a tornado. I fell down twice before I could push myself to my knees.

"Christ, Spik, what are you, crazy?" I heard Coffman shout. "There's nothing you can do about this now. It's too fucking late. Don't you get it, Spik? It's too fucking late. If you keep this up we'll have to kill you, too."

Everything stopped. The violent motions of the catwalk subsided. I heard Pete sobbing and gasping. Coffman and Pozere each had hold of one of his arms. Still, Pete's a big man. It looked to me as if he could have fought them off if he'd really wanted to.

"Jeez, jeez! This is awful, awful, awful!" he moaned.

A hell of a lot worse for me than for you, I thought. I knew then whatever he'd tried to do for me, he'd given up on it. The man wasn't going to save me. He was just going to stand there looking forlorn while his pals fed me to the fish.

"Coffman, push her in now," Pozere said. He didn't even look at me. All I could see was his hawk nose, his thin-lipped profile. "Let's get it over with. The sooner it's done the sooner Pete here will stop shedding crocodile tears and acting like Our Lady of the Tender Conscience."

"Check my jacket first."

At the sound of my voice, all three men stared at me as if I'd just erupted from the earth. I understood the reason for their surprise. They'd stopped thinking of me as human. To them I had become an object to be disposed of. I was still kneeling at the edge of the catwalk. At my back was the tank and its sharks. Pete, Coffman, and Pozere blocked the exit. Delaying their plan was my only chance.

I took a deep breath and repeated my command. "Before you do something stupid, check my jacket."

"You heard the lady," Pozere said to Coffman. "Check her damned jacket."

Grimly, Coffman came forward and ripped the jacket off me. He did it fast and rough. It was as if he didn't want to touch me, to acknowledge that I was warm and still alive.

Seconds later he'd found the printout of Frank's letter. "Jesus Christ, look at this."

Still holding one of Pete's arms, Pozere scanned the paper and then glared at me. "Where'd you get this?"

I regretted giving away Frank's letter. But that had seemed preferable to a swim in the shark tank. Since it was my only leverage, I certainly wasn't going to answer Pozere's question.

All at once he was on top of me, swarming all over me, punching and kicking, raining blows. I yelled and snapped my arms up to protect my face.

"Tell me, you bitch!" He slapped me so hard I would have toppled backward into the water if he hadn't grabbed my arm. Probably he was the one who'd screwed with my brakes and sent Chrissy to a flaming death.

"Stop that," Pete yelled. "Don't hit her like that!"

Pozere paused long enough to heap scorn on his cohort. "Why not? Isn't it gentlemanly? Listen, it won't matter if she's bruised when they find her. They'll think the kid knocked her around before she fell in."

"Jesus, will you stop talking like that? Will you just stop it!"

My mouth was full of blood. I could barely open my eyes. I'd clamped my hands to my face and doubled up on myself like a fetus.

"Calm down, Pete," Coffman said with heavy irony. "You know the guy always had a grisly sense of humor."

"Both of you always had a grisly sense of humor. I just never knew it wasn't funny."

Ignoring that, Pozere said to Coffman, "I told you I heard a dot matrix going when we got into the auditorium. She must have printed this piece of shit in the library. We've got to go back and check the computer."

"Shit! Go all the fucking way back downstairs?" Coffman sounded frustrated to the breaking point by this unconscionable inconvenience. "What about these two?"

I could feel their eyes on my huddled form. "We can't leave Pete here to guard them, that's for sure," Pozere commented caustically. "The wuss would probably turn 'em loose. Okay, this is what we'll do. We'll cuff them both to the catwalk. Then all three of us will go down. That way we can keep an eye on each other. I'm not going to have any finking out by Our Lady of Regrets at this point."

After a brief flurry, I found myself sharing Jamal's handcuffs. Pozere had locked the short chain to a rod on the catwalk. The left-hand ring shackled Jamal. I wore the right-hand ring.

As soon as the three men disappeared, I tested the strength of my restraints. The catwalk rattled when I yanked against it, but it wasn't going to give. I groaned. I'd ratted on Frank's letter for nothing. Now Pozere's scheme might just work. Of course, chances were Frank's diskette would probably never have been found anyway. Decades might go by before anyone would bother opening that big, dusty book.

"Ms. Dunphy?" Jamal was looking at me.

"How long have you been conscious?"

"Long enough."

"Are you okay?" That was a silly question.

"I've been better. Ms. Dunphy, I can't move my right hand. I think my arm is broke or something. Can you reach into the front of my pants?"

"What?"

"I got a gun in there."

My heart leapt. "You're kidding."

"This ain't no joke." Jamal wasn't looking at me. He'd rolled his head to the right so he could stare at the water. Beneath us a gray torpedo shape cruised back and forth. With my free hand I touched my cheek. Blood slicked it. Probably some had already found its way into the water.

I rolled my left shoulder and used my free hand to grab Jamal's belt. "Where have you got it?"

"It's in the waistband of my underpants."

"Jeez, Jamal!" Awkwardly, I undid the buckle and then the snap on his pants. "Nothing personal," I said. I felt the solid shape of the grip and wrapped my blood-smeared fingers around it. "Is it loaded?"

"Yes, ma'am."

"Jesus, what if I shoot you while I'm trying to pull it out?"

"Don't do that."

"I'm trying not to. What are you doing with a gun in your pants, anyhow? I thought you were going to give this sort of thing up."

"I was supposed to take my girlfriend to a party after work. Nowadays I don't go to no parties without protection. Stop beatin' on me. Right now you should be thankful. Maybe with this gun we got a chance."

I wrestled the revolver free of Jamal's belt. "There's not much I can do with it while we're handcuffed like this."

"Maybe you could shoot the lock off the handcuffs. I'd do it myself if my right arm wasn't broke."

"The angle is so awkward and I'm not left-handed. I'll probably blow one of our hands off in the process. Besides, a bullet might bring them running back up here."

"They won't hear all the way downstairs. We gotta get ourselves out of this shit."

He was right about that. I was just taking aim at the chain on the cuffs when Coffman came striding through the door. He jogged across the concrete pad toward the catwalk. Just in time, I rolled my body so he couldn't see the gun.

"Pozere can't find anything on the computer. That means you used a diskette. It's not in the box. Where is it?" He jumped onto the catwalk and lunged for me. "Hey, what have you got?. . ."

I aimed the gun at his chest. It's interesting how I knew what to say. It must be all those cowboy movies I watched when I was a kid. "Make a wrong move and I'll blow a hole right through you."

Coffman's face was within inches of mine. His pale eyes bored into me. For the first time tonight I had the feeling he was really seeing me. "Where'd you get that?"

"Unlock the cuffs."

"What?"

"You heard me. I know you've got the key in your pocket. Unlock the cuffs."

"You wouldn't shoot."

When he straightened and started to pull back, I shot a hole in his shoulder. The noise deafened me and, since I did it one-handed with my weaker hand, the recoil nearly sprained my wrist. I didn't even hear him yell. For several seconds he just stood there staring down in disbelief. Then he covered the wound with his hand. A red stain oozed around his fingers.

"Right on, Ms. Dunphy!" Jamal cried. "Kill the honkie!"

Coffman didn't even spare the kid a look. He was gazing at me in stunned disbelief. "You shot me."

"Now unlock these cuffs or I'll blow your head off. Do it now!" My insides quaked but my voice stayed tough.

To my relief, Coffman took his hand away from the wound and reached into his pocket. Blood coated his fingers. Drops fell onto the catwalk. Below us the water was beginning to churn with gray shapes. I couldn't look at them, but I could hear them.

Beside me, Jamal did look and whispered in horrified awe. "Man, eyeball them motherfuckers. They're ready to eat them some dinner. We better make fuckin' sure the fast-food delight isn't us."

"This wasn't anything personal," Coffman said as if that were going to square things. He knelt and started working at the lock. I held the gun steady and tried not to look at what he was doing. I knew, close as he was to me, so close I could smell his hair tonic and the acrid odor of my own nervous sweat, I couldn't let myself get distracted. If I allowed my attention wander for a split second, he'd take the gun away from me. That was just the kind of macho move he'd eat up.

"I have nothing against you personally. It's just that you couldn't stop interfering."

I couldn't believe what I was hearing. Just how stupid did he think I was? Just how stupid did Duke and Pete think I was? "Shut up and unlock the cuffs." The gun was heavy and my wrist throbbed. I could barely hold it steady.

Coffman unlocked Jamal first. Then, too quick for me, he pulled the boy's body in front of him.

Jamal screamed. "Get your fuckin' hands off me, you motherfucker! My fuckin' arm is broke."

Using Jamal as a human shield, Coffman mocked a grin. "You won't shoot now, will you? You wouldn't want to hurt Little Black Sambo here."

He'd underestimated Jamal. The boy rolled left and slammed his hip into Coffman's groin. The two fell backward together and into the water.

Horrified, I watched them go over. Their screams flooded the narrow chamber and bounced off the pipes poking out from the cement walls. Their flailing arms and legs churned the water into a grayish froth. The rest of the tank came alive. Torpedo shapes rocketed from every direction, surfing through the foamed water like missiles. As they converged on the two swimmers, I thought of the blood seeping from Coffman's shoulder and began to gasp, literally choking with dread. I dropped the gun, unable to hold onto it any longer and jerked at the chain like a madwoman. It came unwrapped as a strong, brown hand curled over the edge of the catwalk.

"Help me, Ms. Dunphy. I can't use my other arm." Behind him, Coffman cursed and howled. He was a blur of motion, squirming and spanking the water while his head whirled wildly from side to side. His screams were high-pitched, birdlike. My God, I thought, he can't swim!

With all my strength, I grabbed onto Jamal's hand and heaved. To his left I spotted a brown shark's head. Its slit of a mouth was open, it's tiny expressionless eyes staring straight ahead in a mindless feeding fever. Its triangular razor teeth gleamed with intent.

The knowledge that he was about to make a serious pass pumped up my strength. I managed to pull Jamal halfway onto the platform. With a gymnast's spring, he flipped his legs up and over to safety. "Fuck, oh, fuck," he muttered between gasps.

My attention went back to Coffman, still thrashing in the middle of the tank. I cast around for some way to help him. The pole the shark keeper used during feeding time was hanging on a hook. It didn't look to be long enough to do any good. Yet I stood up to reach for it.

"Ms. Dunphy, we gotta get out of here." Jamal surged to his feet and clutched at my arm.

"We can't just leave him in that tank."

"We got no choice. Either we're outta here, or we'll be in that tank alongside him. Now grab up my gun and come on."

I glanced over my shoulder. Coffman had disappeared beneath the water. I saw tails and fins. Jamal thrust his gun into my hand and then began to drag me along the catwalk.

"We could shoot the sharks."

"Then the ones left alive would really go crazy. Besides, how we not going to shoot the honky? He's shot already." I stumbled along behind him, drowning in horror myself. "Jamal," I cried, "we can't . . ."

"Please, Ms. Dunphy, shut your mouth. I think I just heard the elevator. We've got to try and get out the entrance before they come up here."

We hurried onto the ramp that wound down through the ring tanks. We were almost into the shark-viewing area when we heard voices.

"Jesus Christ," Pozere shouted. "That's Coffman floating in there."

Wordlessly, Jamal whirled me around. We started sprinting in the opposite direction. Behind us we heard Pete and Pozere's wild shouts and then their running feet.

"Where to?" I panted as we negotiated the tight coil of the coral-reef tank.

"The rainforest." Jamal steered me toward the escalator that climbed to the top of the building.

"We'll get trapped."

"Man, we're already trapped. They'll catch us now if we start down. There's places to hide in the rainforest and you got my gun. Maybe if they come up the front, we can go down the back."

The escalator had been shut off for the night. We pushed our way through the revolving glass door that protected the rainforest's artificially maintained tropical atmosphere and ran up the motionless, steel-ribbed steps. The air was thick and warm, laden with moisture sprayed by humidifiers and the musky fragrance of tropical growth. My lungs ached from stress. By the time we reached the top Jamal, too, was panting.

"Dark up here," he said.

"Yes."

"I never seen it at night before with all the lights off."

"Me, neither."

"You think when they come up here after us, they'll turn on the lights?"

"They'd be foolish to do that. It would attract too much attention." On second thought, I wasn't so sure. Organizations sometimes throw parties at the aquarium at night. They leave lights on and nobody pays attention.

We stood in a square stone-paved plaza. Above us, moonlight filtered through the glass pyramid that roofs the rainforest and is the aquarium's distinguishing architectural feature. To our right a path meandered through layered levels of lush tropical plantings, a piranha pool, and one for tetras and angelfish. Directly ahead, the fat leaves of a chocolate tree reflected streaks of moonlight. I knew the area as a favorite spot for scarlet ibis. Visitors always oohed and aahed when they spotted them. Now I saw no sign of the brilliantly colored, long-legged birds.

"We got to find us someplace to hide," Jamal whispered.

"Maybe on top of the observation platform."

"We'll get cornered up there. Maybe we can hide underneath. It's close to the exit."

Jamal and I trotted down the path. In the dark it felt like an authentic jungle trail. Water dripped down from vines and epiphytes. A piranha splashed in its pool. The leaves of the palm and banana trees rustled from stealthy movements.

"I never worked up here. They got snakes loose?" Jamal asked.

"No snakes, just frogs and birds."

"What about that iguana? I hear he's a big mama."

"I don't know what he does at night. During the day he's very shy. He just hides."

A shadow inched across a patch of moonlight on the floor. We looked up and saw a body clinging to netting stretched across one side of the glass pyramid.

"Jesus, what's that?"

"One of the two-toed sloths. He's shy, too."

"Man, I hope he stays that way."

We reached the platform and stood looking at it. "What do you think?" I asked.

"I don't want to get trapped up there."

"Then maybe we can hide in the center part, or even by the bridge where they keep the Amazon parrots and snapping turtles."

"I don't want to fuss with parrots or snapping turtles. Tell you what, we'll wait here. If they come up the escalator we'll head out the other exit. That way maybe we can get out of the building before they catch us."

I nodded and, despite the heat, shivered. We stood waiting in silence. Fifteen or twenty minutes crawled past. It seemed like years. "Jamal," I finally whispered, "how's your arm? Does it hurt?"

"It don't feel good." Gingerly, he touched his shoulder. "Guess I'm lucky it's still stuck on. Not like that dude downstairs. What do you suppose happened to him? You think he's still breathing?"

We stood looking at each other. "I think they must have fished him out," I finally said. "That's what's taking them so long. Even if he's dead, they'd have to get him out of the water."

"Why's that?"

"If they're still planning on shooting you and throwing me in, they can't have one of them floating around with me. That would really confuse the police."

I started to giggle wildly, then clapped my hand over my mouth. My hysterical cackle bounced around in the humid air. A shot cracked the darkness. Next to me I heard a groan and then a thud. I looked down and saw a dark mass. Jamal lay at my feet.

A second shot snicked close to my left hip. I wanted to help Jamal, but I was already sprinting up the stairs. At the top, I flattened myself on the wood boards as a third bullet whizzed past my ear. Gazing out between the slats of the wood rail fencing the platform, I tried to make out moving shadows in the dense plantings. To my right, a bird disturbed by the bullets flew into the top leaves of a banana tree. The harsh whirr of its wings sent my heart leaping like a hooked trout.

Footsteps pounded below me. Then they died away and I heard nothing except my breath rasping in my throat. I arranged both my hands around the grip on Jamal's gun and pointed the barrel out into the dark jungle.

Crazily, I found myself wanting to fire all the bullets into the menacing thickets of shadow. "No, no Sally," I kept muttering under my breath in a kind of mantra. It was as if one part of my stressed-out brain was trying to communicate with another more primal and far less rational part. I couldn't start popping away because the hysteric in me wanted to make a statement. I didn't know how many bullets I had left, and Jamal was still lying down there, hurt and vulnerable.

Shouts. I went rigid, my eyes darting everywhere. Another shot. Then my straining ears picked up grunts. Close by men were scuffling. I heard the crunch of a heavy blow. Then another. Muttered curses. The lights went on. My shadow world coalesced into a blurry green landscape of trees. To the left and out of sight an angry parrot screamed its rage.

Below and to my right, I saw Pete and Pozere. My stomach tightened. Sweat slicked my palms. Pete had Pozere's arms locked behind his back and was dragging him over to a tree. Suddenly, Duke emerged from the bend in the path. Staring down at him, I felt as I were going to split apart. I wanted to howl out my rage and pain.

Duke kneeled and helped Pete handcuff Pozere's hands to a tree trunk. Ignoring the man's curses, he stood and looked around. "Sally?" Then he spotted Jamal. "Hey, there's the kid. He's hurt."

When Pete and Duke started walking toward Jamal, I worked my thumb to cock the revolver. The faint click stopped both big blond brothers in their tracks. Duke's head jerked up. Through the slat on the platform, our eyes met. "Sally?"

"Don't touch him." I squeezed the words through my teeth.

"What?"

"I said don't touch him. Take another step toward Jamal and I'll shoot both of you."

"Sally, it's okay," Pete said. His voice sounded light, too light for his size. "Coffman's dead and Pozere's out of commission. Duke's here now. He's put a stop to all this. He knows everything. He's here to help."

"I don't believe you."

"What?" Pete looked aghast. His blue eyes squinted up into mine like a hurt boy's.

"I'll never believe you again, Pete. You were ready to see your pals kill me."

"No, Sally, no. I was trying to save you."

"Not very hard, Pete. Why did you bring them here in the first place?"

"I couldn't help that. They heard your message on my answering machine."

"Bullshit." I'd never believe another word he said. And I couldn't let him touch Jamal. Once he got hold of Jamal, he could use him as a hostage and I'd be helpless.

Pete shot a look of consternation at his brother. "Tell her," he said. "Explain how you've been trying to help me get things straightened out.

Duke just stood there silently staring at me.

Pete returned his attention to me. "Even if you don't trust me, anymore, Sally, Duke is here."

"So?"

"So, you trust Duke."

My jaw was rigid. My teeth were locked together so tight my raspy breaths made them chatter. Somehow I unclenched them. "No Pete, I don't trust Duke. I don't trust either of you. I think you and your big brother and your pal Pozere have just put on a little charade for me. Until I see a dozen cops in uniform up here, I'm not letting you or anybody else near me or Jamal."

"Sally, this is dumb." Duke's gruff voice boomed in my ears, competing with the sledgehammer drums of my heart. "You know I'd never hurt you."

I wanted to believe him. Lord, how I wanted to believe him. "I don't know that at all," I said. "I don't even know why you're here. How would you know to come if you weren't in cahoots with them?"

"Tyrone got tired of waiting. He walked Mopsy back to your house. I was sitting in front in my car because Mike Theologus had called the police. When he didn't find you at home and your door was unlocked, he got worried. Tyrone told me where you were and that you might be in trouble. Naturally, I came running."

My brain was too tired to unravel this. Did it mean Mike wasn't in with them, after all? Or what if it was all a lie? "Maybe you're here to help Pozere and your brother kill me. I know you know their pal, Coffman. I found his brochure in your pocket. Is he one of Pete's fraternity brothers? He is, isn't he?"

My voice sounded ridiculously high, like a terrified child's. As I spoke, I aimed my gun at Duke and sited down its barrel. Was I prepared to shoot the man? I didn't know. I only knew that I needed to defend myself and Jamal and that I couldn't be a fool and trust the wrong person again.

"Sally," Pete said, "I gave that brochure to Duke the night your car blew up. I went to him because Coffman and Pozere tried blackmailing me into joining them. They and another guy who works for Coffman were my fraternity brothers, but I swear when they proposed this whole notion a year ago I thought it was all a joke. When Lowecki had an accident and I was then able to run for his spot, I never dreamed they'd arranged it. When they told me, laughing like it was a big joke, I was horrified. They said if I didn't go along, they'd implicate me. I didn't know what to do. Then Joe and Frank were killed and I realized I had to do something. I was going crazy. I felt as if I was trapped in a nightmare. Finally, after your accident, I told Duke. He said he'd try to get to the bottom of this without implicating me."

"Blood is thicker than water, right?"

"Right." Pete nodded vigorously. "Sally, you understand."

"I understand that now I'm the one who can put you on the spot. Maybe your big brother will fix things up for you by getting rid of me."

For another couple of minutes the two brothers stood there gazing at me. "She can't mean it," Pete finally said.

"I think she does." Duke sounded infinitely weary.

"Sally," Pete called, "we have to help this boy here. He's been wounded. He's bleeding."

I risked a glance at Jamal. He lay crumpled on the ground where he'd fallen, but I didn't see blood. A bird flew through my line of sight. Turning the lights on had upset them. They were darting around overhead, calling to each other in indignant shrieks and whistles.

Pete started walking toward Jamal and my finger squeezed the trigger. My bullet chinked at a stone just in front of his foot. He stopped dead, gazing at me in disbelief.

"I told you she meant it," Duke said. "Stay put while I use the phone." He turned and called up to me. "Will a squad in uniforms satisfy you?"

"Maybe."

"Well, it had better satisfy you because that's the best I can do."

"Make it quick, Duke."

Nevertheless, he hesitated another second or two. We gazed at each other. Duke's green eyes were bleak as the Atlantic rolling in on a frozen beach in December. "So long, lover," he said.

"So long," I answered.

Epilogue

Three weeks later I went to my mother's wedding. She wore a wreath of baby's breath in her hair, and a pink lace sheath over a pink silk underslip. I wore blue. Jeffie sported a rented pearl gray tux.

Believe it or not, after the ceremony everyone piled into their cars and drove over to Mama's. The wedding guests spent the rest of the afternoon stuffing themselves there with Polish sausage, grilled hamburgers, and corn on the cob.

Two minutes after I walked through the gate, Mama separated me from my escort and whispered in my ear, "Now, I want you to stop this sulking and say something nice to Duke. He feels real bad that you're not speaking to him. When you consider he saved your life, the least you owe him is a kind word. See him over there by the roses? He's pretending he doesn't see you. Go and make up."

She patted my shoulder, all the while her gaze swiveling to keep track of the thirty or so guests funneled into her tiny backyard. "Oh, look at that. Greg is sticking his finger into the cake. That boy!"

I watched Mama scurry over to the table set up next to the peonies. People filed up to set offerings of food on it. Potato and macaroni salad, heaps of fruit, frothy pink mixtures of Jell-O and whipped cream, baked beans in crocks, a guacamole dip with chips. Dressed up in a miniature pale blue suit, Pete's towheaded son danced before the three-tier cake taking up the central place of honor.

As Mama grabbed his elbow, I shifted my gaze to the right and spotted Pete and Joyce shoulder to shoulder. Hey, did you think Pete would be in jail by now? Not a chance.

This is Pete's story. When his fraternity brothers talked about easing their move up the corporate ladder by assassinating their bosses, he thought it was just a joke. He didn't learn they had been responsible for Lowecki's accidental death until after Frank Leftwich's fatal tumble into the shark tank. Then Coffman and Pozere tried blackmailing Pete into joining their operation. He resisted every way he knew how, he claims. Finally, when he realized the full extent of what was going on, he went to his brother for assistance.

Duke backs up this story. So, legally speaking, that makes Pete nothing worse than an accomplice after the fact. I mean, the poor guy's only a lawyer. So how can we expect him to have a good handle on what's a crime and what isn't? Given his cooperative attitude, and his part in saving my life, the DA probably won't press charges. But Pete's political career is over. Ironically, this saved his marriage and made Mama a happy grandma.

Now that Pete has withdrawn from the city council race, he's spending all his nights in Columbia. Joyce has agreed to bring the kids into the city to see their grandmother more often and even to let them stay overnight sometimes. Mama is delighted. So, as far as she's concerned the Departure Society was a blessing. Have I said anything to persuade her of my belief that her baby boy's role in all this was a little less innocent than advertised? No. How could I say or do anything that would hurt Mama?

As for the others—Pozere is being investigated by a Baltimore grand jury on suspicion of criminal conspiracy and murder. The Bureau of Tobacco, Alcohol, and Firearms is looking into the explosion in Frederick of Mona Leftwich's house. They're investigating not only the arson, but the conspiracy to destroy evidence of federal crimes.

Maybe you're wondering who the fourth fraternity brother was. Well, it wasn't Mike Theologus. Mike graduated from Temple and was never in a fraternity. Despite the dark suspicions that sent me running from my house, it turned out that Colin Frostberg's father died in a real car accident. His Jaguar was in a head-on collision with a car piloted by a drunk driver. Mike had nothing to do with the Departure Society. What's going to happen to Hoyt Coffman's associate, a man named Peter Diehl, the fourth fraternity brother and the man who scared me on the subway? Right now, since Diehl didn't actually do anything to me and is claiming he wasn't involved in the others' schemes, that's unclear.

Pozere wouldn't implicate Diehl or Pete, but he did tell police exactly how Coffman killed Leftwich. Though I never saw Coffman at the aquarium, it turns out he was on the board of directors and thoroughly familiar with the facility. It was easy for him to lure Frank to the catwalk.

I believe that Coffman murdered Joe and Pozere killed Coffman's boss McCahan. Who was responsible for fixing my brakes, or even if they were sabotaged, is still a mystery. In fact, a lot of questions remain unanswered. Maybe the grand jury will uncover all the answers. The cynic in me thinks they probably won't.

"Sally, sweetie, you look beautiful! And that guy you're with is the most gorgeous thing I've ever seen." My mother grabbed my hand and clung to it.

"Oh, no, Mom, you're the beautiful one with the gorgeous guy today." The first part of this was no lie. I guess there's no tonic like true love. I'd never seen my mother look more radiant. Instead of wilting her, the hot July sun beating down on all our heads only made her glow.

"Ain't this the prettiest little lady you ever did see?" Jeffie exclaimed proudly. He and Mom beamed at each other. Then, after I introduced her to my escort formally, she smothered me with a perfumed hug and planted a damp kiss on my cheek.

"Your mama's one happy lady today, Sally."

"I know. I can see that. It becomes you."

"Be happy for me, Sally."

"I am, Mom. Of course, I am. I wish you and Jeffie all the best."

"We're going to cut the cake soon. You should get yourself something to eat."

"Sounds like a good idea. Looks like quite a spread over there."

Shaking hands and smiling all the way, I threaded my way through the crowd. The yard had become a heaving sea of chattering humanity. I speculated that not much of Mama's grass would survive the festivities. After loading a paper plate with salads and pouring myself a stiff wine punch, I asked my date to wait for me. He agreed and I meandered over to the corner by the rose trellis.

"Hello Duke."

He turned away from the elderly neighbor he'd been shooting the breeze with and rested his beer on the fence post. "I wondered if you were going to speak to me."

"Why wouldn't I speak to you? This is a happy day. Your mother is doing mine a big favor. Hey, you're looking extremely handsome today. New threads?"

He glanced down at his cream linen slacks and matching pale beige jacket. "In honor of the occasion."

"You look great."

"So do you, Sally. Your eyebrows are back."

"I guess I looked pretty funny without them."

"You'd have to work to look anything but beautiful. Still, I'd keep the eyebrows if I were you."

"That's what Scott Winder said when I had lunch with him the other day."

"Joe's boy? How's he doing? Did he take it hard when he found out how his father was murdered?"

"Not as hard as he did when he thought Joe had committed suicide. Now, at least, Scott's stopped feeling guilty. He's changed his plans about college, though."

"Oh? How's that?"

"Instead of majoring in business, he's decided on environmental science instead."

When Duke chuckled, I looked away and asked, "Have they got a line on Chrissy's identity yet?"

He shifted his weight and shook his head. "Not yet. Turned out, she had perfect teeth. No dental records to check. What about Jamal? How's he doing?"

"Fine, he's doing fine. Kids that age heal fast. And

there's good news at the aquarium. He's not going to lose his job, even though he did break the rules."

We looked at each other, that last line about rules hanging between us. "Sally," Duke said heavily, "do you understand why I couldn't tell you?"

"Sure I understand." I took a deep breath. The smell from the roses was thick on the hot summer air and painfully sweet.

"When Pete came to me he was so scared he was babbling. I had to look for ways to get him out of that mess before he ruined his life. The man has a wife and kids, a career that matters. Until I'd done my best to see he wasn't going to lose that, I couldn't tell anyone. But you've got to believe me. No matter what, I wouldn't have let any harm come to you. That's why I took you home with me. That's why I wanted you to stay there. If you had stayed at my place, things would have come out okay. I would have talked Pete into going to the authorities on his own. Do you believe me?"

"Certainly. Pete's your little brother. Naturally, your loyalty had to be to him."

Duke sighed. "Up there in the rainforest, you wouldn't trust me. I see you're with Mike Theologus today." He gestured with his head at where Mike stood smiling down at my flushed and excited mother. "Mama tells me you and he are quite an item these days."

"We've been seeing a certain amount of each other. When you get to know him, Mike's a hell of a nice guy."

"Oh, I'm sure. Tell me something, Sal. If I had tried taking that gun away from you, would you have put a bullet in me?"

"I honestly don't know, Duke. I was kind of crazy up there."

Duke smiled, but the expression in his eyes was sad. "I think you would have. Things will never be the same between us again, will they Sally? It's all over, isn't it?"

I put my hand on his shoulder. "You and Pete and Mama will always be my family, Duke. That will never change."

A roar of excitement went up from the people behind us. Mike was striding toward us, his gaze going from my face to Duke's. "Oh, look," I exclaimed brightly. "Mom is getting ready to cut the cake."

Whirling, I plunged into the crowd and headed toward Mike. As I pushed my way through the guests, I didn't look to see if Duke was following. I knew he wasn't, but that was just as well. I didn't want him to see the tears in my eyes.

COMING NEXT MONTH

THE COURT OF THREE SISTERS by Marianne Willman
An enthralling historical romance from the award-winning author of *Yesterday's Shadows* and *Silver Shadows*. The Court of Three Sisters was a hauntingly beautiful Italian villa where a prominent archaeologist took his three daughters: Thea, Summer, and Fanny. Into their circle came Col McCallum, who was determined to discover the real story behind the mysterious death of his mentor. Soon Col and Summer, in a race to unearth the fabulous ancient treasure that lay buried on the island, found the meaning of true love.

OUTRAGEOUS by Christina Dodd
The flamboyant Lady Marian Wenthaven, who cared nothing for the opinions of society, proudly claimed two-year-old Lionel as her illegitimate son. When she learned that Sir Griffith ap Powel, who came to visit her father's manor, was actually a spy sent by King Henry VII to watch her, she took Lionel and fled. But there was no escaping from Griffith and the powerful attraction between them.

CRAZY FOR LOVIN' YOU by Lisa G. Brown
The acclaimed author of *Billy Bob Walker Got Married* spins a tale of life and love in a small Tennessee town. After four years of exile, Terrill Carroll returns home when she learns of her mother's serious illness. Clashing with her stepfather, grieving over her mother, and trying to find a place in her family again, she turns to Jubal Kane, a man from the opposite side of the tracks who has a prison record, a bad reputation, and the face of a dark angel.

TAMING MARIAH by Lee Scofield
When Mariah kissed a stranger at the train station, everyone in the small town of Mead, Colorado, called her a hellion, but her grandfather knew she only needed to meet the right man. The black sheep son of a titled English family, Hank had come to the American West seeking adventure . . . until he kissed Mariah.

FLASH AND FIRE by Marie Ferrarella
Amanda Foster, who has learned the hard way how to make it on her own, finally lands the coveted anchor position on the five o'clock news. But when she falls for Pierce Alexander, the station's resident womanizer, is she ready to trust love again?

INDISCRETIONS by Penelope Thomas
The spellbinding story of a murder, a ghost, and a love that conquered all. During a visit to the home of enigmatic Edmund Llewelyn, Hilary Carewe uncovered a decade-old murder through rousing the spirit of Edmund's stepmother, Lily Llewelyn. As Edmund and Hilary were drawn together, the spirit grew stronger and more vindictive. No one was more affected by her presence than Hilary, whom Lily seemed determined to possess.

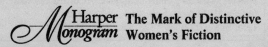

Harper Monogram   **The Mark of Distinctive Women's Fiction**